BREAKUP

A Kate Shugak
Mystery

DANA STABENOW

BREAKUP

G. P. PUTNAM'S SONS
NEW YORK

G. P. Putnam's Sons
Publishers Since 1838
a member of
Penguin Putnam Inc.
200 Madison Avenue
New York, NY 10016

Library of Congress Cataloging-in-Publication Data

Stabenow, Dana.
    Breakup/Dana Stabenow.
        p. cm.— (A Kate Shugak mystery)
    ISBN 0-399-14250-9
    1. Shugak, Kate (Fictitious character)—Fiction. 2. Women detectives—
Alaska—Fiction. 3. Alaska—Fiction. I. Title. II. Series: Stabenow, Dana.
Kate Shugak mystery.   NEBF
PS3569.T1249B74   1997   96-38195   CIP
813'.54—dc20

Printed in the United States of America

10   9   8   7   6   5   4   3   2   1

This book is printed on acid-free paper. ∞

Book design by Kate Nichols

my thanks to Tope Equipment
for the ride on the D-6

and to Mary Ann
for the great line

and to Dad and Hank
for the bear stories

for my girls
Angelique, Tanya, Marie and Monica
sunshine on a cloudy day

BREAKUP

1

Kate surveyed the yard in front of her cabin and uttered one word. *"Breakup."*

Affection for the season was lacking in the tone of her voice.

Ah yes, breakup, that halcyon season including but not necessarily limited to March and April, when all of Alaska melts into a 586,412-square-mile pile of slush. The temperature reaches the double digits and for a miracle stays there, daylight increases by five minutes and forty-four seconds every twenty-four hours, and after a winter's worth of five-hour days all you want to do is go outside and stay there for the rest of your natural life. But it's too late for the snow machine and too early for the truck, and meltoff is swelling the rivers until flooding threatens banks, bars and all downstream communities—muskrat, beaver and man. The meat cache is almost empty and the salmon aren't up the creek yet. All you can do is sit and watch your yard reappear, along with a winter's worth of debris until now hidden by an artistic layer of snow, all of which used to be frozen so it didn't smell.

"The best thing about breakup," Kate said, "is that it's after winter and before summer."

Mutt wasn't paying attention. There was a flash of tail fur on the other side of the yard and the 140-pound half-husky, half-wolf was off with a crunch of brush to chase down the careless hare who had made it. Breakup for Mutt meant bigger breakfasts. Breakup for Mutt meant outside instead of inside. Breakup for Mutt meant a possible close encounter with the gray timber wolf with the roving eye who had beguiled her two springs before, then left her flat with a litter of pups. All five had been turned over to Mandy a nanosecond after weaning. One had been on the second-place team into Nome the month before.

Kate tried not to feel resentful at being abandoned. It was just that it seemed someone ought to have been present, looking on with sympathy as she plodded through the million and one tasks produced by the season's first chinook, which had blown in from the Gulf of Alaska the night before at sixty-two miles per hour and toppled the woodpile into the meat cache, so that the miniature cabin on stilts looked knock-kneed.

The chinook had also awakened the female grizzly wintering in a den on a knoll across the creek. Kate had heard her grousing at five that morning. She was hungry, no doubt, and a knock-kneed cache was probably just the ticket to fill her belly until the first salmon hit fresh water.

And speaking of water, before Kate started work on the truck she had to check on the creek out back. With the coming of the chinook the ice had broken, and the subsequent roar of runoff was clearly audible from her doorstep. The previous fall had brought record rain, and the boulders that shored up her side of the creek had been loosened to the point of destabilizing the creek bank, but before she could do anything about it she'd had to go to Anchorage, and by the time she got back the creek had been frozen over.

Before her lumbar vertebrae could start to protest at the mere prospect of such abuse, she went to take a look, shoving her way through the underbrush that closed in around the back of the cabin to the top of the short cliff overlooking the course of the stream.

From the top of the bank at least, the situation did not look that bad. The tumble of boulders, some of them as tall as she was, broke the current, supported the bank and excavated and maintained a small backwater just downstream within the arm of the outcropping, good for salmon tickling and skinny-dipping.

The thought of skinny-dipping called up a memory from the previous summer, one that included Jack Morgan, whose behind had suffered from sunburn that evening. He hadn't complained.

She flapped the collar of her shirt. It had to be forty degrees. A veritable heat wave. No wonder she was feeling flushed. There was a length of three-quarter-inch polypro fastened to evenly spaced posts leading down the side of the bank, and she went down backwards, breathless not just from the exertion, light of foot and heart.

Up close she was happy to see that the situation looked even less dire. The two boulders that formed the point of the mini-peninsula had shifted, but it looked now as if they had merely to settle in even more firmly than before. No collapsed banks, no rocks sucked into midstream. She scaled the natural breakwater and to her delight found that the alteration had caused the backwater to increase in size and depth, just a little, just enough to increase her crawl from four overhand strokes to five, and Jack's from two to three.

Or just enough to catch her.

"Get a grip," she said, shifting inside clothes that had fit perfectly well when she put them on that morning. It was her own fault for reading Robert Herrick and Andrew Marvell late into the previous night. Those damn Cavalier poets were always headfirst in love with somebody, and none of them had the least sense of moderation. Charles II had a lot to answer for.

It was Jack's fault, too, for not being here, right here where she could get her hands on him.

A rueful grin spread across her face. If Jack had the least idea of her mood he'd be on the next plane.

The water at her feet was so clear it was almost invisible, crisped at the edges with a layer of frosty ice, and she bent over to scoop up a handful. It was tart and oh so cold all the way down. Smiling, she splashed a second handful over her face.

Over the rush of water came a kind of snuffling grunt. Her hand stilled in the act of scooping up more water, and very, very slowly she looked up.

Fifty feet away, standing in midstream, thick, silvered hide spiked with water, a female grizzly stared back.

Ten feet downstream of mama came the bawl of a cub.

Five more feet downstream came the answering bawl of its twin. Neither of them looked more than a day out of the den.

Involuntarily, Kate stood straight up and reached for her shotgun.

It wasn't there.

The grizzly allowed Kate just enough time to remember exactly where it was—in the gun rack above the door of the cabin—before she dropped down to all fours in the water and charged.

There was a bark and a scrambling sound from the top of the bank. "NO, Mutt!" Kate roared, a shaft of pure terror spearing through her. "STAY!"

The bear stopped abruptly in midstream and reared up on her hind legs, so immediately on the heels of Kate's command to Mutt that a bubble of hysterical laughter caught at the back of her throat. The bear's lips peeled back to reveal a gleaming set of very sharp teeth that snapped in her direction. When they came together it sounded like the bite of an axe blade sinking into wood.

All thought of laughter gone, Kate backed up a step, casting a quick glance at the bank behind her. It wasn't as tall or as steep as the bank down to the outcropping, but it was still taller than she was and lined along its edge with a tangled section of alder and diamond willow, with no line to aid her ascent. Mutt barked again, and again Kate yelled, "NO! STAY!" without turning around, because she purely hated turning her back on a bear. She took another step back and began to speak in what she hoped was a soothing monotone. "It's okay, girl, it's all right, you're between me and your cubs, I can't get to them, it's all right, I mean you no harm, settle down now and I'll get out of your face, just calm down and—"

There was another roar from the grizzly and she dropped down on all four feet with a tremendous splash and charged again, water fountaining up on either side.

"Oh shit," Kate said, and on the spot invented a technique for climbing a steep creek bank backwards that might not have been recognized by any international mountaineering organization but got her up and over the lip of the bank a split second before the bear, moving too fast now to stop, crashed headfirst into the wall of dirt with such force that a large section of it caved in on her.

It didn't improve her disposition any, but Kate wasn't hanging around to watch. On hands and knees she wriggled through the undergrowth, branches scraping at her face and tugging at her hair, nails broken, knuckles split and bleeding, all the while listening to the outraged roaring of the grizzly behind her. The sound provided unlimited fuel for forward motion. Kate broke through the other side of the brush and collapsed, only to be pounced upon by an anxious Mutt, who thrust a nose beneath Kate's side and flipped her like a landed halibut, sniffing her from head to toe in between bellowing threats to the grizzly. Between the growling of the infuriated grizzly, the bawling of the terrified cubs and Mutt's challenging howls, Kate's eardrums would never be the same.

"It's okay, girl," Kate said, as Mutt nosed her over for the second time. "It's all right. Calm down, now. Come on, calm down. Mutt, dammit, knock it off!"

Mutt ceased triage with a hurt look. Unhindered, Kate managed to get to her feet and stagger to the cabin to retrieve the shotgun. She got back in time to listen as the grizzly proceeded to tear up an additional six feet of creek bank, which from the sound of it included the felling of a great deal of timber, before taking her frightened offspring in charge and marching them off in the opposite direction. They heard her baying defiance for a good fifteen minutes, and then it faded only as she put distance between her family and Kate's homestead.

It took every second of that fifteen minutes for Kate to swallow her heart, control her respiration and amass sufficient authority over her muscles to still her knees. Her jeans were soaked through with snowmelt, her shirt with perspiration. Her blood thudded against her eardrums and the walls of her veins. With every indrawn breath oxygen fizzed along her pulmonary arteries. She felt ten feet tall and covered with hair. She felt as naked and defenseless as a newborn babe. She was terrified, she was exhilarated, she was most definitely alive.

Returning to the yard, she stood the shotgun butt down next to the cabin door, ready for action. Inside, she noticed with a sense of detachment that her hands were filthy from clawing up the creek bank. She looked up and caught sight of her image in the mirror hanging over the sink. Her waist-length, straight black hair, which had started out the day confined in its usual neat French braid, had been yanked into an untidy bush. The pupils of her almond-shaped eyes took up most of the hazel iris, and her skin, usually a warm golden brown, had paled to the point that the roped scar bisecting her throat was almost invisible.

She noticed further, with that same sense of detachment, that everything within range of her vision seemed to be outlined with a rim of light that shimmered in the crisp morning air, giving it an air of unfamiliarity. It was almost as if she were seeing everything for the first time.

The cabin was a single room twenty-five feet square, with a sleeping loft beneath a high-peaked roof. To the left of the door was the kitchen, containing a sink with an old-fashioned, long-handled water pump, an oil stove for cooking, a woodstove for heat, a table and three old and mismatched but serviceable chairs. A built-in, L-shaped couch upholstered in deep blue canvas filled up the corner to the right of the door, and the rest of the wall space was taken up by bookshelves crammed with books, tape deck and cassette tapes. A dusty guitar hung on one side of the door, a set of caribou antlers on the other side with a down jacket and a fur parka hanging from it. The ladder to the sleeping loft rose up from the center of the room. On nails driven into the sides of the ladder hung two beaver traps, a sliming knife with a white plastic handle in a hard plastic sheath, a couple of rings of keys, a wool muffler and a philodendron she was in the process of killing.

Kate's heartbeat began to settle and the room once again to look like home. It seemed so amazingly unchanged from when she had left it, was it really only twenty minutes before? Strange, when she felt so, so . . . well, she didn't know quite what she felt, except that her knees were still experiencing technical difficulties and as she moved to the stove to pour herself a cup of coffee she kept tripping over objects that weren't there.

The coffee, the last in the pot and strong enough to smelt iron, booted the kick start with a satisfyingly solid jolt. Kate rinsed out the mug, scrubbed her hands, clipped her broken nails and changed into dry clothes, which gave her at least the outward semblance of normality, in spite of the little electric shocks that kept darting beneath her skin. Back outside, she narrowed her eyes against the sun. Never had it seemed more golden in color, never the sky so blue or the trees such a dark, deep, rich green. The air sizzled with life and death and everything in between. She gulped it in, greedy for more.

Jack Morgan's face flashed in front of her, and she knew an immediate, visceral need for his presence, his mouth, his hands, his body. Her skin radiated a sudden and unexpected heat, and she pulled at the front of her plaid shirt, popping one of the buttons in her haste, rolling up her sleeves to bare her skin to the cool, clean air. When she realized what was happening she gave a snort of laughter. Mutt, on self-appointed sentry duty, looked around, ears cocked inquiringly. "It's all right, girl," Kate said, still laughing, albeit somewhat shakily. "Breakup's making your roomie a little needy, is all."

The ears remained cocked, as if to say, So what else is new? or maybe, Get in line. Kate laughed again, and then pulled herself together. There was work to do. Priority one was a truck tune-up. She'd left the supply run to Ahtna until too late to take the snow machine.

The truck was an '84 Isuzu diesel with 150,000 miles on it that still got twenty-six miles per gallon on the straight stretch of former railroad roadbed between Kate's homestead and the village of Niniltna. She had high hopes of it going another hundred and fifty thousand, until either she or the truck died of old age. She sorted through the toolbox for a wrench, pausing when something halfway between a pig squeal and a jackass bray wafted into the clearing on a stray breeze. It wasn't the female this time. Probably the grizzly male one mountain over. Probably the father of the two cubs. She reached down to feel for the 12-gauge and found it right where she'd left it, leaning against the front bumper.

By ten a.m. she had pulled the battery and put it on the trickle charger, drained the water out of the fuel filters, checked the oil, checked the coolant in the radiator, checked the tire pressure all around and investigated the possibility of porcupines in the fan belt. Porcupines were pests damn near as bad as bears, born troublemakers; they would go for anything rubber for the salt in it—the fan belt, the tires, once Kate had seen a porcupine chewing through the track of a Nodwell tractor.

During the tune-up she managed to acquire a metal splinter under the nail of her right forefinger that looked about a quarter of an inch long and felt as if it ran all the way up to her elbow. She startled Mutt out of her nap with a loud oath and went into the cabin to perform emergency surgery. She daubed the resulting gash with antiseptic, and tried to remember the last time she'd had a tetanus shot. Niniltna had no health clinic. Each year the public health nurse came through with an immunization card for every student in Niniltna Public School, kindergarten through twelfth grade, but once you graduated, you were on your own. If Kate needed a tetanus shot, she'd have to drive to Ahtna. Convenient, if that was the right word, since she had to drive to Ahtna for supplies anyway.

The whistle of the kettle interrupted her reverie. A cup of hot cocoa sounded like heaven on earth. Unfortunately, she'd used up her last can of milk the week before, and this morning's coffee had been the end of the Starbucks Christmas blend, which she bought five pounds at a time, when she had money in December. She rummaged around for something else, surfacing eventually with an elderly box of Lemon Zinger. There was some honey left. Hallelujah. She spooned it into the thick white porcelain mug with a heavy hand. The resulting brew was tangy and sweet and scalded her insides.

It was noon and she was hungry, but she'd forgotten to get any meat out of the cache the night before. She added more honey to her tea and put Jimmy Buffett on the tape deck, forgetting how dangerous Jimmy was to listen to during breakup. Kate, too, wanted to go beyond the end, find one particular harbor, be somewhere over China, take another road, any road, especially today, preferably to a place where there were no bears. It was an act of self-defense when she replaced Jimmy with Cyndi Lauper. Girls just wanna have fun. Which of course brought Jack Morgan back to mind with an immediacy that set her teeth on edge. She changed Cyndi Lauper for *Les Miserables*, sat down on the couch and leaned back with a contented sigh. Mutt, who had overseen the operation with a critical eye, flopped down with an equally contented sigh.

Fifteen minutes later Kate jerked awake, the now cool tea sloshing over the side of the heavy white porcelain mug onto her hand and knee. Mutt was on her feet, nose to the door, a steady, rumbling growl issuing from deep in her chest.

"Oh shit," Kate said, and got to her feet.

The .30-06 slid comfortably into her hands, and she flicked off the safety and took a step back as she opened the door. "Stay," she told Mutt, whose growl had grown in volume.

There was a bear in the yard, and to add insult to injury, it wasn't the sow she'd encountered that morning, it wasn't even the boar from the next mountain over. This was an entirely new neighbor, a youngster, two, three years maybe, and small, no more than three hundred pounds and change. His brown coat was long and thick and shining from six months of doing nothing but growing it out underground.

He had managed to bump into the cache, with the result that it was now on the verge of total collapse, so that the frozen meat inside had shifted enough to force open the door. Half a dozen packages littered the ground beneath, and a seventh was at present being finished off with a single gulp, two layers of butcher paper over two layers of Saran wrap and all. He lifted his lip in their direction and attacked another package.

Kneeing Mutt, who had expressed a sincere wish to rid the homestead of its uninvited guest and all his kin, back inside, Kate jacked a round into the .30-06's chamber. "Get out of here!" she yelled. "Go on! Git, you big pest, before I turn you into a rug!" Mutt raised her voice in agreement, sounding considerably more threatening.

The bear stood up on his hind legs and waved his claws, snarling. His mom had taught him that much before she booted him out, and it worked pretty well on other mammals and most humans. Kate shot a round into the ground in front of him. The bear let out a shriek of fear and dropped forward on all four legs, in the process bumping once more into the cache.

"Oh hell," Kate said.

The much-abused knock-kneed leg folded like a pleat in an accordion and the other three legs couldn't stand the strain and the cache began a graceful tilt forward, during which the rest of the meat store fell out and rained down on the grizzly's head—a roast, a package of ptarmigan breasts, another roast, a package of mooseburger, five pounds of caribou ribs. The bewildered grizzly gave a bellow of consternation and bolted like lightning into the east.

A bear in high gear is a sight to evoke awe and admiration, and Kate would undoubtedly have experienced both those emotions but for one thing. The open door of the garage was in the bear's way. His right shoulder clipped it in passing and it ripped easily from its hinges, whirled merrily around on one corner and flopped down with a squishy splat as the grizzly, barely checking, crashed through a stand of alders and was gone.

Kate looked from the garage door lying flat on the ground to the cache crumpled up on the opposite side of the yard and sat down hard on the doorstep, the rifle clutched in her hands, waiting for her heart rate to drop below 200.

"*Breakup*," she said.

2

One bear encounter per life was one too many. Two in the space of eight hours seemed, at the very least, excessive.

Still, any number of bears in one's life was preferable to what waited for her on the kitchen table, a task she'd been putting off for three months, a task she could no longer delay.

That evening she took a deep breath, got out her self-control and marched over to the kitchen table, where the booklet entitled "Instructions for Form 1040" waited for her with a superior smirk on its government-issue face.

An hour later she felt as she always did on this day at this time of the year, frustrated and angry and convinced she was destined to spend the rest of her life in a federal prison in Illinois run by Ida Lupino.

"Income," as usual, was proving to be a problem.

On page 15 of the booklet the IRS had provided a helpful guide to just what kind of income must be reported. Earned income was easy; her brief but intense employment with RPetCo at Prudhoe Bay the previous year had pulled in $17,500 in fees and expenses. That went on line 7, no problem there. There was the mushroom money from last June as well, but it had been paid in cash and Kate decided what the IRS didn't know wouldn't hurt them, or her, either.

She tried to remember where the $17,500 was now. A big chunk of it had gone for Axenia's classes at UAA, although now that Axenia was married her husband would be taking over his wife's bills. She didn't approve of Axenia's choice of husband but at least he'd gotten rich at the government trough and would relieve her of the burden of Axenia's school fees. Or so Kate sincerely hoped.

Too much of it had gone for that damn dress-up outfit for that party in Anchorage last winter. The outfit was hanging in Jack's closet in town, encased in plastic, and if she had anything to say about it, never to be worn again. She still begrudged every dime.

Of course, once she'd put it on, Jack Morgan's chief object in life became a determination to get her out of it as quickly as possible, not necessarily the worst finale to a forced march through Nordstrom's. She smiled to herself, and then made an effort and pulled her wayward imagination back to the subject at hand. Most of what was left of the Slope income had financed Emaa's potlatch. The rest was in the one-pound Darigold butter can on the table in front of her.

Kate still wasn't sure if her grandmother had had legal title to the Niniltna house on the river, but whether she did or not Martha Barnes and her children lived there now, and possession was nine-tenths of the law. She decided the IRS didn't need to know about that, either.

Ekaterina's possessions had been distributed among family and friends at the potlatch. So far as Kate knew, Ekaterina had never had a bank account. For that matter, Kate didn't think her grandmother had ever applied for a Social Security number. She'd never had to pay for much; no family member or friend ever came to her house not bearing gifts. Kate had found seven hundred dollars in small bills and change in the butter can the twin of Kate's sitting on Emaa's kitchen table, a moose hindquarter hanging out back, a chest freezer stuffed with salmon in the round, ptarmigan breasts frozen a dozen per Ziploc bag and enough caribou to keep the entire village in stew for a week in the upright freezer next to it. The pantry had yielded up ten cases of salmon, plain and smoked and kippered, case lots of canned goods and pilot bread, a case of homemade nagoonberry jelly, another of strawberry jam, a fifty-pound sack of potatoes, a fifty-pound sack of onions and two fifty-pound sacks of flour. In the closet hung flowered housedresses, worn Levi's and half a dozen kuspuks, richly embroidered and trimmed with fur, all gifts from loving and/or grateful family, friends, tribal members and shareholders. Money and food both had gone to the potlatch, the kuspuks to female relatives of the right size, and now Kate was wondering if she'd inherited all of it and if she had, if she was supposed to pay taxes on it.

She decided the IRS would never know.

Farm income, now. Would that mean the potatoes Mandy grew and sacked and traded with Kate for salmon to feed Mandy's dogs? Or would that be farm income for Mandy and barter income for her? But it wasn't income if it was an even trade, was it? Kate consulted the booklet. Bartering income was defined as "fair market value of goods or services you received in return for your services."

What the hell was that supposed to mean? Salmon weren't services. Potatoes weren't services, either. They were probably goods, though. How much did potatoes cost nowadays? She had no idea. She never bought potatoes, she either grew them herself or traded with Mandy for them. She wondered if there was some way the IRS could find out about that. She wondered how Mandy had filled out her IRS form, if she had included Kate's salmon as income from barter.

The vision of the federal prison in Illinois faded, to be replaced by one of a chain gang in Mississippi, bossed by Strother Martin.

She made herself another cup of tea and dosed it liberally with the last of the honey. She sat back down at the table and drew a pad and pencil to her and started making out a grocery list, paperwork that was more her speed, but then Kate had always had a tendency to think with her stomach. Coffee, flour, butter, salt, seasonings, milk, canned goods, she was out of everything.

Breakup. If she could just go to sleep at the end of February and wake up on Memorial Day, the truck running and the cupboards full—and taxes filed—life would be so much easier.

She dawdled over the list until the sun had gone down and it was time to light the lamps. She drew out the task as long as she could, checking the fuel, trimming the wicks, polishing the chimneys until they shone like crystal. When she was finished, the interior of the cabin was filled with a warm and welcoming golden glow. She stood admiring it for a while, and her thoughts wandered to her next-door neighbor. She wondered if Mandy's parents had arrived on schedule. She wondered if Mr. and Mrs. Baker had tax problems. Probably not. They probably had a fleet of tax attorneys on retainer. Them that has, gets.

The distant whine of a jet engine broke the silence. Probably an F-14 on maneuvers from Elmendorf or Eielson. Even on a remote site in the Alaskan bush, you couldn't get away from the sonuvabitchin' feds. The reminder drove her back to the kitchen table, before they parachuted an IRS auditor down into her front yard.

She had just resumed her seat when Mutt, dozing next to the stove, woke up with a snort and lunged to her feet.

Startled, Kate said, "What's wrong, girl? What's going on?"

Mutt made a troubled sound halfway between a growl and a whimper. Her rangy body tense, she stood with her head cocked, ears up, yellow eyes narrowed, attention fixed on something Kate could neither hear nor see.

Kate didn't like it, not one little bit. Very carefully, she put her pencil down and rose to her feet. "What's wrong, girl?"

A second half-growl, half-whine was her only answer. It was a sound unlike anything else Kate had ever heard from Mutt, and a prickle of unease rippled up her spine. She walked to the window. Through it, the yard looked much as she had left it, a half-circle of buildings surrounding a clearing with a small, filthy red-and-white truck with a homemade toolbox in the back, a snow machine, a collapsed cache and a scattered woodpile, all well illuminated in that maddening half-light of an Arctic spring evening when the sun was down but not out. A breeze toyed with the tops of the trees, and far above cumulus clouds scudded across the sky, attesting to much stronger winds at the higher elevations.

"What is it, girl?" Kate said softly. "What do you hear? Did that baby grizz come back for more of what he got this afternoon?" She reached for the shotgun and eased the door open. This time she would just shoot the little bastard.

But for now, no bears, no bogeymen, not even any porcupines. Mutt came to stand next to Kate in the doorway. Against her knee, Kate could feel her quivering with unease. She knotted her fingers in the stiff gray ruff and gave it a reassuring tug. "What's wrong, girl?"

Mutt was looking up. Kate looked from her anxious yellow eyes to the sky. The hum of the jet engine was still there, although it sounded odd, a kind of increasing whine. "There's nothing out here, girl," she told Mutt. "Just your imagination working overtime."

Still, she took a long last look around before pulling the door shut, and she didn't rack the rifle, standing it instead against the doorjamb.

She was just turning back to the kitchen table when she became aware of an increasingly loud whistling sound, and then it hit.

It was a thump to end all thumps, a tremendous CRUNCH! of earth and metal. The ground shook beneath the impact, violently enough to knock Kate off her feet.

"Earthquake!" she shouted on the way down. She twisted to land on all fours and headed for the space under the table, knocking a chair out of the way and snaking out an arm to grab Mutt.

Both windows facing the yard shattered and several somethings whizzed over her head and kaCHUNKed into the opposite wall. Books fell to the table and from there to the floor, scattering tax papers everywhere. Mutt, squealing like a frightened puppy, tore free of Kate's grasp and fled across the floor to dive beneath the couch. Since the bottom of the couch was only six inches off the floor and Mutt stood three feet at the shoulder, this was no mean feat.

A split second later there was another CRUNCH! and a piece of the cabin's roof fell in and onto the couch. Another distressed squeal and Mutt shot out, streaked across the room and straight up the ladder to the loft, her paws barely touching the rungs.

The couch fell in.

Well. Not all of it.

Just the section where Kate usually sat to read. The spot where she'd worn a Kate-shaped groove into the stuffing over the years. The spot where she'd fallen in sequential love with Wilfred Wetherall and Lazarus Long and Jamie Fraser.

She looked up.

The roof had fallen in, too.

Well. Not all of it.

Ears ringing, sense of balance iffy, Kate stumbled to her feet and put out a hand to grasp at nothing. "What the hell was that?" Her voice sounded distant and tinny. Nobody answered her. She blinked at the opposite wall, at what had impacted there. It seemed like a long thin piece of gray metal, several of them.

She shook her head, bemused, and made her way across the floor, knees wobbling as if she'd just gotten off a boat after six weeks at sea. The hole in the roof was jagged around the edges. She peered inside the matching hole in the couch below, to find a piece of oily gray metal, all knobs and nuts and bolts and flanges, resting squarely, even neatly inside the Olympia beer box where she stored those cassette tapes she couldn't find room for on her shelves. There wasn't much left of them but plastic splinters and snarled brown tape.

"What the hell?" she said, even more blankly than before. She staggered to the door and wrenched it open, only to find herself nose to rivet with another shard of the metal, quivering with the motion of the opening door. "What the *hell?*"

It was a strip of gray metal nearly identical to the ones in the far wall, driven solidly into the wood of the door. She ducked gingerly beneath it, put one foot outside and froze.

Her truck was gone.

Well. That wasn't exactly true.

It was there, all right, or what was left of it. About all she could recognize were the four tires, evidently still attached to the axles, although all four of them were canted over, and all were ruptured and flat. The doors had burst open and were lying on the ground at odd angles. She couldn't even see the toolbox or the bed.

Because lying squarely on top of it was a jet engine.

Impossible.

Kate blinked and looked again.

It was a jet engine, all right. An enormous jet engine, or what was left of one.

Her mind fought a battle between denial and acceptance. She'd just managed to grasp the fact of the engine's existence when a second observation managed to insert itself into the turmoil of her thoughts.

It was a very large jet engine.

It must have come off a very large jet.

Now there was a comforting thought. She raised her head to look warily up into the darkening sky. If the rest of the plane was coming down she would see it before she heard it, because her ears were still ringing.

Long moments passed. No plane fell on her.

She let herself relax some, not much, just enough to unlock her knees and approach the wreckage, almost hopefully, as if closer examination might make it all go away.

No such luck. The engine wasn't round anymore, it wasn't even egg-shaped, it was a scrap heap of aluminum and steel or whatever they made jet engines out of nowadays. She craned her neck up over the lip of the thing and peered inside. Well over half of the turbine blades seemed to be missing.

The shard of metal in her front door was one of them. So, she discovered as she stumbled numbly around the semicircle of buildings, were the shards of metal embedded in the bookshelves on the far wall of the cabin, in the outhouse door and inside the garage on the wall from which her tools hung (one of which had neatly severed the power cord to the hand drill), piercing the side of the snow machine, from which a trickle of gas ran to mingle with the slush beneath, and the roof of the cabin and in various tree trunks around the clearing.

Kate emerged from the garage and faltered to a halt, drawing in a shaken breath. The acrid smell of diesel fuel filled the air, from either the airplane engine or Ichiban or both. Or, no, of course not, jet engines ran on jet fuel. The diesel smell must be from the truck. In some detached portion of her mind, she was thankful there was no fire.

She looked up to see stars twinkling in the sky. The breeze ruffled the tops of the trees. A torn wisp of cloud slid to one side to reveal the moon, almost full, silver rays shining down, all the better to illuminate the complete shambles of Kate's yard. Her ears were still ringing with the sound of metal crashing into the earth, and she became aware that, yet again, her knees were trembling.

"*Breakup*," she said, with loathing.

3

The sun came up at 4:57 a.m. the next morning, or it would have if the sky hadn't been overcast.

By 4:58 a.m., the homestead was crawling with people.

Kate had progressed from speechless shock to speechless rage.

Mutt was still up in the loft, under the bed.

"Jesus, what a mess." A man of medium height, clad in jeans and a jacket with National Transportation Safety Board insignia on it stared around the clearing, at the turbine blades embedded in garage, greenhouse, cabin, outhouse and trees, at the hole in the cabin roof, at the flattened truck still obscured by the engine, at the severed and shattered tools in the garage, at the pierced gas tank on the snow machine, at the collapsed cache.

"I've seen worse, though." He saw Kate's expression. "No, really. Happens more often than you might think, a lot more often than the airlines like to admit. Big chunks of frozen sewage, access panels, doors and hatches, cowling, cones, turbine blades, they've all fallen off a plane at one time or another. It's kind of like a car losing a hubcap or a muffler."

Kate said nothing.

"Although," he said with a rueful smile, "generally speaking mufflers don't have time to accelerate at thirty-two feet per second per second." He paused expectantly, but something in her eyes must have told him not to explain that this was the acceleration of gravity, so he contented himself with adding, "Must have been one hell of a bang."

Kate said nothing. The line of her jaw was very tight.

He pursed his lips in a judicious expression. "You're lucky."

She looked at him.

"Yeah, believe it or not, you are. Outside, there are so many planes in the air at any given moment that it's next to impossible to track down the offending aircraft. In Alaska it's easier. Last night, there was only one 747 in the right place at the right time." He shrugged. "Easy to identify, and easier for you to demand restitution. By the way, the plane made it back to Fairbanks safely. Nobody hurt."

"You," Kate said, very carefully, "have obviously mistaken me for someone who gives a shit."

The speechlessness was beginning to wear off.

The NTSB man raised a quizzical eyebrow. "I'm sure you'll be reimbursed for damages."

"You bet your ass I will."

He offered his hand. She didn't take it. "I'm John Stewman, National Transportation Safety Board. I'm the head of the go team." When she didn't ask, he explained. "That's what we call our response-to-crash teams, Ms. . . . er," and he smiled, revealing deep dimples and a slight gap between his two front teeth. His eyes were brown and crinkled at the corners. Dark hair fell untidily over his forehead, increasing the resemblance to Tom Sawyer.

Alarmed and annoyed at this sudden awareness, she snapped,

"Shugak." It was nothing more than a biological response to a nearly fatal experience, she told herself sternly. Ask any soldier left standing after a battle. Ask any pilot who walked away from a crash. Between the bear encounters and the jet engine, she was feeling a little rough around the edges, that was all. It would fade.

"Shuyak?" Stewman repeated in a louder voice, and she started and swore to herself. "Like the island?"

"S-H-U-G-A-K, Shugak, Kate." Besides, Stewman wasn't all that attractive, he just thought he was. "Make sure you spell the name right on the check."

The NTSB would not be writing her a check, Earlybird Air Freight would, maybe, but "S-H-U-G-A-K," he repeated, imperturbable, writing it down on the top of a form, "Kate. You live here alone?"

"No." She didn't elaborate.

His gaze lingered for a moment on the scar on her throat. "You married?"

"No."

"Children?"

"What are you, the census taker? No."

He sighed. "Ms. Shugak, we need to know who else lives here, so we can—"

She looked behind him and the taut lines of her face eased. "I've got a roommate."

He pivoted.

Mutt stood in the open door of the cabin, a distrustful expression on her face. The man extracting the turbine blade from the snow machine caught sight of her and stood straight up. "John," he said.

The man next to Kate said, "Yes, Brandon."

"Um, there's a wolf? Over there?" He pointed at Mutt, who regarded his pointing finger for a moment and then slowly, deliberately and thoroughly licked her chops.

Stewman looked at Kate for confirmation. "Is it? A wolf?"

He didn't look more than wary at the prospect, and Kate, damn his eyes, liked him for it. She gave a casual shrug and Jack Morgan's standard answer to that comment. "Nah. Only half."

This time the smile did more than crinkle his eyes. "Only half, Brandon," he said.

Brandon, a gaunt, pinch-faced albino blond, was not noticeably reassured.

"Mutt," Kate said. Mutt looked over at her but made no move. "Come on, girl. It's all right."

Mutt had her doubts about that. She took a long, careful look around the clearing. The half dozen men and women in it slowed their work to a halt, equally wary expressions on their faces. Brandon's nervousness was catching. "Come on, girl," Kate repeated. "It's okay now. Come on, come here." She patted her leg.

Mutt could face down a bull moose in rut, a brown bear waking up cranky from his winter nap, a mass murderer armed with a shotgun. The engine off a 747 falling from the sky was beyond her ken, and it was taking her a while to adapt. Her speculative gaze fell on a woman in an FAA jacket standing next to what had been Kate's truck. The woman took an involuntary step backward. Satisfied that, jet engine or not, she hadn't lost her touch, Mutt strolled over to stand next to Kate. She looked up and cocked an ear, as if to say, What's all the fuss?

Kate caught Stewman's eye. He was grinning, and she almost laughed but caught it in time. There was no point in giving an inch until the check cleared the bank.

"John!" somebody yelled. "Come here, will you?"

"In a minute, Tim," he yelled back, and looked from Kate to Mutt and back again. "This your roomie?" She nodded. "And will she be filing a claim as well?"

Kate showed her teeth. "I'll be filing one for her."

He grinned again. Kate thought of the fence and the whitewash and resisted the charm in that smile.

"Introduce us," Stewman said.

"Huh?"

"Introduce us, so she doesn't take a bite out of me the next time I make a move in your direction."

Kate wasn't altogether sure that that was such a good idea, but she said, "Make a fist, hold your hand out, palm down."

He did so without hesitation. Mutt sniffed at it, sneezed once and looked up at Kate for approval, her plume of a tail waving back and forth in a gentle arc. Kate scratched behind her ears.

"That it?" the NTSB investigator asked.

"That's it."

He retrieved his hand and closed the notebook. "Look, Kate, I know this is tough, but we'll be out of your hair before you know it. We're really very good at putting the pieces back together."

"How long before you clear all this crap out of here?"

"One day, maybe two."

"How long before I'm reimbursed?"

"You'll have to take that up with the Earlybird representative."

"Which one is he?"

He pointed at a skinny man with a thin, harried face standing on the other side of the wreckage. "The name's Kevin Bickford. He's Earlybird's director of operations for the state."

"Thanks," Kate said, and walked around the wreckage to tap Bickford on the shoulder. He turned and stared at her uncomprehendingly.

"Kate Shugak, Mr. Bickford." He looked blank, and she added pointedly, "This is my homestead your jet engine just trashed."

He cringed inside his oversize parka, reminding her of nothing so much as a parky squirrel diving down the nearest hole. He even looked a little like a parky squirrel, with small, bright eyes set close on either side of an insignificant little nose that didn't look as if it could suck in enough oxygen to keep a gnat alive. His teeth, bared in a failed attempt at an ingratiating smile, were little and white, with the exception of the front two, which were big and buck. "Mr. Bickford, as far as I'm concerned, this could not have happened at a worse time. I need my truck. When will I be reimbursed for the damage done by your engine?"

He couldn't hide his look of surprise, and Kate wondered sourly if he thought broken gutturals would have been more appropriate to her brown skin, black braids and Bush lifestyle.

Bickford cleared his throat nervously. Kate raised her brows and waited. His gaze fell on the scar at her throat and widened. "Holy—"

"About restitution, Mr. Bickford," Kate said.

He flushed and his eyes slid past her guiltily. "Well, Ms. Sha-geluk—"

"Shugak," she said, patiently for her. "SHOO-gack."

"Of course." His smile was weak. It matched his chin. "Well, Ms. Shungnak." Close, but no cigar. Kate left it for another day. "I don't rightly know when you can expect restitution. We have to assess the damage first, of course. Get an estimate on the replacement value of your truck, that sort of thing."

"Including delivery here," she said.

"Of course, of course," he said hurriedly.

"And not forgetting the collateral damage done to the tools in the garage."

"No," he said obediently.

"Or the interior of my cabin, and the contents therein, not to mention the roof."

"Certainly not."

What the hell. "And the meat cache."

He took it without a blink. "Of course."

"Fine," she said. "I'll start a list. One more thing."

Relieved that it was only one more thing, he said almost eagerly, "Yes?"

"I don't want a check."

He blinked. "No check?"

"No. Cash. Nothing bigger than a hundred, please. Fifties if you can manage it." Cash because the nearest bank was Ahtna, and fifties because it was next to impossible to get change for a hundred in the Bush during breakup anywhere except maybe the Roadhouse. Everybody was broke, even Bernie, who let customers drink on tab until they made their first set of the year.

She saw no need to explain herself to Bickford, who looked a little dazed by the request, but such was the force of her personality that he found himself mumbling agreement.

The go team went about its business, locating, identifying and cataloging the various pieces off the engine around the clearing and marking their location on a map they had drawn of the site five minutes after they had arrived. Other than requesting, very politely, that she touch nothing, they hadn't bothered Kate much. Except for the photographer, whose flash had to be about ready to wear out. Kate would be seeing spots for the rest of the week.

She left Mutt to supervise the debris collection process from a post next to the woodpile and went back to her cabin. The interior looked as if the second chinook of the year had passed directly through it, books and canned goods and cassette tapes alternating with glass shards and wood splinters all over the floor. She couldn't even put on any music to drown out the sounds of the people outside because one of the turbine blades had skewered the cassette deck, an electronic shish kebab. Not that there was anything to play after the piece off the engine squashed most of her tapes.

A can of stewed tomatoes looked like breakfast, and she dumped it into a bowl and ate to the accompaniment of a low hum of conversation and an occasional clang of metal from the yard. She did her best to ignore both, but as she was scraping the bottom of the bowl, rain began to patter on the roof, and through the hole onto the couch and the box of crushed tapes beneath it. She heaved a sigh, went out to the garage, located the ladder among the wreckage and set it up against the eaves of the cabin.

The hole was about a foot and a half in diameter. The good news was that it appeared to have missed all the rafters. Kate went back to the garage, started the generator, plugged in the power saw, mercifully intact, and cut a piece of plywood to fit the outside and a piece of Sheetrock to fit the inside and scrounged up enough pink insulation to stuff in between. Caulking, tar paper and shingles followed. A quantity of Spackle later and the job was done, except for painting. Kate had a dreary suspicion that she'd have to paint the entire inside of the roof to make it match, but that was for tomorrow, when the Spackle had dried.

O joy, o rapture, it was time for lunch. A can of refried beans heated up and seasoned with garlic powder and oregano was better than cold stewed tomatoes. She cleaned up the kitchen, tossing the ventilated canned goods and restoring the rest to the shelves above and below the counter, adding as she did so to the grocery list, which was beginning to resemble the provisional logistics for D-Day.

After that it was time to start a list of everything Earlybird was going to replace whether they wanted to or not. She started with the tape deck and the box of tapes beneath the couch. The list was over fifty titles before she was done.

She moved on to the books, where the news was even worse. The copy of *The Wind in the Willows* with the wonderful Michael Hague illustrations had been pierced through the center, stabbed to the heart, a fatal wound. Next to it, Louise Erdrich's *Tracks* had the cover peeled back like an onion. "Goddammit," she said, and started another list.

Halfway down it came the sound of raised voices from the yard. They got louder. She marched over to the door and yanked it open, ready to kick ass.

The go team were clustered in a group in the center of the clearing, around two of their own, a man and a woman. Stewman, his back to the cabin, heard the door open and turned.

She glared at him. "What's with all the noise?"

He glanced back at the group. "We've, ah, we've run into a little, uh, well, I guess you could call it a snag." He tried to smile but it didn't take.

The woman, a slender redhead with freckles, looked as if she was going to throw up. The man next to her, the albino blond, looked terrified. Kate took a step forward. "What's going on?"

Stewman glanced back around the circle, and back at Kate. "We, uh, well, we found a body."

Kate stared at him. "I beg your pardon?"

He shoved back his cap to scratch his head, and resettled it firmly. "There's usually a pattern to the way debris scatters in an incident like this one. I sent Selina and Brandon"— he indicated the terrified man and the nauseous woman —"out to canvass." He paused. "They found a body instead."

"They found a *what?*"

"A dead body," John Stewman said for the third time. He had regained his composure and he was patient and apologetic but firm. "The body of a dead man." He glanced back at Selina and Brandon. "I gather it's not in the best of shape."

Kate stared at him. He wasn't joking. She sat down heavily upon the doorstep. Mutt, concerned, deserted her post near the woodpile and trotted forward to nose at her cheek. Kate put an arm around her neck and rested her forehead against the thick gray fur. "You're not kidding, are you," she said into Mutt's ruff.

"No."

"Why me?" Kate said.

"If not you, who?" Stewman said brightly. "If not now, when?" She raised her head to look at him. Just look. He sobered. "Sorry."

"Where?" she said, mostly just to be saying something. Ex–DA's investigator on automatic.

Stewman pulled off his cap again and smoothed back his shaggy mane of hair, a nervous habit. "About three miles that way." He pointed roughly southwest, away from the Yukon Territory and toward Valdez.

The Earlybird man said apprehensively, "How did he die? Did you see any parts off the engine nearby?"

Stewman raised an eyebrow and said sardonically, "Don't worry, Bickford, this guy's been there longer than last night."

Brandon shuddered his agreement. Selina made a stifled sound and clapped her hand over her mouth. She staggered off a few steps and lost her lunch on the ground right next to the snow machine.

"Did you send for the trooper?" Kate said.

Stewman held up a two-way radio. "We called it in on Channel 9. Talked to somebody in Niniltna, a ham operator—"

"Bobby Clark."

He nodded. "That's the guy. He said he'd call the trooper in Tok."

"Good," Kate said without enthusiasm. Just what she needed, on today of all days, a smartass trooper with the mating instincts of a tomcat and the come-on repertoire of Casanova. A thought occurred. "You said three miles? That way?" She pointed.

"More or less. Selina and Brandon said it was pretty rough going. My guess is it's closer rather than farther away."

What with one thing and another, it had been a very long twenty-four hours, even for breakup. Not one but two close encounters of the ursine kind, a jet engine falling out of the sky to smash flat her primary means of summer transportation, a hole in the roof and, oh yes, let us not forget, income tax.

And now, on top of everything else, a body. "You know what?" Kate said brightly. "If you found the body three miles that way, it isn't on my homestead, so it's not my problem." She got to her feet and dusted her hands. "It's not my problem," she repeated firmly, willing herself to believe it. "You can leave, and you can take your pieces of engine and your bodies and your go team with you." She looked at Bickford. "Now."

Stewman had the audacity to laugh out loud. "Is this what they call the bum's rush?"

"Off," she said to Bickford, pointing in the general direction of Seattle.

Bickford had donned a too-big gimme cap whose brim came down to the end of his nose. It had a patch with a red-and-white jet on a robin's egg blue background and a border reading "Around the Clock, Around the World." The name Earlybird Air Freight was inscribed on the bill. He snatched the cap off to wring it between his hands. "I'm sorry, Ms. Shungnak," he said, searching desperately for understanding, forgiveness and even a trace of fellow feeling in Kate's stony expression, "but I'm afraid it'll be a while before we get the equipment in here to do that." He nodded at Kate's squashed truck and the engine on top of it. "Sucker weighs more than four tons."

Four tons? Eight thousand pounds? A shiver ran down Kate's spine as she realized again just how close the world had come to losing her. For some reason it made her even angrier and she rallied, her chin coming up and taking aim. "I don't give a shit about any problems you might have, Bickford. You're in the air freight business. Find a Herc or a helicopter and fly it out, or mush it out on a dogsled, or haul it out on a horse-drawn cart." Her voice rose. "I don't give a good goddam how you do it. I want you people off my land. You got that?" She rose to her feet. "You're trespassing. I want you off my land." She fumbled behind her for the door handle.

"Ms. Shungnak, please, be reasonable. We can't—"

"Git!" she said. "Don't even fly over here anymore!" As she turned to go back inside the cabin, Mutt spoiled her grand exit with an anxious whine. "What!" Kate said furiously. "What now!"

Mutt had her ears cocked, and she was looking east. At least this time it couldn't be a jet engine falling off; jet engines didn't fall horizontally. It was something, though, because, now that Kate had stopped yelling they could all hear an approaching sound like a herd of elephants crashing through the underbrush. A second later and the herd of elephants smashed through into the clearing and resolved itself into a bull moose, young, his antlers mere beginning spikes.

This barely had time to register, as he was moving like he was up against Secretariat in the Kentucky Derby, a flat-out, no-holds-barred, down-the-straightaway gallop. He pounded through the clearing and people leapt out of the way and into trees, with the sole exception of the Earlybird man, who appeared to possess no self-protective instincts whatsoever. The moose ran right over the top of him and charged out the other side of the clearing, crashing through the underbrush with a fine disregard for the scenery.

Kate put one foot out to see if Bickford was all right—she didn't want him damaged before she had the cash in hand—and in the next instant drew it back smartly. The race was not limited to a single contestant. No indeed, hard on the heels of the bull moose was a grizzly bear, the same cache-robbing youngster Kate had run off the day before. She opened her mouth to shout a warning but there was no need, g-men diving for cover for the second time in as many minutes. She reached for the rifle over the door, but there was no need for that, either, as she had just enough time to see the harried expression on his face before the bear ran straight across the clearing and on through the brush, taking the trail the moose had broken for him.

Three bear encounters in two days was almost enemy action, and Kate was inclined to be indignant. So was Mutt, who took off in pursuit, barking excitedly.

"Mutt!" Kate yelled.

Mutt skidded to a halt, and was giving Kate a reproachful look as the bear's backside disappeared, when the sound of gas engines going flat out approached, again from the east.

"What the fuck's going on?" somebody yelled.

"Dive, dive!" somebody else yelled, and they did, everyone who had just picked themselves out of the mud and the slush dove for cover yet again, with the exception, of course, of the Earlybird man, who gazed about him with a bewildered air. The stranger in a strange land.

Two four-wheelers, driven by two big men in black-and-red-checked mackinaws and deerstalker caps, burst into the clearing. Mutt, balked from bear chasing, took off after the four-wheelers instead, barking with enthusiasm and adding to the general uproar.

One of the four-wheeler drivers had a rifle in his right hand with the sling wrapped around his forearm and a bottle in his left. "Whoopee!" he shouted.

"Powder River, let 'er buck!" yelled his friend.

They roared in a circle around the Earlybird man, frozen in the center of the clearing, only to finish up, after Whoopee clipped a section of the jet engine and swerved, with a grand front-end finale, hard enough to catapult both drivers from their seats. They met head to head with a Crack! that could be heard all across the clearing. One of the four-wheelers managed to climb over its sister ship, turn hard right rudder and run straight into Kate's garage, impacting, in order, Kate's old-fashioned but until then still-working wringer washing machine, the trickle charger and the far wall with enough force to send all the remaining tools on the wall crashing to the floor. The washer, dancing frantically around on one caster, lost the battle for balance to gravity and tipped over, landing on its barrel side. For not having achieved thirty-two feet per second per second, it made a splendid crash.

Kevin Bickford stood where he was, white face streaked with mud and oversize parka stained with slush, looking as if he couldn't believe he was still alive and in one piece. Kate didn't blame him, but she had other things on her mind, like murder.

She started forward and a third four-wheeler leapt out of the brush, this one driven by Dan O'Brian. Skidding to a stop in the center of the clearing, he killed the engine and was one step ahead of Kate to the four-wheeler drivers, who were sitting up and beginning to take hilarious notice of their surroundings. Whoopee had lost his bottle, so Powder River hoisted himself up and fished a silver flask from a hip pocket. Whoopee greeted this with a loud cheer and a wet, noisy kiss on Powder River's cheek.

They had just enough time for a gulp apiece before Dan fastened a hand in each collar and jerked them to their feet, causing them to spray whiskey all over the Earlybird man, for whom Kate, against her will, was beginning to feel a little sorry.

"GOTCHA," Dan roared, "you drunk-driving, wildlife-poaching, great-white-hunter-wannabe sonsaBITCHES!"

He slung Whoopee down ungently at the base of a tree and fastened his wrists together with a plastic restraint. Powder River received the same treatment. They recovered enough to protest.

"SHADDUP!" Dan roared again.

They shaddup.

Dan, quivering with outrage, smoothed a trembling hand over the red hair standing straight up all over his head and turned a wrathful gaze on Kate to say one infuriated word.

"Breakup."

4

At that moment the sound of another engine was heard, and with a single bound Mutt gained the center of the clearing, where she stood barking up at the sky, tail wagging furiously. Kate didn't look. She, too, knew the sound of that engine.

Sure enough, over the tops of the trees came a Bell Jet Ranger, a small helicopter with the insignia of the Alaska Department of Public Safety emblazoned on the doors. It set down a little to one side of the center of the clearing, rotors only just missing the top of the wrecked engine and the eaves of Kate's garage, cabin, greenhouse and outhouse. It would have taken a chunk out of the cache's roof had the cache still been standing, but it wasn't, and if Kate had been in a fair mood, she would have admired the artistry of the landing.

She wasn't. She didn't.

Seconds later the trooper emerged in all his blue-and-gold glory. He conferred first with Dan, then with Stewman, then with Brandon and Selina, while Kate watched from her front doorstep, scowling and keeping her distance. Wasn't her land. Wasn't her body. Weren't her hunters. She didn't want anything to do with any of it, and she was prepared to tell Jim Chopin so, at length, but she never got the chance, because he loaded Selina into the chopper and took off.

Well. It was obvious that her help was neither wanted nor needed. Fine. She stamped inside and made a fresh pot of hot water, just in time to pour out for Dan O'Brian, who had calmed down enough to stare into his mug and say incredulously, "Since when do you drink tea?"

"Since I ran out of coffee and a jet engine fell on the only transportation I've got to get me to the store for supplies."

He caught the ferocity behind the misleadingly mild words, and said hastily, "Hey, I live for tea. Serve it up. Got any sugar?" It was immediately obvious that that was the wrong thing to say too, so he fell back on something he knew for certain she would agree with. "I hate this time of year."

"I heard that," Kate said, with feeling.

He nodded at the wreckage in the yard. "Looks like Chicken Little was right."

"Looks like."

"Jim says they found a body."

"That's the rumor," Kate said, studying the swirling liquid in her mug with absorption.

He grinned. "Amazing how you don't have to go looking for work, Shugak, how it comes looking for you."

"I wasn't looking," she stated. "I'm not looking. It's breakup, for crissake, I've got nineteen different things to do without taking on trying to figure out why some doofus wound up dead wandering around the back of beyond."

His grin faded. "I thought he got brained by a piece off that engine."

"I don't know," Kate said stubbornly, stifling the memory of Stewman saying, *This guy's been there longer than last night.* "I don't know anything about it. I don't want to know anything about it. All I know is the engine missed me."

He got up to look out the window, measuring the distance between the engine and her front door. "Barely."

She was tired of the subject, or so she told herself, and nodded through the cabin's open door at the two men sitting at the base of the tree. They had stopped shouting obscenities with the arrival of the trooper. Now they were silent and glum. "What's with Rocky and Rambo?"

"Couple of Arco engineers from Anchorage." Dan turned to raise an eyebrow in her direction. "On a hunting trip," he added blandly.

"In a manner of speaking," Kate agreed dryly. "How'd you get onto them so fast?"

It was a legitimate question. The Park comprised twenty million acres and the year-round ranger staff was so small that most of the time irresponsible hunters did their damage and were long gone by the time Dan caught up with them.

"You'll like this." He drank tea, repressing a shudder. "They flew into Niniltna in a Cessna 180, loaded—you should pardon the expression—for bear. They got a ride to the Roadhouse last night and started asking around for the best place to go hunting."

Kate laughed. She couldn't help it.

Dan grinned. "Yeah, I know. Like anybody at the Roadhouse would steer them toward a bear they'd already marked out for themselves. So somebody told them Fish and Game hasn't issued permits for a bear hunt in ten years, the grizz population in the Park being down to what it is and all."

Kate was of the newly formed opinion that the Park's grizzly population was in definite need of a brisk culling, but the Park's chief ranger was highly unlikely to enter into her feelings on the subject. "I guess they didn't take the warning to heart, did they?"

"Nope." Dan shook his head. "First they got drunk, and then they got a couple of four-wheelers—"

"Where from?"

Dan looked at her out of the corner of his eye and said, "Bought them off Dandy Mike. Cash on the barrelhead. Twice what they were worth."

"Ouch." Like all Park rats open to opportunity, Kate prudently refrained from asking him if the four-wheelers had belonged to Dandy in the first place, and, like a good friend, Dan avoided burdening her with that information. "Anyway, Dandy counted the cash, twice, made a few suggestions as to where they might look for bear, and as soon as they were out of sight he called me. I flew down and borrowed Billy Mike's four-wheeler, and here I am."

Kate sat up straight. "Dandy sent them up here?" Dan grinned again, an answer in itself. "That son of a bitch!"

"Now, Kate," Dan said soothingly. "To be fair, I'd rather they tangle with you than anyone else in the Park, and Dandy knows it. Hell, they all do."

Kate looked around at the shambles of her homestead, and her burst of anger died away. "I don't feel all that formidable today, Dan."

The ranger raised his mug in salute. "A temporary setback, Shugak. You'll have all this up and running again in no time, I guarantee it. These go teams move fast, from what I hear."

They watched the NTSB work in silence for a moment. "So if he didn't get brained by a piece off your engine—"

"It's not my engine."

"—what was he doing out here anyway? Hunting bear, do you think? That's the only thing worth hunting this time of year."

"Don't know how long he has been there," Kate said, and shrugged. Okay, she'd play. "If he really has been out there over the winter, he could have gotten lost hunting, got hurt. Happens all the time."

"Maybe a bear ate him," Dan suggested.

Kate thought of Mama Bear coming at her flat out across the creek the morning before. Maybe the sow's eagerness and speed hadn't entirely been due to her protective instincts, but to the sight of what she had already found to be an easy snack. Ursine finger food. Kate repressed a shiver. "Maybe. Although it's not like a hungry bear to leave enough to show whether a body is male or female, and Stewman was definite that it was a man." She shrugged again.

"Aren't you even curious?" Dan was joking when he added, "What kind of sleuth are you anyway, Shugak?"

She wasn't when she snapped out her reply. "A retired one."

Dan looked as if he'd like to argue the point but Chopper Jim's return spared her. The helicopter settled into the clearing in the exact same spot as before, this time with a body bag strapped to one of the skids and a stretcher with a sandbag strapped to the other for ballast. Selina got out the instant the skids touched down and walked away very fast without looking back. Dan went to retrieve Whoopee and Powder River. Jim waved Kate over. She went, reluctantly.

He opened the door as she approached, his earphones around his neck. "What you got?" Kate shouted over the noise of the engine, the rotors whapping at the air over her head.

He grinned at her. "Looking for business, Kate?"

Her expression told him what she thought of that question and he laughed, kind of heartlessly, she thought, given she was standing like Dido in the middle of Carthage after the sack. He nodded at the jet engine. "It seems Chicken Little was right."

"So they tell me." She jerked her chin at the body bag. "What'd he get hit with?"

"What do you mean, what'd he get hit with?"

"Didn't he get clobbered by a piece off that engine?"

"Kate. We found him three miles from here."

"When you drop an airplane engine from thirty thousand feet, I imagine the parts tend to scatter just a tad."

"True, but he didn't get hit with a piece of your engine. He's been there all winter."

Shit, she thought. "Who is he?" she said out loud, adding immediately, "Not that I'm all that interested."

"No ID left on him. For sure he isn't my missing hiker."

It took her a minute. "You mean the guy you were looking for last June? The one up in the Mentastas?"

He nodded.

She almost smiled. "Come on, Jim. The Mentastas are seventy miles north of here. That would have been one hell of a hike."

Jim grinned again, unrepentant. "I hate open cases. And he almost fits the description."

Kate nodded at the body bag. "How long's he been dead?"

"Longer than last night. Long enough for the critters to chow down some on him." He raised an inquiring eyebrow. "Mutt bring home any suspicious-looking femurs lately? He's only got one left, and it looks kind of gnawed on."

"Yuck," said Dan O'Brian, in the process of forcing the Great White Hunters into the back of the chopper. Whoopee started to complain that his butt was wet. The trooper turned his head and gave him a narrow-eyed look that reminded Whoopee that he was soon to be two thousand feet up with one potential witness dead and the other already snoring in a drunken stupor. He shut up.

Kate heard a faint staticky noise and Jim raised one of the earphones to his ear. "Roger that," he said into the microphone. "I'm on my way."

He resettled the headset in place. "Gotta run," he said, raising his voice over the increasing whine of the helicopter's engine. "A Nizina fisherman just shot his father over a Prince William Sound drift permit. Seems he thought it was time for Dad to retire, only Dad disagreed." He adjusted something on the dash and raised his voice over the increasing whine of the engine. "I just *love* breakup, don't you?"

Kate and Dan duckwalked beneath the props to one side of the clearing as the rotors spun into a blur. A tossed salute through the windscreen and Jim was gone.

The sound of the chopper faded into the distance. "Well," Dan said, "time I moved like I had a purpose." He surveyed her trashed yard one more time and cocked an eye at Kate. "You going to be okay?"

"Yeah."

"We got a bunk up on the Step with your name on it, if you need it."

She relaxed enough to smile, and mean it. "Thanks, Dan. I'll keep it in mind."

"Come to that, there's a bed with my name on it you're welcome to, when you've a mind to it." He waggled his eyebrows suggestively.

The attempt to commit lechery was tempered with too much humor to take offense. It always was, but today found her wondering what Dan would do if she took him up on his offer. The thought of his probable reaction made her laugh out loud and she waved him off with a shooing gesture. He mounted Billy Mike's four-wheeler with a swagger, pressed the starter and was off in a roar of sound.

It faded just in time for her to hear a truck grind to a halt at her trailhead, a quarter of a mile through the woods. She heard Dan shout something, and a voice she recognized shout back. All amusement gone, Kate swore out loud.

John Stewman, writing something on his clipboard, looked around. "Like Grand Central Station around here today."

Mutt took off up the trail to investigate, and returned shortly with three people in tow. One was Amanda Winthrop Baker, known to friends as Mandy, to mushing fans as the Brahmin Bullet and to the couple behind her as Amanda dear.

"Amanda dear," the woman said, "do you have to walk quite so fast?"

"Yes," the man said, "your mother isn't used to—what did you call it?—bushwhacking. Try to keep it down to just under a gallop, if you don't mind."

Only a friend who called her Mandy would have noticed the look of quiet desperation that gleamed in her eyes. Only a friend who called her Mandy would not have remarked on it. Kate, a very good friend, bade a mental goodbye to any prospect of peace this day and with true nobility—because she'd been listening to Mandy's stories of her parents for years—stepped once more into the breach, holding out a hand and saying heartily, "Hi, Mandy. And these must be your parents. Nice to meet you, folks, I've heard a lot about you."

She didn't add what she'd heard. With the innate wisdom of all parents everywhere, they didn't ask.

• • •

Mandy's parents huddled as close together as they could get without actually sitting in each other's lap, not because there wasn't room on the one undamaged arm of Kate's couch to spread out, but because they were mesmerized by the unwavering yellow eyes of the 140-pound half-husky, half-wolf lying in the middle of the floor. The expression on their thin-boned, aristocratic East Coast faces was identical, and if each hair of the immaculately groomed, distinguished white caps on both their heads wasn't standing straight up, it was only because their fear of letting down the side exceeded their fear of being ripped to shreds by a wild animal.

Medusa had nothing on Mutt, Kate decided, and declined to reassure the Bakers for the third time that since she had introduced them as friends they had nothing to fear.

Mandy was staring, fascinated, out the kitchen window at the lump of gray metal reposing in the yard. She'd finally noticed the shambles of Kate's homestead, and had been sufficiently jolted from her self-absorption to demand details. "Jesus, Kate. Forty feet north and you'd have been bear bait."

"I am aware of that, Mandy," Kate said testily. She turned to the parents. "Would you like something to drink? Some tea?

Lemon Zinger? Although I haven't managed a spring run for supplies yet, so I'm out of anything to put in it."

"Thank you," Mr. Baker said, still hypnotized by Mutt's eyes.

"That would be lovely," Mrs. Baker said, just as mechanically. Mutt stretched and let out a little whuff of a groan. Mrs. Baker inched closer to her husband. Mutt rolled a yellow eye in Kate's direction. Kate bit her lip and turned to pump up a kettle of water.

Mrs. Baker said, "Amanda dear, we appear to have imposed upon Ms. Shugak at a rather unfortunate time. Perhaps we should just—"

Mandy aimed a broad, insincere smile in the general direction of the couch. "Just a moment, Mother. Kate, take a look at this." Mandy grabbed Kate's arm and crowded her toward the window.

Kate peered through the shards of shattered glass. The go team was going about its business. The jet engine was still there. Her truck was still flattened. She gave up the hopeful notion that Mandy had made it all go away and said, "What?"

Mandy dropped her voice. "My folks want to see the mine. Can you take them?"

Kate stared at her friend as if she'd lost her mind. "What?"

"I told the folks about the copper mining the Astors and the Carnegies did up here around the turn of the century, and they want to take a look."

Kate took a deep, steadying breath. "Then I suggest you take them yourself. For crying out loud, Mandy—"

"Shhh!" Mr. and Mrs. Baker stirred restively. Mutt opened one eye, and they stilled.

"I just had a jet engine flatten my homestead and you want me to take the afternoon off?"

"What is there for you to do until they get all that crap hauled out of here? They're driving Chick nuts, Kate," Mandy whispered.

"Chick," Kate said, spacing her words with precision, "is a grown man."

"Oh, all right, they're driving me nuts, too. Just get them out of my house for a little while, please?"

"How long have they been here?" Kate demanded.

"Thirty-eight hours," Mandy said. She checked her watch. "And forty minutes."

"Not even two days?" In spite of herself, Kate's shoulders shook. "Jesus, Mandy, get a grip." She waved a hand toward the window. "Besides, what used to be my transportation is buried beneath four tons of scrap metal. And it's breakup, I've got a thousand things to do."

"Like what?"

"Like finish my income taxes."

Momentarily diverted, Mandy said, "You left it to the last minute again this year?"

Kate bristled. "You got a problem with that?"

"No, it's just that last year you swore—" At Kate's expression Mandy floundered. "It's just that you're usually such a planner, Shugak, I'd think—" She looked at Kate again and steered the conversation back to where she wanted it in the first place. "You can use my truck to ferry them up to the mine, and drop me off at my trailhead on the way."

Kate's expression did not noticeably soften, and Mandy dropped her voice a persuasive octave. "Look, if you could just show them around the place, tell them some of the good old stories. Shove them off the edge of the glacier. Just kidding," she added quickly when Kate's brows rose. "Ha. Ha ha ha. Seriously, Kate. If you could just get them off our backs for three or four hours, I'd sacrifice a goat in your honor. Please, Kate."

Kate put her hands on her hips and demanded, "Did you hear a word I said?"

Mandy glanced over at her parents and lowered her voice further to a whisper, as if she thought that if she did her parents couldn't hear every word she said in a twenty-five-foot-square cabin. "They actually think I'm going to come home. Can you believe it? It's like they're deaf, Kate! When am I coming home, Amanda dear, Dad says, and I say, I *am* home, Dad. Next fall, perhaps? he says, and I say, I *am* home, Dad. There's this man at home, Amanda dear, Mother says, he's a Cabot and so suitable, and I say, I'm not getting married, Mother, and I'm sure as hell not coming home to get married, and Mother says, He's so charming, Amanda dear, you'll adore him. You'd think I was some kind of witless little deb, fresh from her coming-out party!"

Her voice, having risen over the last words, stopped abruptly as Mandy waged an obvious battle for self-control. Kate looked at her, at the weathered skin that made her look older than Kate, though she was two years younger, at the neatly trimmed cap of thick brown hair, the deeply set gray eyes surrounded by wrinkles that came from years of squinting into an Arctic sun from the back of a dogsled. She was mostly muscle and bone, and she was dressed in a fashion to wring her mother's heart, or much as Kate was, in plaid flannel shirt, jeans and tennis shoes. She didn't look much like a Boston Brahmin debutante, and in fact she wasn't one, but only because she had made her escape the instant she was of legal age.

Mandy had been born in Hyannis, Massachusetts, on Valentine's Day thirty-two years before. The day after her birth her father, a banker who inherited one fortune from a Carnegie forebear and made a second lending overpriced money to Israel and Argentina, put her name down for Vassar, eighteen years hence. That same day her mother, a great-niece of Henry Cabot Lodge, began making plans for her daughter's coming-out party, also eighteen years hence. The interim was taken up with piano and ballroom dance and French lessons, instruction at a private, exclusive girls' school and private, exclusive parties given in private, exclusive homes to which children of only the most private, exclusive families were invited.

Somewhere along the line the Bakers must have slipped up in their indoctrination. No one knew it better than Mandy, who during childhood and adolescence was able to conceal her deplorable preference for L. L. Bean over Halston (who had been dressing Mrs. Baker since her coming out), Robert Service over Robert Lowell (a second cousin once removed) and hiking the Appalachian Trail over sailing off Cape Cod (Mr. Baker maintained a sloop in Newport), but the day she turned twenty-one and came into her trust fund she came out of the closet. "I'm moving to Alaska," she announced at breakfast.

Their maid Carlotta nearly dropped the bowl of muesli she was handing around.

Her father laughed comfortably from behind his paper. "Don't be silly, Amanda dear, you're graduating from Vassar next year."

"I'm moving to Alaska instead," she said, and her mother said, "What do you think of this shade of taffeta for your ball gown, Amanda dear? Too pink?"

"I don't know and I don't care, Mother," Mandy said. "I won't be wearing it. I'll be in Alaska."

"It *is* too pink," her mother decided. "I'll have to ask Roy for more swatches."

"Whatever, Mother, but you'd better get it sized to fit you, because I'll be in Alaska when they strike up the first waltz."

Carlotta, who had been with them since before Mandy was born and who at that point knew her rather better than her parents did, burst into tears, threw her apron over her head and ran from the room. Mandy went upstairs to pack.

They trailed after her all the way to Logan International Airport, she in a Yellow Cab and they in the Bentley, driven by Carlotta's husband, Alfonso (a Bentley because Mrs. Baker said that Rolls-Royces were getting positively common when bourgeois entrepreneurs like Donald Trump drove around in one). They protested her decision in louder and louder voices right up to the time the hatch on the jet shut in their faces.

Mandy changed planes in Seattle and arrived in Anchorage on a cold, snowy day in March. She transferred her trust fund to an account at a local bank, found a real estate agent with a pilot's license and began flying into remote properties in the Bush. It took her two months to find exactly what she wanted. When she did find it, an abandoned lodge on Silver Bottom Creek and 130 acres, she bought it, along with three nearly feral dogs, without haggling. She knew from the real estate agent's face that she'd overpaid. "I don't care," she told Kate. "At least for the first time in my life that damn trust fund is being used for something besides bachelor bait." It took her the whole first summer just to clean up the mess the previous owners had left and take inventory, her first winter included a record snowfall that caved in a corner of the roof, and she learned the hard way how not to attract the attention of hungry grizzlies. But she did survive, which was more than most wannabe frontiersmen could say. And out in the Great Alone, with a silence she almost could hear, she was truly and deeply content for the first time in her life.

The following year, attending the World Championship Sled Dog Races during Anchorage's Fur Rendezvous, she met Chick Noyukpuk, also known as the Billiken Bullet, a two-time world champion dogsled racer and part-time drunk. The attraction was instantaneous and mutual, and she brought him back to the homestead with her. When he'd sobered up he made friends with her huskies, half-wild half-wolf creatures that slunk around the lodge and would approach close enough to snatch food from her hand and no closer. Two were females and came into heat almost immediately, followed by two litters, one of five and the other of seven. Chick had them in traces before they were three months old. He found an old sled in the pile of debris behind the cabin, mended it and hitched up the team. Mandy, skinning her first beaver in the front yard, paused to watch them parade back and forth, the short, stocky man with the black hair and the big grin kicking off behind a tiny forest of dangling tongues and plumed tails. "Hey," she said finally, laying down her knife. "Let me try that."

Eventually she became the fourth woman to win the Iditarod and the third to win the Yukon Quest. They traded off the team, Chick racing the dogs one year, she the next, and the newspapers started calling her the Brahmin Bullet. When they weren't racing they came home and oversaw their breeding and training program, trapped mink and beaver, hunted moose, caribou and black-tailed deer, dip-netted salmon out of the creek and did a little desultory gold panning, more out of the wish to maintain an Alaskan tradition than out of any real desire to strike it rich. It was a good life. She didn't ask for more.

Except, perhaps, Kate thought, to be left alone by her parents, and for perhaps the first time in her life realized that being the only child of deceased parents wasn't necessarily all bad. "Look, Mandy, make Chick give your parents the tour. He's mushed over every inch of the Park, he probably knows it better than I do."

"Kate," Mandy hissed, desperate now, "these are people whose closest approach to a Native American has been a benefit revival of *Nanook of the North* at the Boston Museum of Art. Mother asked Chick if he did rain dances."

"What did Chick say?" Kate couldn't resist asking.

"Only if there was a forest fire that needed putting out. It's not funny, Kate!"

Kate, choking, whispered back, "Mandy, in case you hadn't noticed, I'm an Aleut. What makes you think they'll take to me any better than they did Chick?"

"You haven't had carnal knowledge of their one and only daughter," Mandy said grimly. She brightened at a new thought. "I'll pay you."

"Good," Kate said, surrendering with a sigh to the unconcealed panic in her friend's eyes. "Now we're getting somewhere."

"How much?"

"One million dollars."

"It's yours."

Kate laughed. "Or alternatively, the loan of your truck for a supply run into Ahtna."

"You can have the million," Mandy said earnestly, "just as soon as they die and I inherit."

She didn't add, The sooner the better, but they both thought it. "I'll settle for the loan of the truck," Kate said dryly. "I'll need it anyway if I'm going to ferry your parents around."

"It's yours," Mandy said, holding up both hands flat out. A

done deal. "You can have it. I'll buy another. No problem. My dividends are up this year from last." Obviously afraid Kate would change her mind, Mandy dug in her pocket and handed over the keys forthwith.

Accepting them, Kate wondered if the IRS would call this exchange barter and subject to tax.

5

An hour later, she was wondering if there was any insanity in her family.

To the barely concealed relief of her two guests, Mutt remained behind to keep the fear of God in the go team. Mandy had been dropped off at the top of the trail leading to her lodge, and Kate had driven the twenty-five miles of ice, slush, pothole, washboard and washout to Niniltna in a loquacious babble of information about Alaska in general, the Park in particular, and the Kanuyaq Copper Mine's life and death.

There followed a complete history of the building of the Kanuyaq River and Northwestern Railroad, beginning in 1900 with the probably apocryphal story of two old Ninety-niners prospecting for gold with a couple of hungry pack mules. Casting about for graze, they looked up and saw a green mountain, only to find upon arrival that the mountain was not covered with grass, it was made of copper. They carried the news Outside, and a couple of the robber barons of the time, Carnegie and Mellon, or maybe it was John Jacob Astor, Kate couldn't remember and by this time didn't much care—

"Guggenheim and Morgan," Mr. Baker said.

Startled, Kate looked over at him, and then had to grab the steering wheel with both hands when the right front tire lurched into a pothole and Mandy's brand-new, bright red, four-wheel-drive Ford Ranger XL long-bed Supercab bottomed out. When they regained the horizontal—was the play in the steering wheel just a trifle looser than before?—Mr. Baker said, almost apologetically, "The Guggenheims are cousins."

"Oh."

"Distant cousins," Mrs. Baker added in austere reproof, and Kate wondered how the Guggenheims had managed to offend Mrs. Baker's delicate sensibilities. In the end, she decided that Mrs. Baker's beef probably had more to do with money than sex; maybe the Guggenheims had rooked the Bakers on a deal that rooked the shareholders even more. It had to be one or the other; in Kate's experience, sex and money were the prime motivating factors in every human quarrel. Look at God's fight with Adam and Eve, and that was probably over sex only because money hadn't been invented yet.

Or maybe it was just that she had sex on the brain this spring. She brought herself firmly back into the present and her tour guide duties. Guggenheim and Morgan, then, purchased leases from the federal government, as Alaska was at that time a territory, finished the railroad from Kanuyaq (*kanuyaq* was Aleut for copper) to Cordova by 1911 and ran raw copper ore down it for twenty-seven years. The ore played out at about the same time the price of copper went into the toilet, and it was abandoned in 1938, except by Park rats searching for useful fixtures such as stoves, ice-boxes and toilets, and by the ever heavy hand of time.

Kate's voice, a broken husk of sound to begin with as a result of the scar that nearly bisected her throat, a reminder of her former job in the investigator's office of the Anchorage DA, was just about gone. Mr. and Mrs. Baker had noticed the scar and ignored it, thereby demonstrating how very well they had been brought up. They were a polite and attentive audience, she'd grant them that. Still, the journey seemed interminable. They passed Niniltna without stopping, Kate thinking that Auntie Vi would be good for cocoa and fry bread on the way back and that her passengers would need it then more than they did now. There were only a few homesteads and a few lone cabins on the road between the village and the mine, and the surface had deteriorated conspicuously because of the lack of traffic to pound it into some semblance of shape. Mandy's pickup bounced and jounced from pothole to pothole, so that riding inside the cab was like riding inside a washing machine on the heavy-duty cycle. Mr. and Mrs. Baker attached hands like limpets to the dash and hung on for dear life.

It didn't help when Kate jammed on the brakes and no one was wearing a seat belt.

"What—" Mr. Baker started to say.

There was an audible gasp from Mrs. Baker, and Mr. Baker looked around to see a grizzly explode out of the brush onto the road, catch sight of the big red truck, apply its own brakes by application of hindquarters to the surface and slide to a halt six inches off the front bumper.

"Big one," Kate observed, trying to sound a little bored and succeeding, she was pleased to note, fairly well.

Mr. Baker swallowed audibly. Mrs. Baker might have whimpered. Neither was in any state of mind to hear the breathless quality in their fearless guide's voice. A casual glance over her shoulder reassured Kate that Mandy's .30-06 was hanging on the gun rack in the back window as usual. Good to know.

The bear was a female in the prime of life, with a thick, glossy brown coat, loose around her body after her winter nap. In the very short space of time granted for reflection, Kate estimated the bear's weight at approximately seven hundred pounds.

Picking herself up briskly out of a puddle of slush, the bear let forth a roar of outrage, lowered her head and charged with a force and speed unpleasantly reminiscent to Kate of the previous morning. All seven hundred pounds hit hard. A high-pitched scream sounded from Mrs. Baker. "Oh my God!" cried Mr. Baker, and a grim Kate, who had automatically thrown out the clutch when she slammed on the brake, held on to the steering wheel with both hands as the truck skidded back at least four feet.

The grizzly roared and rammed again. The truck slid back again, but the second ramming was less enthusiastic, and this time Kate had managed to shift into second before the bear hit, so the backward motion was only three feet and change. The grizzly bawled defiance a third time, reared up on her hind legs and made one swipe with a paw at the front bumper, which resulted in a screech of tearing metal. She placed her forepaws on the hood of the truck and did a violent push-up. Her claws left parallel grooves behind on the brand-new truck's brand-new paint job. The whole front end sank two feet, the shock absorbers groaning beneath the strain, and bounced back up again, so that Kate's head nearly ricocheted off the ceiling. As he was a foot taller than she was, Mr. Baker's did.

Kate heard his curse as if from a great distance. Time seemed to have decelerated somehow, as if they and the bear were passing through deep water, the weight of it slowing action as well as reaction. There was no time to be afraid, but there was all the time in the world to observe. This bear was a beauty, standing eight feet or so at the shoulder. Her hump was the size of a small mountain, well formed and mature. There were dark red stains around her nose, mouth and throat, indicating a recent feeding, in which case Kate couldn't see what she had to be so cranky about. The silver tips of her coat caught the rays of the morning sun.

There were no signs of a cub, which would have gone a long way toward explaining her throwing down the gauntlet to a top-of-the-line Ford four-wheel-drive, one of the few mobile things in the Park that outweighed her. She reared up on her hind legs again, front legs curving in classic confrontational stance. Kate examined the claws revealed thereby with detached interest. Shreds of something pale were caught between the claws of the right paw.

The bear gnashed her teeth at them. The clicking sound of incisor upon incisor was clearly audible inside the cab. It sounded just like an axe chopping wood, in fact just like yesterday's visitor, only louder, more solid and somehow infinitely more threatening. Someone whimpered.

The bear gave a fourth and final bellow, dropped to all fours, whirled and charged headfirst through a thick stand of mountain hemlock, which proved less unyielding than the Ford's front end. The green branches crashed together, and as they quivered to an indignant standstill in the grizzly's wake, time returned to its normal steady passage.

It was quiet in the cab of the truck for quite a while. At last Mr. Baker stirred. "What," he said, striving for an even tone despite the beads of sweat popping out on his forehead, "may I ask, was that extraordinary creature?"

"That?" Kate said, and had to clear her throat. "Oh. That would be your basic brown, or grizzly, bear. *Ursus arctos horribilis.* An omnivorous North American mammal with a plantigrade gait. Plantigrade," she explained kindly, "means it uses the entire sole of its foot in walking. *Homo sapiens* is also a plantigrade mammal." It was difficult to shake off the pedant, Kate discovered, once she got hold of the scruff of your neck.

"Indeed."

"It's warming up," she added, "so they're waking up."

Mr. Baker refrained from remarking on the superfluity of Kate's last statement and turned to his wife. "Are you quite all right, my dear?"

Mrs. Baker shifted in her seat. Her voice was thin but steady. "Ms. Shugak, don't you think we should, perhaps, drive on?"

"Certainly," Kate said, because the West Coast has its end to hold up, too. She let out the clutch and set off once again up the road to the mine, only very slightly grinding the gears. "The indigenous population of this area is largely Athabascan, but there has been a good deal of immigration from other parts of the state over the years—"

A mile later the road mercifully ended in a cluster of shabby clapboard buildings, all painted the same fading red with white trim. Kate parked the truck in front of what had been the old mess hall and they got out to look at the view.

It was sensational. The overcast had cleared and they were fifteen hundred feet up, with the blue-white peaks of the Quilak Mountains at their backs, stretching southeast to northwest, uncompromisingly beautiful and, Kate was pleased to see, effortlessly outhaughtying the Bakers. "Prince William Sound is that way," Kate said, pointing south. "And this"— a sweep of arm indicated a wedge of area that stretched from horizon to horizon—"is the Park. This valley is pretty much the Park's center, and where most of the people in it live. Just around that bluff, you can't see it from here, is a little plateau, we call it the Step. That's where Park Headquarters is. And see the glaciers?"

It would have been hard to miss them. There were half a dozen in sight, beginning with the Kanuyaq, a sheet of translucent blue ice a hundred feet tall that formed the head of the Kanuyaq River. Water opaque with gray glacial silt roared downstream at the base of the cliff on which they stood. The glacier calved as they watched, an immense shard of blue-green crystal detaching from the main body of ice to fall ponderously into the river. A few seconds later the *Crack! boom! crash! splash!* reached them.

The swift-moving surface of the river swelled into a wave that slammed into both banks at the same time. It uprooted a clump of small alders and washed out a boulder the size of Gibraltar, rolling it downstream as if it were of no more consequence than a glass marble.

Even the Bakers seemed impressed. "Spectacular, really," said Mr. Baker.

It was better than nothing, and Kate had begun to shepherd them toward the mill when Mrs. Baker said, "Why, who is that, do you suppose?"

Kate heard a sobbing kind of shout and turned to see a man stumble out from behind what had been the company store. He fell practically at their feet. "Help me," he said, clawing at Kate's legs. "Help me." He fell forward, gasping for breath.

She knelt and took hold of the man's shoulders. "What is it, mister? What's wrong?"

"My wife, my wife!"

"What about your wife?"

His voice rose to a scream. "My wife! My wife!"

"What about your wife!" Kate bellowed, shaking him. "What happened?"

"Bear," he said, pointing back in the direction from which he'd run. "Grizzly attacked us. She's on the roof. Help her!"

"The roof of what?"

"One of the houses! Help her!"

The memory of the grizzly female they had encountered on the road up flashed through Kate's mind. The hairs prickling on the back of her neck, she cast a quick look around, saw no bears and stood to haul the man bodily to his feet. "Help me get him into the truck," she snapped at Mr. Baker.

Together they got him into the truck, Mrs. Baker close behind. Kate reached for Mandy's rifle. "You two stay here with him," she said, checking the chamber. "I'll go round up the wife."

"Ms. Shugak—" he began.

"Stay here!" she barked. Without waiting for a reply she pivoted on one heel and headed down the road between the mine buildings at a trot, head up, eyes alert, a fine sweat of nervous perspiration breaking out along her spine. She had the edge on vision and weaponry but the bear would have the edge on smell, size, strength, quickness and claws. She knew who she'd have put her money on.

Bears were odd beasts, she reminded herself; ninety-nine times out of a hundred they'd pass ten feet in front of you, ignoring you, at most roaring a challenge or faking a charge to satisfy honor. Yesterday morning at the creek had been the exception, the young male she'd run off from the meat cache far more the rule.

And the female with the stained muzzle? In which category did she belong?

Kate checked the safety a second time. It was still off. Good. She held the rifle in front of her, right finger inside the trigger guard. Always prepared. She and the Boy Scouts.

She cursed the couple who had picked this day to come up to the mine, cursed them for making her a hero, cursed herself for being in the wrong place at the wrong time and cursed them again for evidently coming unarmed into a region well known for its active bear population. Just the summer before, a grizzly had taken an eight-year-old boy in Skolai. Didn't people read? Didn't they watch the news? Did they think all bears were funny and cuddly like Baloo? Like Charles II, Walt Disney had a lot to answer for.

The road turned right up the hill behind the mill. She followed it, mouth dry, into the cluster of houses the mine owners had provided for the manager and the senior staff and their families, ones with real running hot and cold water, electricity and plumbing. There were plenty of places all over America in 1911 that didn't have as much, but in 1911, with the price of copper what it was, money was no object, and Morgan-Mellon-Astor-Carnegie-Guggenheim-whoever had wanted to keep their upper-echelon employees happy and productive. The lower-echelon employees, i.e., the ones who got the copper out of the ground and loaded it on the railroad cars, stayed in the bunkhouse farther down the side of the hill and shared the bathroom with ninety-nine others.

The houses were small affairs built of the same faded, peeling red clapboard as the main buildings. There wasn't anyone on the roof of the first house in line, and the soft, slushy, rapidly melting snow hid what tracks there had been. She didn't hear the growl of an infuriated grizzly, either, and she was listening for it pretty hard. All that was audible was the roar of the Kanuyaq River, loud

56   DANA STABENOW

enough to drown out the sound of an approaching bear until it was right on her.

"Lady?" she called. "Lady? I've got a gun, I'm here to help. Your husband's okay. It's safe to come down now." She walked forward.

One house. Around a corner and another. A cluster of scrub spruce and a third house, a fourth and a fifth without incident.

"Lady?" she called again, and cursed herself again, this time for not asking for the name. "Lady, can you hear me? My name is Kate Shugak. I've got a rifle. Don't be afraid, you can come down now."

A sixth, a seventh, an eighth. The road wound around the ninth and Kate halted abruptly.

The woman lay in the middle of the road, soaked to the skin from the rapid melt of a winter's worth of snow, staring sightlessly at the sky.

Or she would have been, if she'd had any face left.

Her left arm was missing below the elbow, as was most of her belly and thighs. Bears were notorious for exerting the least effort for the most result and went for the soft meat and the viscera first. The arm had most probably been lost in trying to fight off the inevitable.

Blood was everywhere, the salty copper smell of it strong in her nostrils, and the melting snow had kept it bright red, redder than the fading walls of the little house in the background. The resulting slush had mixed with the dirt track beneath and the area was a sea of churned-up mud in which the paw prints of a very large bear were prominent. The muddy, bloody prints led into the brush on the downhill side of the road.

She couldn't move.

This could have been me, she thought.

If I hadn't moved fast enough, gotten up the bank when I did, this could be me lying here. If the brush hadn't slowed her down coming after me, if Mutt hadn't been barking, if her cubs hadn't been bawling for her.

This could have been me.

She could almost see herself, sprawled on her back in the little swimming hole, sightless eyes staring up, the dark blood drifting out of the backwater to be snatched into the swift, midstream current and washed downstream, into the river and the gulf beyond. How long before anyone would have known, if ever?

Her hands cramped, making her aware of how hard she was gripping the rifle. She swallowed and forced herself to move forward, focusing fiercely on one of the clearer prints, in which a puddle of reddish water was already beginning to form. About six or seven hundred pounds, she estimated, standing six to eight feet.

The pink shreds in the grizzly's claws had been human flesh.

She looked away, at the fading wall of the house, long strips of paint peeling from its sides, and swallowed hard. Dimly, her own words echoed in her head. It was that hundredth bear you had to watch out for.

She heard a sound behind her and spun around, rifle at the ready, to find Mrs. Baker retching emptily on one side of the road. Mr. Baker, white to the lips, was patting her shoulders soothingly.

"Oh great," Kate said before she thought. "Mandy is going to *kill* me."

6

George Perry ground-looped 50 Papa on a short final into Niniltna.

Two circumstances contributed to this unfortunate occurrence.

One, there was a fourteen-inch rut halfway down the icy surface of the 4,800-foot airstrip, which the latest grader pass had missed and which the left front tire on 50 Papa had the misfortune to catch precisely at touchdown.

Two, Ben Bingley was barfing down the back of his neck at the time.

Kate drove up with the Bakers and the bereaved husband in time to see the red and white two-seater pull sharply to the left, losing its center of gravity just long enough to lean over and catch the ground with the tip of the left wing. Newton and inertia took care of the rest as the plane completed a snap roll so perfect it would have brought tears to the eyes of an

Air Force flight instructor if only it hadn't been performed at zero altitude.

In short, the plane flipped over and pancaked flat on its back. Under the beneficent rays of the spring sun, the surface of the airstrip had been reduced to a foot of packed snow, submerged beneath an inch of water, providing a marvelous surface for a nice long gliding slide. Five-zero Papa slid very well indeed, on a direct line heading for Mandy's truck as it pulled to a halt in front of the post office. It was a combination skid and spin; in fact 50 Papa was going around on its back like a slow top for the second time, the ripping sound of tearing wing fabric clearly audible to the stupefied witnesses in the cab of Mandy's truck, just as the plane ran into them. Kate looked down, fascinated, as one wing slid smoothly between the front and back tires, and looked up just in time to see the wheel of one landing gear hit the top of the driver's-side door with a solid thud that shook the cab and rattled the passengers in it, although not as much as the grizzly had done earlier.

The window bowed inward but did not break. There was the unmistakable groan of bending metal, though. Kate, a little light-headed, thought that Mandy might not notice the dented bumper and the clawed finish and the need for a front-end alignment on her brand new truck after all.

Her second thought was to wonder how full the Super Cub's tanks were, one of which was at present resting directly beneath her ass.

Foolishly, she grabbed for the handle and shoved. The door, the right gear of the plane jammed solidly against it, unsurprisingly did not budge. "Out!" she roared. "Out! OUT! OUT!" Mr. Baker fumbled with the passenger door and stumbled to the ground. Kate, not standing on ceremony, shoved Mrs. Baker and the husband out after him and scrambled out herself to run around the truck. She sniffed, tense. No smell of gasoline.

She went around to the Cub's right side and squatted to fold up the door. A smell hit her in the face like a blow, powerful enough to knock her on her butt. It wasn't gasoline, it was vomit. She took a couple of deep, gasping breaths, muffled her face with a sleeve and spoke through it. "George, are you okay?"

George looked at her, still suspended upside down in his seat harness, bits of brown something spattered across the back of his head and neck. "I *hate* breakup," he said.

"Never a dull moment," Kate agreed.

A rustle and the snap of a buckle came from the seat behind him. "No!" George said. "Ben, don't—"

But Ben did, releasing the buckle on his seat belt. He fell heavily on his head and shoulders against the ceiling of the fuselage. A cry of pain and some futile thrashing around followed, after which George contributed some acerbic commentary, because he now could not slide his seat back to get out. Matters did not improve when Ben threw up again.

"AUGGHHH!" said George. He braced his feet up against the dash, reached for the lever and shoved with all his might. The seat slid back and hit Ben in the butt. Ben tumbled backwards in a corkscrew somersault into the pile of U.S. Postal Service mail sacks that had been piled on the floor in back of his seat and were now piled on the ceiling. It was too much for him and he threw up for the third time.

George braced himself on one arm, popped his harness buckle and was outside and on his feet a moment later. Thin-lipped and furious, he addressed the area in language suitable to the situation. George was an ex-helicopter pilot who had learned his trade under fire in Vietnam and perfected it on the TransAlaska Pipeline before deserting the rotor for fixed wing and starting an air taxi in the Park. He was also one of five ex-husbands of Ramona Halford, the right-wing state senator representing the area of Alaska that included the Park, which all by itself had been an education in expletive deleted.

Over his shoulder, Kate caught sight of the widower, staring down into the bed of the truck at the body, cocooned in a blue plastic tarp. A few feet away stood the Bakers, color back in their faces and by the wideness of their eyes evidently improving their vocabulary with George's able assistance.

Cravenly, Kate ducked down again to help Ben Bingley out of the plane. This wasn't easy, as Ben had heard George's lengthy and comprehensive address and somehow received the impression that George might hold him in some small measure accountable for the ground loop. He was of course absolutely innocent of anything of the kind, but he had decided he would stay in the plane for a while, like maybe until George went home, or perhaps left the Park forever.

So he held on to the back of the pilot's seat, refusing to let Kate pull it forward, until she had to kneel down in the slush. The aroma of beer-based puke was gagging and Kate lost her temper. "Ben, stop being such a big baby and get your ass out of this friggin' plane."

Ben was more scared of a mildly pissed Kate Shugak than he was of George Perry at full volume and he wavered. "You promise you won't let him hurt me?"

"I'll kill you, you stupid little shit!" George said from above.

"I promise," Kate said, more temperate now. Somebody had to be. "Come on out, Ben."

"I don't know," Ben said doubtfully, "he sounds awful mad."

"He's just shook up from dinging the plane. Come on out, Ben."

"I'll rip your fucking guts out and use them for crab bait!"

"Maybe you could just bring me a beer," Ben said hopefully.

"I'll feed your sorry ass to the first bear to come down the pike!"

Kate winced, and was glad that in her current position she couldn't see the expression on her three passengers' faces.

George ran out of breath and threats and Ben finally did come out, standing so as to keep Kate between himself and the enraged pilot at all times.

Kate began negotiations toward a truce and was making some headway when Ben's wife appeared on the airstrip. It became immediately apparent that he had way worse problems to deal with than a plane wreck, an enraged bush pilot and vomit down the front of his shirt.

Cindy had left the house without her jacket but not without her 9mm Smith and Wesson, which she held in a business-like grip with the business end pointed at Ben.

"Whoa!" George said, startled out of his wrath.

"You little prick," Cindy said.

"Now, Cindy," Kate said, eyes almost crossed on the barrel beneath her nose, trying to see if the pistol was loaded. She could tell it was an automatic, but the way Cindy kept waving it around she couldn't tell if there was a clip in the butt. Might be one in the chamber anyway, so she wasn't safe whether she could see the clip or not, and stopped trying.

"Now, honey," Ben said, peering fearfully over Kate's shoulder.

"I *hate* breakup," George said.

"Get out of my way, Kate!" Cindy snarled. "That son of a bitch stole the kids' quarterly dividends and probably drank up every last damn dime! Why the hell don't you people do something so he can't get his hands on the money!"

"I'm not on the board," Kate said.

Cindy dismissed this spineless and specious attempt at diversion with a contemptuous wave of the pistol that brought George into the line of fire. George took a hasty step backward, slipped and sat down hard in a puddle. "You're Ekaterina's granddaughter, you say jump, they say how high, who cares about titles! How am I going to feed the kids until the salmon start running? Huh? How?"

Kate had no answer for her, and Cindy's smoldering gaze fixed upon her cringing husband. "I told you, Ben, I told you if you ever did that again I'd kill you!"

She meant it, too. *Bang!* went the pistol. The bullet went into the driver's side door of Mandy's truck with a clang, missing the right tire on the Super Cub by an inch.

Definitely loaded, Kate thought, orchestrating a graceful swan dive.

"Hey!" George roared indignantly. "Watch out for my god-dam plane!"

Bang! went the pistol again, and George decided better the Cub than him and dove after Kate.

Ben was left standing all alone, a sickly smile spreading across his face. "Now, honey—" he began. *Bang!* went the pistol again, and he broke and ran. *Bang! Bang!* and Cindy took off in pursuit.

Their thudding footsteps faded, followed by some crashing of brush and yelps of pain. Kate, sandwiched between the Cub's wing and the pickup's differential, raised her head to survey the area. Nobody shooting in her immediate vicinity. This was good. She looked over at George. His eyes were squeezed shut and he'd managed to jam himself almost all the way beneath the truck, the bed of which had been ventilated at least twice that Kate could see from her prone position. Kate wasn't worried. At this point Mandy would barely notice the bullet holes.

"So, George," she said, "you think we should go after them?"

"Nope," George said, opening his eyes.

"Me neither," she decided. It was breakup, and she had nineteen other things to do without adding the arbitration of Ben and Cindy Bingley's marital spats to the list.

Bang! went the distant sound of the pistol a sixth time.

Especially when Cindy was so well armed.

George gave a long, shaky breath and climbed to his feet. "She's empty, now, anyway."

"It was an automatic," Kate said, wriggling free and standing up. Her Nikes were wet, dammit. Kate hated getting her feet wet. It ranked right up there with turning her back on a bear.

Three more shots sounded in rapid succession, followed by a whoop of triumph from Ben, a snarl of frustration from Cindy and the snapping of tree limbs. "Now she's empty," Kate said, relieved.

"Unless it was a staggered clip," George said. "Staggered clips have fourteen rounds."

"Shit," Kate said, with feeling. They both listened intently, but there were no more shots. Kate bent to brush ineffectually at the mud clinging to her knees. "Let's just hope she didn't have a spare clip."

"Gee, thanks for sharing, Shugak. You're always such a comfort to me."

"Mr. and Mrs. Baker?" Kate said belatedly. "Are you all right?" There was no immediate answer. Alarmed, she started around the truck, where she found Mr. and Mrs. Baker and the widower seated in a row on the ground. The widower's hands were over his ears, Mr. Baker's over his eyes, Mrs. Baker's over her mouth. Kate, reprehensibly, laughed.

Mr. Baker sensed movement and uncovered his eyes. He blinked up at Kate, rose a little unsteadily to his feet and assisted his wife to hers. Kate rearranged her face into a solemn expression and waited for it. It wasn't long in coming. "Are you quite all right, Ms. Shugak?"

"Quite all right, Mr. Baker," she replied, with admirable gravity. "And yourselves?"

"Oh, quite," he said. He brushed at his once impeccably creased chinos. The seat was soaked through to where you could see what he was wearing beneath. Boxers. Only in Boston. "Who, may I ask, was that most extraordinary young woman?"

"Ah," Kate said. "That was Cindy Bingley."

"And the young man was her husband."

"Yes."

"Who appears to have committed some sort of transgression."

Kate was beginning to be amused. "Some sort."

Mrs. Baker weighed in. "She certainly seems to have a temper."

"She certainly does," Mr. Baker agreed, and if Kate was not demented, there was even something approaching a twinkle in his eye.

That was it? Evidently that was it. Kate didn't see any wounds or blood, and by this time they had acquired an interested crowd, everyone from inside the post office as well as most of the residents of the village and a few AWOL high school students, about three hundred in all and all clustered around George's pancaked plane.

There was much shaking of heads, a great deal of sagacious commentary, which George bore with gritted teeth, and a few offers of real help, which Kate promptly accepted on his behalf. They slid the plane sideways until the wing was free of the truck, and George, outrage evident in every line of his thin, angular body, marched off to fetch the crane truck while the rest of them unloaded everything they could out of the plane.

Between the crane and a dozen willing pairs of hands, the plane was right side up again thirty minutes later. "Thanks," George said in a gruff voice. The prop was bent into an artistic curve but the wing tip wasn't and nothing else looked much hurt, although Kate knew that the bent prop alone meant a complete teardown of the engine. George was a certified A and P mechanic, but it wasn't much consolation, as he would be spending a lot of hours on the ground when he should have been in the air making money.

Everyone in the crowd was thinking the same thing, and Demetri Totemoff cleared his throat. "George, you need a plane to keep the business going. I'll trade you hours on my 172. It's got the Lycoming conversion, so you can get in and out most of the places you do with the Cub."

George's expression lightened. "When's your annual due?"

"September."

"What about you? What will you be flying in the meantime?"

"The Tripacer's at Tyson's in Anchorage. He says the annual's done and the plane's ready for pickup. You know that cantankerous bastard, he wants it off the lot yesterday. We could take the 172 in, I can fly the Tripacer back, and you can take the 172."

George considered. Demetri was proposing an hour of maintenance in exchange for every hour in the air, the bulk of which would not be payable for another five months, and he could work on the Cub when he wasn't in the air. "Deal." He stuck out his hand. "Thanks, Demetri."

They shook on it. Kyle Kirkus, one of the schoolteachers who had only been in the Bush since the school year began the previous September, blurted, "You're going to loan him your plane? He just wrecked his own!"

Demetri looked at Kirkus with his usual impassive stare and said flatly, "At this moment, George is the safest pilot in Alaska."

Kirkus looked around for support, found none and wandered off, shaking his head.

The Cub was rolled across the airstrip to George's hangar, the rest of the crowd following with the seats. Once inside, it became obvious that the inside of the Cub and its seats were in urgent need of immediate swabbing down, preferably with an ammonia-based, industrial-strength cleaner, but this task the helpers seemed to feel George was capable of handling on his own, and scattered for home.

Kate crossed the strip and discovered that the Bakers had wandered into the post office, presumably to see if the same wanted posters hung on the walls there as in the post office on Beacon Hill, although now that she thought of it, she was pretty sure the Bakers didn't do anything as plebeian as post their own mail. The widower stood next to the truck, staring vacantly off into some never-never land, surrounded by several villagers who had by some subtle osmosis become aware of the bear attack and clustered around in an awkward attempt at condolence.

She headed up the single road that connected the houses of the village to the riverbank. The NorthCom shack was fifty feet up from the Niniltna school, and it was just that, a shack made of plywood stapled to a two-by-four frame and covered with tar paper. Behind it stood a 112-foot steel tower surmounted by a satellite dish.

Inside, unfinished interior walls leaked pink insulation all over the plywood floor and a tiny woodstove burned red-hot. A counter divided the work space from the living space, if you could call one room with a camp cot and no running water living space. The work area was a counter with a bank of electronic gear stacked on it, surrounded by a litter of notepads and a scattering of ballpoint pens. A thin curtain of faded, fraying flowered cotton divided the two. The air was redolent of hot grease. "Mel?" Kate said. "You in here?"

A head crowned with shaggy dishwater-blond hair poked around the curtain. "Well, hey, Kate, how you doing?" The rest of his slight frame, clad in jeans and bright red aloha shirt, followed, one hand holding a plate of chicken-fried caribou steaks. Kate's mouth watered. She must have looked extremely needy, because Mel grinned and held out the plate.

Melvin Haney was young, the only kind of people Northern Communications, Inc., could bribe to stay this long at remote Bush earth stations with their primitive living conditions, although working a month on and a month off eased the pain somewhat. So did the salary, which astronomical sum Mel considered barely adequate compensation for having to use a chemical toilet he had to empty himself. A graduate of East High in Anchorage, where he'd spent a thoroughly enjoyable five years majoring mostly in trouble, his father, a NorthCom executive, had given him a choice: the job in Niniltna offering the Park population communication with the outside world via satellite, or a one-way ticket Outside. Mel had been to Disneyland, and after one look at the L.A. freeways had decided that while Outside was a nice place to visit, no sane person would want to live there. To his own surprise and to his father's amazement he had proved a success at the Niniltna site, and the rest, along with a succession of girlfriends provided by Kate's extended family, was history.

Kate liked him, scrawny, cheeky little squirt that he was. "Hey, Mel," she said, around a mouthful of steak. "Good stuff."

"The best." A generous and kindhearted young man, he put the plate on the counter between them. "What can I do you for?"

"You can marry me if you can cook this good," Kate mumbled around another mouthful.

"Nah," he said, snagging his own steak before they were all gone. "I know you, you'd be the jealous type, you wouldn't let me play the field."

"True." She swallowed. "Can you raise the trooper's office in Tok?"

"Really, Kate." He licked his fingers and did his best to look hurt. "I can raise the Viking 1 Lander on this thing if I have to."

"You've been spending way too much time with Bobby Clark," Kate said.

Mel laughed and didn't deny it. "What's going on?"

"Bear attack up to the mine."

He made a face. "Is it bad?"

"She's dead." Remembering how dead, Kate lost her appetite and shoved the plate of steaks to one side.

"I'd call that bad, all right," he said soberly. "Who was it?"

"Don't know. Even if I did know her, I probably couldn't say now." In answer to his look, she added, "There's not much of her face left."

He shuddered, and moved to adjust a switch on a bank of electronic equipment. He punched some numbers into a keypad and gave her the handset. It rang twice before the other end picked up. "Alaska State Troopers, Tok."

Kate recognized the voice. "Elaine, this is Kate Shugak in Niniltna."

"Well, hey, Kate. Long time no see. You survive the winter okay?"

"The winter was fine. I may not make it through breakup."

"Oh, yeah? What's up?"

"Bear attack. One woman dead."

"They're up, are they?"

"They're up and grouchy," Kate said. "Can you tell Jim to rod on over here with a body bag?"

"Wasn't he just over there picking up another body?"

"Yes."

"*Breakup*," Elaine said. "Hang on." She muffled the receiver for a moment before coming back on. "He's on his way, Kate. Don't you just love this time of year?"

"I downright adore it, Elaine. Tell Jim I've got the remains rolled in a tarp in the back of a truck parked on the Niniltna airstrip next to the post office."

"Okay. He'll be there inside the hour."

Mel accepted the handset and signed off. "Want me to call Dan O'Brian next?"

In Alaska, every accidental death required an investigation and an autopsy, and the ones involving close and fatal encounters with wildlife usually involved a fish hawk or a ranger as well. "Might as well."

She visited with Mel for a while before returning to the airstrip. In the post office she checked her mail, avoided looking at the ubiquitous piles of tax forms stacked on the counter and went back outside in time to see Dan's Super Cub lining up on final. He landed, taxied to the head of the runway and got out. "Just couldn't wait to see me again, could you, Kate?" he said cheerfully.

"It's not pretty," she warned him as he began to unroll the tarp.

"It never is," he agreed, but when the body was bared the muscles in his face shifted. Kate watched him in silence. She had been too preoccupied with her own problems that morning to take a good look at him, which was a shame, because the view was not bad.

Armed with a degree in forestry, Dan O'Brian had come into the Parks Service by way of the Everglades in Florida, where he discovered an aversion to snakes, and Volcanoes National Park on Hawaii, where he discovered an even greater aversion to lava.

He transferred to Alaska just in time for the d-2 lands bill, which doubled the size of the Park. He'd been chief ranger for fourteen years, steering a course between the Scylla of the rights of the Natives and homesteaders and miners around whose property the Park had been created, and the Charybdis of his responsibilities as custodian of twenty million acres of public property. He succeeded so well that not once had he ever been shot at on duty, which had to be some kind of record for a federal employee in the Alaskan bush. Off duty was another matter. As much of a skirt chaser as Chopper Jim, he was less successful at it, and thus less irritating to local husbands, but they couldn't shoot at a state trooper. A park ranger made a not disgraceful second-best.

About the time Kate started comparing the blue of his eyes with the blue of Chopper Jim's, she came to her senses and pulled herself together. She'd always had a healthy respect for the sexual urge but fantasizing over a man she'd known as a friend for more than fourteen years veered dangerously close to the ridiculous. She was angry with herself, and deep down, a little afraid. Control was very important to Kate Shugak, and over the last two days control seemed to be slipping from her grasp.

"Nope," Dan said heavily, "not pretty at all." He quietly refolded the tarp around the body. He looked up and surprised a look of fierce concentration on her face. "What?"

"Nothing."

He waited, but that was all she was going to say. "So." He nodded at the still figure in the tarp. "When did you find her?"

With a slight shock Kate realized that it was almost six o'clock. "Less than two hours ago. Her husband said they went up to take a look at the mine this morning, and the bear attacked them."

Dan frowned. "Tourists?"

"I don't know. That's him." Kate nodded at the man leaning up against the post office wall just out of earshot. The little crowd of sympathizers had dispersed once the mail started being sorted, and he was alone again, head back against the logs, hands in his pockets, eyes closed. "He hasn't said much."

"The bear just attacked them? Without provocation?"

"I don't know," Kate said. "I didn't hang around to see if the bear wanted to make it two for two. And I've got Mandy's parents with me."

Dan brightened. "You've got the Original Eastern Establishment Royalty Couple with you?"

"Yes," Kate said, as the two emerged from the post office, bulging bags indicating that the gift shop that took up the right side of the post office had not gone unpatronized. "Allow me to introduce you. Mr. and Mrs. Baker, this is Dan O'Brian, chief ranger of the Park."

"Hello," Dan said, shaking hands and looking over their matching right-off-the-L. L. Bean-rack safari outfits, soaked behinds and all, with an appreciative eye. "Nice to meet you. Hell of a musher, that daughter of yours. Don't often run into that much guts and talent walking around on two legs. You must be proud."

That this was not a thought that had previously occurred to them was obvious from the startled expression on their faces. Kate reflected that both generations of the Baker family had a lot to learn.

Dan's gaze wandered past them to the widower, who had remained apart from the rest of them, face averted. "How's he holding up?"

"He's on his feet," Kate said.

Dan nodded. "Shows something. What's his name?"

"I asked. He hasn't said anything yet."

"Probably in shock, poor bastard." Dan walked over and held out a hand. "Dan O'Brien, chief ranger. I'm sorry about your wife, Mr. . . . ?"

"Stewart." The man stirred and gave a long, heavy sigh. "Mark Stewart."

He shook hands with Dan, and Kate stepped forward. "Kate Shugak."

"Oh. Right. I'm sorry, I—I just couldn't talk before."

"It's all right," Kate said. "I understand."

"Mark Stewart," he repeated unnecessarily. "I guess I should thank you."

"No need," she said, adding, "I just wish I could have gotten there sooner." She didn't mean it, and Dan at least was fully aware that she didn't, but it was the kind of thing one said at times like these.

Stewart's grip was warm and dry and so strong it was almost painful. The man was of medium height with well-defined shoulders topping a rangy frame. He had dark eyes beneath thick dark brows, a wealth of dark hair that fell in a careless swath that must have cost $150 in some Anchorage salon, and a wide, full-lipped mouth that undoubtedly spread into a charming smile. That mouth was held rigidly now in a straight, expressionless line that matched the bleak, unfocused look in his eyes.

At least, bleak and unfocused until they looked at Kate. As their eyes met, a flash of visceral awareness leapt between them. Kate very carefully freed her hand and took what she hoped was an unobtrusive step back. Damn, damn, damn.

"I know you've just been through a horrible experience," Dan said to Stewart, "but can you give us an idea of what happened? If we've got a rogue bear on the roam in the Park, I need to know about it."

Mark Stewart looked down, long, thick lashes shadowing his cheeks. "I— You're right, it was horrible. I—" He paused, and drew in a long breath.

"Mr. Stewart," Dan said, as if he couldn't help himself, "didn't you bring a rifle with you? A pistol, even? Some kind of weapon for your own defense? Surely you must have known that this was an area known for its bear population?"

Stewart looked at the ground. "No," he whispered.

Dan met Kate's eyes and shook his head. Tourists.

"It's all so awful," Stewart muttered. "We came up here to be alone, get away from everything. This morning was so nice, we decided to walk up to the mine with a picnic lunch. And then we got to the mine, and the bear came out of the woods, came right at us, and Carol—"

"You said she was on the roof," Kate said. "When you first saw us."

He nodded miserably. "I gave her a leg up the side of one of those old houses. I told her to stay there while I went for help. It—the bear must have climbed up after her. I never would have left her if I'd thought— I never— Then I heard your truck and—" His face twisted.

"It's okay," Dan said with quick sympathy. "Never mind. We can talk about it later."

Stewart hid his face in his hands.

Dan was right, the poor bastard probably was in shock. Coldly ashamed of her momentary awareness of him as an attractive man, and disregarding his equally obvious appreciation of her as an attractive woman, Kate said, "The trooper's on his way."

Stewart's head snapped up. "Trooper?"

"Chopper Jim?" Dan said, and Kate nodded. "The trooper from Tok," he told Stewart. "Jim Chopin."

"How'd you talk to him?" Stewart said. "I thought— Are there phones in Niniltna?"

"I called him from the NorthCom earth station." Kate indicated the tower just visible over the tops of the trees clustered between the airstrip and the village.

"The troopers are always called in on cases of accidental death," Dan said.

"Of course," Stewart said, head bent again. "Of course they are. Sorry, I'm still a little out of it."

Dan regarded him with a puzzled air. "You know, I could swear— We've met before, haven't we?"

Stewart shook his head. "I don't think so."

Dan's brows came together but he shrugged. "If you say so."

The Bakers had wandered across the strip to watch George swab out the inside of his plane. Kate hoped George had simmered down some, but the rigid set of his shoulders didn't look promising, in which case she hoped the Bakers would restrain any impulse they might have toward commentary. She wondered what Mandy was going to say when she heard the tale of the day's adventures. Somehow she felt that a fatal bear attack, a plane wreck and an attempted homicide were not what Mandy had had in mind when she sent her parents out that afternoon.

Dan strolled a little way down the runway, inviting Kate with a jerk of his head to join him. "So what did Mandy bribe you with to get you to play tour guide?"

She fell into step next to him. "The loan of her truck."

Dan grinned. "That's right, yours is slightly out of commission, isn't it?" He looked at Mandy's brand-new Ford. The windshield had a horizontal crack in it that started in front of the steering wheel and progressed all the way across to the passenger side. The driver's-side door was crumpled in and sported two bullet holes. The black plastic bumper was cracked right down the middle. Dan inspected the claw marks on the hood with a professional eye.

"Yeah," Kate said, "we had our close encounter with the bear, too."

His head snapped up. "Same bear?"

She nodded. "I think so. The way the road switches back, about the time she hit us she could have come straight down the slope from where I found the body." She paused. "She had blood on her face and muzzle, and what looked like flesh between her claws."

"Jesus."

"Not a pretty sight," Kate agreed, and took a deep breath to steady her stomach. "Still, hard to get too upset over bears acting like bears."

"Yeah." He didn't believe it any more than she did, but in the face of nature red in tooth and claw he was damned if he'd let Kate outmacho him. " 'She?' "

"It was a female, a big one, six, seven hundred pounds."

"Which way was she heading?"

"West, last I saw."

Dan's brows snapped together. "West from the mine?"

"West from a mile or so down the mine road."

"Heading away from the village, then."

"Last I saw," Kate repeated. They both knew how futile it was to try to predict the path a bear might take.

"You scare her off her kill?"

"I don't know. Maybe. You know what the road's like, and I had the truck in second gear. We were pretty noisy."

"And bears do tend to get a little cranky when their meals are interrupted," Dan observed.

Kate remembered the enraged grizzly, standing on her hind legs, claws extended, showing off a very long, very sharp, very fine set of teeth and an even finer set of lungs.

Dan stood back and surveyed the truck again. "You're awful goddam hard on trucks, Shugak." He poked a finger into one of the bullet holes, and looked at Kate with a raised eyebrow.

She made a face. "Ben Bingley went on a toot on his kids' corporation dividends, apparently. George had just brought him back—" She told him about the ground loop and from his delighted grin knew his next stop would be George's hangar. "Anyway, they'd just flown in from Ahtna when Cindy showed up. She wanted to discuss the matter. Over a Smith and Wesson."

"My, my," Dan said. "Bet the Bakers enjoyed that." He smiled slowly. "Kate Shugak, tour guide. Wish I could have been along for the whole ride. Did they say if they enjoyed themselves? They signed up for a raft trip down the Kanuyaq yet? You could probably dump them in along about Chitina without half trying, get 'em wet all over, maybe even get 'em drowned. Worth a try, don't you think?"

Chopper Jim's arrival spared her the necessity of a suitably discourteous reply. The Bell Jet Ranger settled down and Jim was out before the rotors stopped turning. To Kate he said, "Just couldn't wait to see me again, could you?"

Dan laughed. "My words exactly."

Jim hitched up his gun belt. "What have we got?"

They told him. He walked over to the truck and unwrapped the body. He looked at it without expression, and listened to Mark Stewart's story with even less expression.

Kate and Dan helped Jim load Carol Stewart's body into the back of the chopper. Stewart got into the passenger seat and the trooper closed it after him. Instead of walking around to the pilot's side, he walked out from beneath the rotors and motioned to Kate. "He say the bear come after him, too?"

"He said something about shoving her up on the roof of one of the staff houses out back of the mine while he went for help. Other than that, he hasn't said much of anything."

Chopper Jim was silent for a moment, staring at the end of the runway, brows knit. "Okay. I'll fly him and the body to Tok. I got an emergency call about a wreck on Sikonsina Pass. Some asshole's boat slid off the trailer and front-ended a tractor-trailer full of liquid oxygen." He adjusted the brim of his hat with a flick of his fingers, in a crisp, somewhat exasperated manner that suggested he'd like to square away life in all of rural Alaska, or at least that part under his jurisdiction, in the same no-nonsense, no-action-wasted fashion. "I just *love* breakup."

They looked at the helicopter, Stewart waiting, silent and staring, the tarp-wrapped body of his wife invisible behind him.

"He said they came up here to get away from it all," Kate said.

Jim's grin was taut and mirthless. "Didn't get quite far enough, did they?"

7

There was a lot more traffic on the road between the village and the Roadhouse than there was on the road between the village and the mine, so it was in better shape, with most of the winter's ice broken up and potholes smoothed out to no more than on average a foot deep. It was twenty-seven miles from Niniltna, and exactly nine feet and three inches outside tribal jurisdiction, which location made it the only legally licensed purveyor of liquor in twenty million acres of Park. A square, solid building with a corrugated tin roof, a satellite dish perched on one corner and a haphazard jumble of tiny rental cabins and Bernie's home out back, it made up in atmosphere what it lacked in architectural aesthetics.

There were no dogsleds and no snow machines visible in the parking lot. There were three rows of vehicles, beginning with a blue Chevy crew cab pickup.

Kate's face brightened. "Great, Bobby's here. Bobby Clark, a friend of Mandy's and mine," she explained to the Bakers.

At the end of the same row there was a fifty-foot Pace Arrow motor home with Pennsylvania plates, proudly displaying the wear and tear of twelve hundred miles of Alcan and another four hundred miles of Alaska dirt road. Kate shook her head. They were coming up earlier every year, and it was getting so you couldn't get them to leave once they'd come. Welcome to Alaska, now go home. Her eye traveled to the vehicle opposite the RV. "That goddam Frank Scully," she said before she thought.

Mr. Baker cleared his throat. "And who is Frank Scully, Ms. Shugak?"

"He moved up from Washington last year, bought Greg Migaiolo's cabin."

Mr. and Mrs. Baker looked inquiring.

Kate pointed. "He drives that Cherokee Chief over there, and he still hasn't got Alaska plates on it. That always ticks me off, people move out into the Bush and think they can get away without paying for a new license and registration."

They pulled in between a rusty black Ranchero and a rustier brown Plymouth sedan with both bumpers missing. Kate put the truck in second and shut off the engine. The Ford was running well even if the driver's-side door still wouldn't open. "Now, folks, remember what I told you, the Roadhouse isn't exactly what you're used to. Are you sure you wouldn't rather head on back to Niniltna? My Auntie Vi makes great cocoa, not to mention fry bread."

"Ms. Shugak," Mrs. Baker said, displaying a hitherto unsuspected firmness, "if you are a friend of Amanda's, you know she doesn't keep liquor at the lodge."

"Yes," Kate said meekly. "I mean, no."

"Well, after what we saw this afternoon, I for one would kill for a drink."

"I for two," Mr. Baker added.

They smiled at Kate. If they weren't careful, they were going to upgrade from stereotypes to real live human beings before the day was over. Kate grinned. "I'd kill for some rational conversation myself. Okay, but don't say I didn't warn you."

But at the door to the Roadhouse, Mr. Baker paused. "Ms. Shugak—"

"Yes, Mr. Baker?"

"That woman at the mine—"

"Yes?"

"Was it our bear that killed her? The one that ran into us on the road?"

Kate briefly considered lying, and quickly discarded the notion. "Probably."

"There was blood on her muzzle."

"Yes."

"That woman's blood."

"Yes."

Mr. and Mrs. Baker exchanged glances. "Will someone go after the bear, try to kill it?"

Kate looked surprised. "Why?"

Mr. Baker blinked. "Well, naturally, I assumed— I've been hunting in Africa, Ms. Shugak. When a lion becomes a man-killer, the only thing to do is to hunt it down and kill it, otherwise it will go on killing men."

Kate sighed. "Mr. Baker, an Alaskan grizzly eats anything that doesn't move out of the way in time, animal, vegetable or mineral. That includes bugs, canned goods, canteens, backpacks and people, as well as any and every other mammal that comes down the pike. Protein is protein. They're a perambulating appetite with a serious advantage in speed and armament. Most of the time they leave us alone. Sometimes they don't."

Mrs. Baker regarded her with a quizzical expression. "It doesn't appear to upset you very much, Ms. Shugak."

Kate shrugged, and repeated what she had said to Dan, this time with more conviction. "Hard to get upset over bears acting like bears. Comes with the territory. It's not pretty, but then nature often isn't."

The Roadhouse door opened abruptly into the conversation, almost catching Mrs. Baker on the nose and smacking into Kate's reflexively upraised hand. A man somersaulted out of the building to roll down the steps and fetch up flat on his back in a puddle of muddy slush. There was a slurred curse.

The Bakers regarded the outcast for an expressionless moment before Mr. Baker reached for the door, which was swinging slowly closed, and pulled it open with a polite inclination of his head. Mrs. Baker swept through, with Kate bringing up the rear, feeling like a very minor courtier in an exceptionally regal retinue.

Inside, the bar was three deep, there wasn't an empty table in the joint, and the floor was jammed with dancers in Pendleton shirts, Levi's and wafflestompers, the men distinguished from the women only by their beards. On a twenty-four-inch television screen suspended from one corner of the roof Steven Seagal was putting out an oil rig fire in a series of actions that would have put his ass into orbit on any oil field other than Hollywood's. An enthusiastic audience led by Old Sam Dementieff was improvising new dialogue. Half a dozen older women sat in a circle quilting, mugs of hot buttered rum at their elbows, Auntie Vi firmly guiding the gathered needles in some complicated knot. She looked up, saw Kate and beckoned. Kate deliberately mistook the gesture and waved back airily.

Another crowd stood around two pool tables in the back, the crack of ball on ball muted by the occasional flush of a distant toilet. Jimmy Buffett was on the jukebox, wanting to go where it's warm, accompanied by half a dozen tone-deaf backup singers who felt the same way, including Frank Scully, evidently suffering no guilt feelings whatever at not contributing his share to the state treasury.

The tourists from Pennsylvania were easy to spot. They sat at a table by themselves, attired in matching plaid polyester pantsuits.

Matching Pittsburgh Steelers windbreakers hung over the backs of their chairs, matching potbellies pushed at their shirts, and matching befuddled smiles spread across their faces as they took in Life in the Alaskan Bush, a point-and-shoot camera at the ready on the table in front of them, right next to a dog-eared copy of the *Milepost*, Everytourist's all-purpose, super-duper utility guide to Alaska. In spite of herself Kate thought they looked kind of cute.

The air smelled of stale beer, roll-your-owns of old tobacco and older marijuana, and wet wool. Eau de breakup.

Kate broke trail to the bar, where Bernie was pouring out drinks with all eight hands. He was a long, gaunt man with a receding hairline in front and a ponytail that reached to his waist in back to make up for it. He looked like an aging hippie only because he was one.

Bernie Koslowski was Chicago-born and Midwest-bred and all flower child. He had been mugged by Daley's finest at the 1968 Democratic convention, had danced in the mud at Woodstock in 1969 and had merrily burned his draft card on the steps of the Capitol in Washington, D.C., in 1970, whereupon Attorney General John Mitchell, unamused, had had Bernie and three thousand other demonstrators thrown behind a chicken-wire fence on the Mall, in direct violation of their Fourth Amendment rights. Bernie took it personally. Upon release, he walked by the White House to flip Nixon the bird and hauled ass for Canada, eventually migrating into Alaska through the Yukon Territories, working construction on the TransAlaska Pipeline. He retired from the pipeline to buy the Roadhouse in 1975. If the Roadhouse wasn't connected by road to the TransAlaska Pipeline's right-of-way, there were other means of transportation an ingenious and thirsty pipeliner could and did promote, including, one glorious day two years before, a D-9 Caterpillar tractor. Business boomed.

Bernie's father, who never let anyone forget he had gone ashore with the first wave at Anzio, had struck Bernie's name from the family Bible and forbidden mention of it in his presence. His mother and sisters sent him surreptitious care packages every year at Christmas, filled with water filters, Swiss Army knives and waterproof compasses ordered from the REI catalog. From time to time they would inquire solicitously as to the state of his health, since blubber couldn't be all that nutritious as a dietary staple, and did his Eskimo friends live in igloos? Bernie had never met an Eskimo in his life, or seen an igloo, and since whales had been put on the endangered species list, muktuk was in short supply, and Aleuts ate seal muktuk anyway. Or the ones he knew did.

One of his Aleut friends who ate seal muktuk jerked her head toward the other end of the bar, where Bobby Clark was, as usual, sitting at the center of a lot of laughter and rude comment. "Life of the party," Bernie said. "How you been, Kate?"

"Don't ask."

"All right," Bernie said agreeably, and poured Kate a Coke without waiting for an order. "Where's Mutt?"

"Guarding the homestead from the federal government."

"What?" There was restive movement behind Kate, and Bernie said, "May I help you?"

"Bernie, this is Mr. and Mrs. Baker. Mandy's parents."

Bernie broke into a smile that lit the deceptively mournful lines of his face with warmth and humor. "Of course. Mr. and Mrs. Baker. I've heard Mandy talk about you." With the diplomatic dexterity of a career bartender, he refrained from repeating precisely what he'd heard Mandy say. "It's nice to meet you. May I pour you a drink?"

"I wish you would," said Mrs. Baker with feeling.

"You certainly may," said Mr. Baker at the same time, with even more feeling.

Bernie glanced at Kate, and was intrigued by the suddenly wooden expression on her face, although true to form he made no comment. "Fine. What would you like?"

The Bakers eyed the assortment of bottles crammed into the shelves on the wall behind the bar. Mr. Baker spotted a tall green bottle and pointed. "Is that Glenlivet?"

"It certainly is."

"I'll have some," Mr. Baker said, in a manner that brooked no contradiction. "Dear? Dear?"

Mrs. Baker's gaze was fixed and staring. Bernie turned to see what she was looking at.

On a small shelf by itself perched a clear, square-sided bottle half filled with golden liquid. It was what was lying on the bottom of the bottle that had caught Mrs. Baker's fascinated attention, and Kate smothered a grin as Bernie said with elaborate nonchalance, "Oh, that. That used to be tequila. Now it's Middle Finger." Mrs. Baker's eyes widened but before Bernie could launch himself on the saga of the unprepared climber who had lost three fingers to frostbite climbing Angqaq Mountain, one of which now reposed at the bottom of the bottle in question, Kate said, "Bernie, these folks have already been through one bear attack, one plane crash and one attempted murder today. Just pour them some booze, okay?"

Drinks in hand, they moved down the bar, gravitating naturally toward the spot generating the most noise. Bobby was accompanied by a wraithlike blonde who caught sight of Kate before he did. "Hey, Kate."

"How you doing, Dinah?"

"Fine," the blonde said, smiling, blue eyes dreamy. "Incredible. Wonderful. Sublime."

Impressed, Kate said, "Must have been one hell of a winter."

The dreamy smile widened. "You have no idea."

Dinah Cookman was a twenty-two-year-old strawberry blonde who, upon graduation from Columbia the previous spring with a degree in photojournalism, had armed herself with a video camera and a pale blue 1969 Ford Econoline van and driven north to Alaska, determined to make her name with a breakthrough celluloid essay on life in the Alaskan bush. By the time she got to Tok she had run out of gas money and stopped off to pick mushrooms to sell to cash buyers from Outside, and also to meet Bobby and Kate, but especially Bobby. Under their expert tutelage, especially Bobby's, she was fast redeeming her cheechako status. This afternoon, for almost the first time since Kate had known her, she was without her video camera. She looked unnatural, almost naked, without it.

The black man with the impressive shoulders put his wheelchair into a 180. "Goddam! Shugak! Long time no see!" A long arm hauled her into a comprehensive embrace, a hard kiss and a not so brotherly pat on the ass. "How was your winter?"

"Not as good as yours, apparently," she said, returning the embrace and the kiss and letting the pat go by without comment. No one else could have patted Kate Shugak's ass in public and gotten away with it, not even Jack Morgan, and the people around the group regarded him with no little awe.

Bobby peered behind Kate. "And you are?"

"Bobby, Dinah, I'd like to introduce Mr. and Mrs. Baker. Mandy's parents."

"The snobs from Nob Hill?" Bobby said, not so sotto voce.

"No, the snobs from Beacon Hill," Kate said under her breath. "Behave." More loudly she said, "Mr. and Mrs. Baker, these are some more of Mandy's friends. Bobby Clark, he's the NOAA observer for the Park, uh, that's National Oceanic and Atmospheric Administration. And this is Dinah Cookman, Bobby's roommate and a photojournalist."

"Documentary filmmaker," Dinah said, the old her surfacing for a moment before the rosy haze enveloped her once more.

Kate regarded Dinah with a wary eye. "I beg her pardon, documentary filmmaker. And you've met Bernie Koslowski. He owns the joint."

Everybody shook hands. "Where's Mandy?" Bernie said.

"She's back at the lodge. I, ah, volunteered to give the folks the grand tour." Nobody believed it, but nobody was brave enough to say so.

"You want a table?" Bernie said.

"You got one?"

"Always got one for you," he said. "Judy!"

"Yo!" A short, wiry woman in jeans and T-shirt whose fringe of thin brown hair was stuck to her forehead with sweat peered at them from behind thick round glasses that made her look like an inquiring insect.

"Save that table for me!"

She stuck up a thumb, and was lifting an overloaded tray without apparent effort by the time Mr. and Mrs. Baker, Kate, Bobby, Dinah and Bernie reached her. There weren't enough chairs, which Bernie rectified by snitching several from nearby tables while their occupants were on the dance floor. "I'm on break," Bernie told Judy.

"Up yours," she replied with a grin. She shoved her oversize glasses up the bridge of her nose and shot off to answer a cry for more beer.

Bernie shook his head. "That Judy, she only knows two speeds, fast and stop. So, Mr. and Mrs. Baker, how are you finding Alaska so far?"

"Quite stimulating," Mr. Baker replied without missing a beat.

Kate choked over her Coke and Bobby demanded details. They took news of the bear attack philosophically, pitying victim and survivor alike without shock or horror. "Dumb to go up there unarmed this time of year," Bobby said, which summed up the general consensus. George's ground loop was received with glee, Cindy's ambush with applause. When they stopped laughing, Kate said, "Yeah, right, hilarious," but she noticed that Mandy's parents were looking much more mellow. Probably the Glenlivet. Whatever worked.

Bernie had been in on the ground floor of Dan O'Brian's hot pursuit of the two Great White Hunters, so the denouement was well received, but it was the story of the 747 engine almost falling on her cabin that got by far the most acclamation. "Jesus, Kate," Bobby said, wiping away tears of mirth, "that's got to be the best story yet. You're getting better and better at lying in your old age." He started to laugh again. "I knew I was a good teacher, but damn, I didn't know I was that good."

"It's true," she insisted.

"Yeah, right, and the *Nimitz* just rammed my boat dock," he said, and everybody laughed again.

"She really is telling the truth," Mr. Baker murmured, but no one was listening.

"Is that what all that air traffic was this morning?" Bernie said.

"Yes," Kate said. "The NTSB and the FAA descended on my place at about five."

Bobby's beer was arrested halfway between table and mouth. "Air traffic?"

"Yeah," Bernie said. "Didn't you hear it? Sounded like the U.S. Air Force was staging an invasion from the Niniltna strip. Early," he added with bitter emphasis. The Roadhouse didn't close until two in the morning, and Bernie usually didn't hit the sack until three-thirty or four o'clock. He was not a morning person.

Bobby looked at Kate. "It really is true? The engine off a 747 really did land in your front yard?"

"Not fifty feet from my front door," Kate said ruefully. Mr. and Mrs. Baker nodded in solemn agreement. Kate noticed their glasses were nearly empty. So did Bernie, and he signaled Judy for a refill.

Bobby stared at her. "Jesus H. Roosevelt Christ," he said finally. "Now that's what I call *breakup*."

The door opened and Mac Devlin came in. He spotted Bobby and bulled his way through the crowd to the table. Kate was sitting a little in back of Bernie and he didn't notice her at first. "Bobby, is it true what I heard? Did a plane crash on Kate Shugak's homestead?"

Bobby raised his eyebrows, not averse to making a good story even better. "Why, I do believe it did, Mac."

Mac Devlin was a short, barrel-shaped man with a red face and redder hair that stood up straight in the standard ex-marine's crew cut. "Jesus! I hear over a hundred people got killed."

Kate leaned farther back into Bernie's shadow, and obligingly he leaned forward on his elbows, the better to keep her hidden. The Bush Telegraph had never been known for its strict adherence to the facts, and it appeared that today it had been working over-time. Bobby was thoroughly enjoying himself, and no one at the table gave him or Kate away. "At least."

"Jesus!" Mac Devlin said again. "I heard Kate was hurt, too."

"Intensive care at Providence in Anchorage," Bobby said.

"Serious," Bernie said solemnly.

"Critical," Dinah said, getting into the act.

"Near death," Bobby said, shaking his head mournfully. Dinah wiped away a tear. Bernie gave a heartfelt sigh. Mr. and Mrs. Baker drank single malt and kept their mouths shut, going up another notch in Mandy's friends' opinion poll.

Mac Devlin thought for a moment. "Listen," he said, dropping his voice to a confidential murmur, "you don't happen to know who Kate's heirs are, do you?"

"I don't believe so," Bobby said gravely. "I'm not sure she had any."

"Other than us," Dinah said, and slid her hand into the crook of Bobby's arm.

"Because then I could approach them about subsurface mineral rights on her homestead," Mac said.

Kate felt Bernie shake next to her, and a responding laugh bubbled up to the back of her throat. She pinched his arm in warning. He pinched her back.

Bobby almost forgot his part. "I've got to hand it to you, Mac, you never give up."

Mac's ruddy skin became even ruddier. "Because you know I've been after Kate for the mineral rights to that ridge above the creek back of her cabin ever since I came into the Park."

Dinah eyed him, enthralled by his every word. "What do you think is there?"

"I think it's where the silver vein that played out in the Lost Wife Mine reappears." Mac's chest puffed out. "I can show you the maps, and the geologic charts."

"Gee," Dinah told Bobby, all earnest persuasion, "maybe we ought to let him take a look."

Kate leaned forward into visual range and raised her voice. "Like hell. I've seen what Mac can do with that D-6 of his. He could move all hundred and sixty of my acres five miles west if he was of a mind to." She met Mac's astounded gaze and smiled. "Thanks, Mac, but no thanks. I'll pass."

Mac's jaw dropped, and the table erupted into laughter. He regained enough self-control to curse them all roundly and bulled off in the direction of the bar.

Still laughing, Bobby said, "There might be silver in them thar hills, Kate. Aren't you even a little excited at the prospect?"

"Oh," she said politely, "you think I don't get enough excitement out at the homestead already?"

"Lay off, Bobby," Dinah said. "Not everybody's in the market to moil for gold."

"I'll moil it for her," Bobby said promptly.

"Thanks anyway," Kate said. "I don't think so."

"Are you sure you're really okay, Kate?" Dinah said, sobering. "Sounds like one hell of a close call to me."

"It was, but I'm fine."

"And may be richer for the experience," Bobby said, lifting his beer in a toast.

"I'd better be," she said gloomily. "The damn thing flattened my truck."

"Not old Ichiban?" Dinah said in dismay.

"Stewart?" Bernie said suddenly. "Did you say Mark Stewart? Kind of looks like Robert Redford, only with black hair?"

Kate blinked at him, lost for a moment. "Who?"

"The guy whose wife got eaten by the bear," Bernie said.

"Sounds like a book by John Straley," an irrepressible Bobby observed.

Bernie ignored him and persevered. "Does Stewart look kind of, I don't know, not Redfordy exactly, but, I guess, sort of deliberately movie star–ish? Lean, black hair?"

She paused with her glass halfway to her lips. Now that she thought about it, she couldn't remember the color of Stewart's hair, the jolt of awareness when their eyes met obscuring every-thing else. She had been trained to observe, and she couldn't come up with something as basic as a physical description. And she had at one time called herself an investigator. She was even more dis-gusted with herself.

"Jesus, Bernie," Bobby said, unknowingly coming to her rescue, "you sound like you're in love with the guy."

Bernie shot him the finger, and Kate was able to say with a laugh, "Now, now, gentlemen. I happen to know the proprietor of this establishment, and he frowns on fisticuffs. Yes, Bernie," she said, turning to him, "that sounds like the guy. Why?"

"They were in here last night."

"'They'?" Bobby said. "You mean the widower and the deceased?"

"Yeah," Bernie said. "They were really lovey-dovey." He paused, and added, "Or at least he was. She didn't look like she was all that excited to me."

Bobby made a rude noise. "Wishful thinking."

"Hey," Bernie said, wounded. "I'm a married man."

Kate was distracted by a burst of noise from the television screen, where a little old Native man was being roughed up by a bunch of big ugly oil field workers in what passed in Hollywood for a bar in the Bush, which was about as accurate as the rig fire scene. Steven Seagal entered the frame. Old Sam Dementieff, who was twice as old and twice as decrepit as the little old Native man on the television screen, raised up a thin, twittering voice. "Oh, please, Mr. Big Strong White Man, save poor, weak, drunk little me from the Big Bad White Guys!" Obediently, Seagal did, with the requisite amounts of testosterone and karate. "Oh, thank you, thank you, Mr. Big Strong White Man!" Old Sam cried. "You saved me! You shall be made a member of my tribe! Forever after you shall be known among us by your secret tribal name, Biggest White Prick!"

Chuckling, Kate turned back to the table.

"He's a big-time Anchorage contractor," Bernie was saying.

"He built the Roadhouse for me. Back when we were both just starting out. He cut his expenses to the bone, I'll say that for him, but he sure was hard on employees. He paid them ten bucks an hour—for Bush work, no less—and made 'em sleep in tents. Oh, and he refused to hire a cook."

"What'd they eat?"

Bernie grinned. "Surplus MREs."

"No fucking way!" Bobby roared in outrage.

"So," Kate said, with a quelling frown in Bobby's direction, "Mr. and Mrs. Baker, how long will you be visiting? Mandy didn't say."

"The jet will be back in Anchorage for us next Saturday," Mr. Baker said, and drained his glass as if it were the last drop of liquid between him and the day of departure. Mrs. Baker wasn't far behind. Bernie signaled for a second refill, as a brief silence, respectful of a private jet, fell.

"It's great that you came up," Kate said. "I know Mandy's been wishing you would for a long time."

Mrs. Baker's lips tightened ever so slightly. "We've been trying to talk her into coming home for a visit for years."

Obviously dangerous ground, and Bobby said briskly, "Enough with the small talk." He straightened in his chair, adjusted the set of the wheels, brushed an imaginary speck of dust off his T-shirt and demanded, "Ask me how my winter was."

"How was your winter?" Kate said obediently.

Bobby stroked his chin and seemed to consider. "Productive," he decided finally. "Yes, I'd say productive was the appropriate word." Dinah smiled again, the same dreamy smile as before. The rest of them sensed a story, and waited in expectant silence. Bobby did not disappoint them. "In fact," he said, regarding the level of beer in his glass with a critical frown, "I'm glad you came in today, Kate, I need to ask you a favor."

"Name it," Kate said, raising her glass.

"Will you be our best man?"

The Coke went down the wrong way and she choked and coughed

and Bobby, a huge grin on his face, wheeled around the table to pound her on the back with more force than was absolutely necessary but she couldn't catch her breath to complain. Meanwhile, Bernie exclaimed, Mr. and Mrs. Baker added dignified congratulations and Dinah smiled her dreamy smile. When Kate got her breath back she said, eyes watering, "You're actually getting married?" She looked from Bobby to Dinah and back again.

"Yeah, I know, sounds a little precipitous, don't it? We haven't even been living together for a year yet. But, well, you know, we thought it best, what with the baby coming and all."

This time the Coke came out her nose. Bernie was rendered speechless, an event so rare it ought to have been recorded in the Park annals, if there had been such a thing. Again, Mr. and Mrs. Baker leapt into the social breach, not by so much as a flicker of an eyelash indicating any disapproval of the sequence of events, or of anyone's relative age, or of the color of anyone's skin, either, which made Kate wonder if perhaps Mandy hadn't misread her parents' reaction to Chick. When she got her breath back the second time, she said, "I'll be best man only if I get to be godmother, too."

"Deal." Bobby stuck out a hand.

She took it and yanked him into a hug. "You lucky bastard," she said into his ear.

He hugged her back hard. "I know." They both admired Dinah, who sat in her chair looking positively angelic, which she was not. "I know," he said again.

She watched him watching Dinah. Bobby's face was square and smooth and black as coal beneath a tight cap of frizzy curls going gray at the temples, his eyes brown and shrewd, his smile in turn charming, seductive and downright wicked. Bobby Clark was a hillbilly turned Park rat from Tennessee who had come to Alaska by way of Vietnam, where he'd left both legs from just above the knee. What he didn't know about surviving in Bible Belt, jungle or Bush wasn't worth knowing. He and Kate had been lovers once and were friends now, and Kate was happy for him and a little sad for herself, although she couldn't have said precisely why.

They discussed names for the baby—Bobby favored Clyde, for Clyde McPhatter, or maybe Chuck, for Chuck Berry, or, alternatively, Ronette, Shirelle or Chiffon. Kate caught Dinah's eye, who shrugged resignedly and said, "He could want to call her Dixie Cup."

"Or Supreme," Kate suggested, getting into the spirit of things.

"Or Jelly Bean," Bernie said with a grin.

They all considered that one for a moment, before saying in unison, "Nah."

Bernie six-packed the table (apple juice for the expectant mother, Coke for the teetotaler) and rose to his feet to toast the imminent arrival of the newest Park rat. They drank, and in the absence of a fireplace to hurl the glasses into thumped them all down onto the table and raised a ragged cheer.

"Katya!" She turned to see Auntie Vi waving at her again. There was no ignoring the summons a second time, and she excused herself temporarily from the celebration.

Auntie Vi was a tiny woman with defiantly pitch black hair cut short and permed into a thousand tiny corkscrew curls around a face like an old apple, red-cheeked and wrinkled but with plenty of juice still left beneath the skin. Widowed, Auntie Vi fished subsistence during the summer and ran a bed-and-breakfast out of her home the rest of the year. She lived in a rambling cabin just outside Niniltna on the road to the Kanuyaq mine. Since hers was the only noncamping place to stay between Bernie's cabins and the pipeline-camp-converted-into-a-hotel in Ahtna, she did a brisk business with hunters, climbers and other assorted phenomena. In the past the latter had included an itinerant art collector scrounging old ivory carvings and baskets and button blankets and halibut lures and fishing visors and glory hallelujah, one time even an entire kayak in astonishingly good condition, which nobody told the collector had been made the previous summer by Gordon Tobeluk and sunk in the river to age for a year, as well as a Stanford sociologist writing his Ph.D. dissertation on the dynamics of subsistence survival in an adulterated rural lifestyle, who jumped a foot in the air every time a twig snapped and refused to go any farther from the village than the last house, and a television reporter from ABC's L.A. affiliate looking for the definitive story on the effect of the *RPetCo Anchorage* oil spill, which he hoped would but did not get him an offer from national.

Auntie Vi rented them all beds made with clean sheets, served up caribou sausage and eggs, homemade toast and nagoonberry jelly the following morning, and charged on a sliding scale according to what she perceived to be her guests' net worth. She was the closest the Park had ever gotten to having their own home-grown entrepreneur. Mac Devlin wasn't even in the same class.

She was also an expert quilter. Close up, the quilt the circle was working on looked even more beautiful than it had at a distance, an organized swirl of shades of blue and white, with flowers made of a combination of embroidery and appliqué spaced at regular intervals. "Forget-me-nots?" Kate said. "My favorite flower."

"You hinting, Katya?"

Kate batted her eyes. "Who, me?"

Enid Koslowski, Bernie's wife, scowled at both of them. "She's not married."

"Nor about to be," Kate agreed, and nodded at Dinah. "She is, though."

"And Bobby's been here a long time," Auntie Joy said happily, knotting a thread.

"I didn't know you were in town, Auntie," Kate said to her.

Auntie Joy heaved a gusty sigh. "I get hungry for family, so I come." Over the tops of her half-glasses, she fixed Kate with a severe eye. "How is it this is first time I see you, Katya? You too good, or maybe just too lazy to come to town to visit your auntie?" Not waiting for Kate to answer the unaswerable, she said, "Break time, Vi?"

Grinning, Auntie Vi nodded and the other five exchanged thimbles and needles for mugs. Auntie Vi rose and stretched and took a few steps from the table, nodding at Kate to follow her.

"So," she said, looking over Kate's shoulder, "I hear you give Mandy's mom and dad the grand tour?"

"You could call it that."

Auntie Vi's eyes twinkled. "Mandy probably never let her folks back in the state, much less the Park."

"Probably not."

"They look like nice people."

"They're coming around," Kate admitted.

"So maybe their shit stink like everybody else's," Auntie Vi said complacently, and Kate had to laugh. "Katya, I need a favor."

"Sure, Auntie," Kate said, displaying about as much sense of self-preservation as Kevin Bickford had that morning on her homestead. "Anything you want, you know that."

"I want you to talk to Harvey."

Kate stiffened. Harvey was Harvey Meganack, one of five board members of the Niniltna Native Association. He was pro-development to the extent that he was willing to open traditional tribal lands up to mining, logging and tourism, a subject over which he and Kate had locked horns the previous October. The board, stable and unchanging for twenty years beneath the firm hand of Kate's grandmother, had recently experienced a sea change, losing three of its members and electing a new chair. It was still sorting itself out, and no one really knew what direction the board might take in the future.

Auntie Vi was only the board secretary, not a member, but she was a tribal elder and as such had tremendous influence with both the board and the shareholders. Kate, who had been waging a life-long battle to stay as far removed from tribal politics as possible, was thrice cursed, first in that she was the granddaughter and only direct descendant of Ekaterina Moonin Shugak, second in that she was smart, capable and a natural leader, and third in that those qualities were recognized and needed by her people. Authority is as often a burden thrust upon the reluctant recipient as it is a prize pursued by the ambitious.

Kate, resolved to serve from outside the circle of power no matter how often her elders tried to extend it far enough to draw her in, said guardedly, "What about Harvey?"

"He's almost convinced Demetri and Billy that the profits we made last year from the logging at Chokosna should go out in a supplementary dividend to the shareholders."

Normally, the dividend check was a quarterly payment representing income and interest earned on funds invested by the Niniltna Native Association, one of hundreds around the state created by ANCSA, the 1972 Alaska Native Claims Settlement Act, which had traded money and land for a right-of-way for the Trans-Alaska Pipeline across aboriginal territory. Sound counsel and some lucky investing on the part of the Niniltna board had produced dividends that had steadily increased over the years so that individual shareholders now received almost a thousand dollars four times a year. One was paid out on December 1, to help put some spirit into Christmas; one in March, to help gear up for the fishing season; one in June to help buy that new impeller the boat needed after it went over the sandbar at the mouth of the Kanuyaq River; and one in September, in case the fishing season had been lousy and there was no money for the fall grocery run to Costco in Anchorage.

It wasn't a bad arrangement. Unfortunately, a quarterly payment was also a fine way to finance a quarterly spree, as Cindy Bingley was all too well aware. And when, as this year, additional income from investments or, in this case, logging leases accumulated and had to be dispersed to the shareholders, there was a great temptation to regard the resulting funds as found money and blow it on a spree, or a third four-wheeler. You can never have too much stuff in the Alaskan Bush. "And?" Kate said.

"And," Auntie Vi said, "Joy says we should maybe earmark a few of those funds for a health clinic instead."

Kate looked at Auntie Joy, another round-shaped elder, whose chubby cheeks gave an impression of youth, especially when two deep dimples creased them, which happened frequently. Her cheerful front hid a deep and abiding concern for her family and friends and for the community as a whole, blood or not. For "Auntie Joy says," Kate thought, read "the majority of the elders in the Association say." She glanced at Old Sam Dementieff, the fifth, eldest and newest board member. "What does Old Sam say?"

Auntie Vi shook her head. "Nothing, yet. Will you talk to Harvey, Katya?"

"What makes you think he'll listen to me? We haven't been on good terms since last October. Hell, we've never been on good terms. He'll blow me off."

"Try."

Kate's hackles instinctively went up at the tone of Auntie Vi's voice. After a brief struggle, she said, "All right, auntie. I'll try."

"Try soon."

Kate took a careful breath, exhaled it. "Yes. As soon as I can."

"Good." Auntie Vi examined her critically. "I hear you almost get flattened by airplane."

"Not a whole airplane. Just one engine."

Auntie Vi's eyes twinkled again. "Oh. Just the engine. That's all right then."

Kate had to smile.

"And woman get killed by bear." Auntie Vi shook her head. "Bad thing."

"Were they staying with you?"

Auntie Vi nodded. "For a week, they said." Her smile was wide and satisfied. "Now I got federal men staying. They pay more."

"Good for you."

"That wife nice lady," Auntie Vi said, smile fading. "She been here before." She gave Kate a sly look. "But she not with him."

At that moment the door to the Roadhouse crashed open and a neon Budweiser sign hanging on the back wall shattered and cascaded to the floor in bits of glass.

In the absolutely still moment of silence that followed, Kate heard the distinct echo of a rifle shot. A .30-30 she thought, but didn't have enough time to make sure.

"Incoming!" Bobby put both hands flat on the table, vaulted across the surface and tackled Dinah, who went over backward in her chair. They both crashed to the floor with Bobby mostly on top. Kate, a nanosecond behind him, caught Auntie Vi in one arm and Auntie Joy in another and used them to take the rest of the quilting bee down. Bernie did his duty by Mr. and Mrs. Baker.

"Well, really," Kate heard Mrs. Baker say when she got her breath back.

Bernie cursed.

Mrs. Baker shut up.

A second shot, a clang and the tin-shaded light over one of the pool tables swung wildly back and forth. A figure loomed up in the open doorway, outlined against the Park's one and only streetlight, and a third shot rang out, followed by a shrill scream.

"Kay!" a man's voice screamed. "Omigod! Kay!"

The figure in the doorway disappeared. The door slammed itself shut, cutting the light off as if someone had thrown a switch.

Bernie's comment came clearly to Kate from halfway across the room.

"Breakup."

8

The door banged open again. "They've shot my wife!" a voice yelled from outside. "Somebody help! They've shot my wife!"

"Everybody stay down," Kate said, and got to her knees.

"Katya!" Auntie Vi said. "No!"

"Shugak!" Bobby yelled. "Now is not the time to play hero, goddammit!"

She ignored both of them and snaked a path toward the back of the room, past bodies hugging the floor, hugging beer glasses, hugging pool cues, and one uninhibited couple hugging each other as they took brazen advantage of their suddenly horizontal position. Kate took a second look. The guy was Dandy Mike. It figured.

There were more unintelligible yells from outside, more shots, more thuds as bullets impacted the wall of the Roadhouse and a lot of panicked shouts and questions from inside, chief among which was, "What the fuck is going on?"

Seemed like all day people had wanted the answer to that question.

Someone was crying and someone was cursing and somebody else was screaming and Kate looked up just in time to see the lady tourist from Pennsylvania aim her camera and take a picture. Her husband, wide grin intact, looked as if he'd gotten a bargain in front-row seats to a John Wayne shoot-out.

"Get down, you damn fools!" Kate shouted.

They took her picture instead.

Kate crawled beneath the television screen, opened the back door a crack and hooked one wary eye over the sill. Nobody shot at her. A belly-scraping slither got her outside and down the steps. She sidled furtively up to the corner and peered around. Nothing, but the yelling was louder. She sidled even more furtively up to the next corner and peered much more cautiously around it.

The yelling resolved itself into words. "You bastards, you shot my wife!" The speaker was kneeling on the steps to the front door, a woman draped over his lap, her left shoulder and breast stained red. He had a pistol in his hand and a feral look in his eye. "You bastards, I'll kill you for this, I'll kill you!"

"You deserve everything you get, you godless heathen!" was the response, a woman's voice, high and shrill and determined. A shot followed and a bullet hit the wall of the Roadhouse not a foot from his head.

"Get down!" Kate snarled. "Goddammit, you asshole, get down!"

He looked her way, half raising his pistol, a .357 magnum. At least it wasn't an automatic; he could only shoot her six times. It wasn't a comforting thought.

Another shot from the parking lot slammed into the building to Kate's left. She jerked back instinctively and banged her head hard enough on a protruding beam to see stars. "Ouch!" There was another shot and another. From the front of the building there was a scrabble of bodies; she hoped it was the man with the pistol hauling his wife beneath the stairs.

Kate, rubbing her aching head, spared a moment to wish that Mutt was with her, so she could have launched an attack on two fronts. In the next moment she was just as glad to be alone, as not even Mutt was immune to bullets. She gathered her courage and peeked around the corner again.

"Mom!" The voice came from a jumble of vehicles a little to her left. "Mom, where are you?"

"I'm over here, Petey!" came the reply. The same woman's shrill voice, hard-edged, coming from somewhere near the Pace Arrow in the parking lot. "Are you okay?"

"Yes! Where's Dad?"

"I don't know! Joe? Joe!"

"Dad! Dad, are you okay? Dad, answer me!"

Under cover of the yelling, Kate slipped out of the shelter of the bar and ducked in between a red Suburban and a construction-orange Dodge pickup. She dropped forward on her hands and looked underneath the Suburban, getting a face full of mud and slush for her pains.

About six vehicles down she saw the bottom half of a body, clad in jeans and shoepacs and holding a rifle into which a pair of hands was feeding bullets. The hands were shaking and dropped every other bullet, but enough were making it into the rifle for the rifle to accomplish its designated task. Shit, Kate thought, and took a detour out to the perimeter of the parking lot. Her feet crunched in the snow and it was only a matter of time before Mom or Petey heard her, not to mention Joe, wherever he was. She had to move fast if she was going to get a handle on the situation before it exploded again.

She jumped when a shot boomed from beneath the front porch of the Roadhouse. Dirty Harry warming up. The other two returned fire, Petey with his rifle, the .30-30 maybe, from the sound of it, more firepower than Kate wanted to go hand to hand against, and Mom with what sounded like a popgun by comparison but was probably a .22 and could kill her just as dead at close range. She used their shots to cover the sound of her movements, duck-walking behind the last row of trucks. Her Nikes, soaked once already that day on the airstrip and just beginning to dry out, were soaked again. There was just no justice in the world.

Nothing to be done about it now, but any feeling of mercy she might have had in dealing with the cause of her wet feet died stillborn. A stumbling rush brought her up behind the last vehicle in the row next to the Pace Arrow, an old white International pickup the size of Rhode Island. Three more booms sounded from the Roadhouse's front porch, during which Kate crossed to the Pace Arrow, followed by a pause. Probably reloading. Kate took the opportunity to peer around the corner. A woman in jeans and sweatshirt was on her knees, leaning against the Pace Arrow, her rifle grasped in both hands.

The RV was twenty-five feet long if it was an inch, too long a distance for Kate to rush without Mom hearing, way too long for Kate to get to her before she swung the rifle around. She cast about her for something to even the odds. Nothing but half-melted snow and rotten ice and gluey mud as far as the eye could see.

She looked back at the surface of the lot. Why not? She scooped up a bunch of snow and packed it down, squeezing the muddy liquid out between her fingers, rounding off the edges, shaping the mass into a solid ball of ice, as fine a projectile as an attacker could hope for. She made half a dozen more, stockpiling her arsenal. She waited until Mom was sighting down the barrel before she raised her right arm and threw a fast, hard ball that hit with a solid thump between Mom's shoulder blades.

"What the hell!" Mom was rocked forward on her knees but she didn't drop the rifle. She turned and Kate threw again, as hard as she could, this time connecting with Mom's shoulder.

"Ouch!" Rocked off her knees, Mom sat down hard in the slush, and Kate threw again, this time adjusting trajectory for wind resistance and gravity, this time putting every ounce of force in her body behind it and this time smacking Mom squarely between the eyes. The rifle dropped into the snow, Mom's eyes rolled up in her head and Mom fell face forward into a puddle of slush, out cold.

Kate was rather pleased with herself. She was slightly less pleased when the .357 opened up again, the bullets tearing into the Pace Arrow.

"Mom?" Petey's voice was sounding quavery, which Kate took to be a good sign. "Mom? What are you doing? What do we do now? I shot somebody, Mom!"

Kate got Mom's face out of the slush before she asphyxiated and unloaded the .22, pocketing the bullets and tossing the rifle into the back of someone's pickup. The .30-30 had opened up again, exchanging desultory fire with the .357 under the porch. Crouching down next to the wheel, trying to make herself as small as possible in case the shooting started coming at her from both directions, she raised her voice. "Petey! Petey, stop shooting! And Wayne, if that's you under the porch, you do the same!"

A bullet hit the tire three feet from her head and the air sighed out of it. "Goddammit, you two, this is Kate Shugak!" she roared furiously. "You two idiots put down your weapons! Do it! NOW!"

A brief silence, into which a shaken voice said, "Mom?"

"Your mom's okay. Put down that rifle before you hurt somebody else, Petey. Do it now."

"He had his gun out first!"

"Like hell I did!"

"I don't care who had whose gun out first," Kate roared again, "I want them both down on the ground! Now!" Too angry for caution she surged to her feet and swarmed down on Petey, a thin, pallid youth with the scraggly beginnings of a beard and an incipient whine. He shrank back against the truck as she approached and, lucky for him, wasn't fool enough to raise the rifle. She yanked it out of his hands and unloaded it. A fist knotted in his collar pulled him to his feet. "You dumb little shit," she said, and kicked his ass all the way across the parking lot. He uttered distressed yelps with every contact, which only made her want to kick him harder.

At the porch, Kate bent down to peer through the risers. "Wayne? Is that you?"

A burly bear of a man some twenty years the boy's senior crawled out from beneath the steps, soaked, shivering and covered with mud, still holding his pistol. Kate delivered a final kick up Petey's behind that propelled him headfirst into the side of the building. There was a thud, a groan, and he slid down on his butt in the mud, his head falling forward, tears streaking his cheeks.

Kate removed the .357 from Wayne's unresisting hand and unloaded it. "Where's the rest of it?" Wayne stared at her, uncomprehending, and she snapped her fingers impatiently. "Come on, Wayne, where's your ammo?" Mute, he produced a yellow cardboard box, half full of rounds. Kate stuffed it into the pouch of her windbreaker, feeling like a pregnant kangaroo, and tucked the pistol into her waistband at the small of her back. "How bad is Kay?"

Recalled to his wife's presence, the burly man dove down and hauled out a body that at first glance looked as if nothing could save it. Kay's entire right side was covered in blood. Kate, who had seen more than enough dead bodies for one day, swore and raised her voice. "Hey! Inside the bar! We need a medic out here on the double!"

Since the Ahtna Native Health Foundation had begun running EMT classes five years before, they had qualified ten Park residents in emergency medical training. As the most serious hunting, fishing and flying accidents tended to be instantly fatal, about the only thing the EMTs got to do was deliver babies, which led to a certain amount of professional frustration. Kate didn't have to ask twice; at least five doctor-wannabes, some the worse for liquor but if anything more enthusiastic because of it tumbled out of the Roadhouse to engulf the victim in TLC. Bernie produced blankets and they formed a makeshift stretcher and carried Kay inside, where three tables had already been cleared to form an operating theater. The lady tourist was hovering on the fringes of the action, camera snapping, face flushed with excitement, her husband at her elbow. Mr. and Mrs. Baker, thankfully, remained in the background out of the way, glasses clutched tightly in their fists. Glasses, Kate noticed in passing, which testified to the consummate professionalism and dedication of their bartender. This was what, their fourth?

Kate was not an EMT and had no desire to become one. She shoved Petey into a chair and Wayne into a chair next to him, and went outside to fetch Mom, just regaining consciousness. When the three of them were lined up in front of her she said, "Okay, what the hell is going on here?"

Wayne, face white and strained and eyes fixed painfully on the crowd surrounding his wife, didn't answer. Mom was groggy but game. "Don't use that foul language around me, if you please."

"I don't please," Kate said unpleasantly. The woman returned no answer, and Petey's eyes slid away.

Behind her Bobby's voice said, "It's about the access road, isn't it, Petey?"

Petey wouldn't look at Bobby, either.

"The access road?" Kate said. "I thought you people got that settled last fall."

Mom, also known as Cheryl Jeppsen, Petey's mother and Joe's wife, raised a hand to her eyes, which were swelling into twin shiners of historic proportion and hue. "Godless heathens," she muttered.

A figure detached itself from the crowd around Kay and crossed the room. "Wayne?"

"Dandy?" Wayne looked up, dazed.

Slim and handsome with laughing brown eyes and an infectious grin, Dandy Mike had been one of the first Park rats to qualify as an EMT, from motives Kate was certain had more to do with getting women's clothes off them than ministering to the sick. He was wiping red-stained hands on a bar rag. Wayne looked at the rag and his face went even whiter.

Dandy took a swift step forward and reached out to keep the big man from sliding off his chair to the floor. "Wayne, it's okay. Kay's going to be fine. The bullet hit her high up in the shoulder, from the looks of it small caliber, so there wasn't much damage." The .22, Kate guessed. "It's a through-and-through. We'll clean it and slap a bandage on it, and she'll be fine. She'll be hurting, but she'll be fine. Lucky thing Cheryl and Petey are such lousy shots."

Petey began to weep, long, sad tears rolling down his face and into his collar.

"Praise God," Cheryl said, although it didn't have quite the pious effect she'd hoped for.

"Oh for Christ's sake," Bernie said wearily, "stop with the ever-lasting Jesus-freaking, will you, Cheryl?"

Stiffening, Cheryl said, "You'll answer to the Almighty for that blasphemy, Bernard."

Dandy used his free hand to chuck Cheryl beneath her chin. "Cheryl honey, why don't you put a lid on it before I tell all these folks just how godless you could be in the old days?"

Cheryl's mouth snapped shut like a live trap and she flushed a deep red. "That life is all behind me now. I have confessed my sins to God and He has forgiven me."

Dandy gave an evil chuckle. "Even the night up on the bridge over Lost Chance Creek?"

Bobby, reprehensibly, grinned. "Tell us, Dandy. Sounds like a tale I'd sit still for."

"Okay?" Wayne said, belatedly fastening on the one word of Dandy's that mattered to him. "Kay's going to be okay?" His eyes fell on the bar rag again. "But I saw her, I—"

Dandy, reminded of his duties, turned back to Wayne and shook him once, gently, to stop the babble. "Wayne, Kay is going to be fine," he repeated. He raised his eyes and looked at Cheryl. Lucky for you, his eyes said. Cheryl's eyes held his for a moment before sliding away. In that moment the family resemblance between her and Petey was very clear.

It sank in, and relief washed over Wayne's face. He got to his feet. "I want to see her."

"Fine," Dandy said soothingly. "Go ahead." They watched Wayne lumber off, and then Dandy turned to look Kate's drenched and muddy self over with a speculative eye. "Shugak, you are a mess." Gentle fingers touched her left temple and came away bloody.

She looked at his hand in surprise. "What's that?"

"Blood. Yours." He turned for a handful of cotton and a bottle of hydrogen peroxide. He dabbed at her temple and examined the result with a critical eye. "Yeah, she grazed you all right. As clean a crease as you'll ever want to see."

"I didn't feel it," Kate said blankly. The room took a half-turn around her. "I didn't even hear it."

Auntie Vi said something in Aleut that was probably better left untranslated, and came forward to grab Kate's arm and sit her firmly down in a chair, where she suffered not in silence beneath Dandy's ministrations.

"Oh, quit your bitching." Dandy shook his head, recapping the bottle. "It's just a scratch. It's not even bleeding now. You always did have more luck than you deserve, Shugak."

"You should talk," Kate retorted.

He looked her over again. "Anything else I should see to while I'm at it?"

Her head ached where she'd banged it against the side of the Roadhouse, but not bad enough to let Dandy Mike anywhere near her. "No way, Dandy. I don't need or want any more nursing."

He patted the air. "Fine, fine. Jesus, anybody'd think you were somebody's maiden aunt. I just wanted to help." The wounded sound of his voice was belied by a wide grin. "It's your loss, after all," he added, and sauntered off to prospect the crowd for a female patient with less resistance.

Kate remembered something still left undone. "I forgot about Joe. Watch these jerks," she said to Bobby, pointing at Cheryl and Petey, who she noticed for the first time was wearing a T-shirt inscribed "I Burn Banned Books." She wondered if she could turn Petey loose up around the Kanuyaq mine. Maybe the bear would get lucky a second time.

"Katya!" Auntie Vi said with indignation. Auntie Joy, who understood Kate better than her sister did, put a restraining hand on Vi's arm, although both aunties watched Kate leave the room in equally disapproving silence.

She found Joe groaning under a flatbed loaded with PVC. He'd tripped and managed to knock some of the PVC loose, which had returned the favor and rolled over on him, whereupon he'd fallen and fractured his tibia. Kate called Dandy out and he pulled an inflatable cast over the break with gentle hands. "There now," he told Joe, patting his shoulder comfortingly, "that'll hold you until you get to the clinic at Ahtna. You ought to be fine so long as you don't make any sudden—"

Kate grabbed Joe by the scruff of the neck and hauled him to his feet. Joe screamed.

"—movements," Dandy finished. "Jesus, Kate," he added, but it was more in resignation than protest.

Inside the bar, Kate slung Joe down next to Cheryl and Petey, who was still sniveling. Kate would have liked to kick the boy again just on general principles.

"What you gonna do with them?" Bobby said, without much interest.

"I'm not doing anything," Kate said. "It's not my problem." Seemed like she'd been hearing herself say that same sentence all day, too. "You can call Chopper Jim if you want."

There was a brief silence.

"Well," Bobby said, "nobody's dead."

He looked at Bernie, who shrugged. No way was he going to swear out a complaint and have to be a witness at some trial in Glenallen or Palmer, or worse yet, Anchorage. Who would fill in behind the bar? He looked across the floor at Enid, and shuddered. She was still pissed about Lisa Gette. Best not to push it.

No one else wanted to get tangled up witnessing and testifying, either, not with fishing season so close to starting. Wayne, asked if he'd like to press charges, shook his head numbly and accepted assistance in getting his wife into their vehicle. No one else stepped forward to lodge a complaint. Mr. Baker squinted into his empty glass. "Well, hell," Bobby said, disgusted. "Better get somebody to drive 'em to their place."

"We can drive ourselves," Cheryl said, sitting up.

"Right, and have you play bumper cars with Wayne and Kay all the way home," Bernie said. Just because he wasn't pressing charges didn't mean he wasn't thoroughly pissed off. "I'd as soon let a drunk out of here with his car keys in hand."

Kate had a fleeting wish that Ben Bingley confined his drinking to the Roadhouse. Bernie was the only bartender she knew who had a real conscience and acted on it. "You know, Cheryl," she couldn't resist saying, even knowing it would do no good, "the Bible says, Love thy neighbor. That's all it says. It doesn't say, Love thy neighbor only if he's a straight white antiabortion meat-eating born-again right-wing Republican foot-washing Baptist. Love thy neighbor. That's all it says. You miss that verse, or what?"

"I didn't miss the verse that says even the devil can quote Scripture for his purpose," Cheryl snapped.

Feet wet, her head aching, Kate had to smile. "That's not in the Bible, Cheryl, it's in *The Merchant of Venice*."

She repaired to the bar, intercepted along the way by Frank Scully, who insisted on grasping her hand and shaking it warmly. "Goddam, if it isn't our trusty Eskimo protector! You do good work, Shugak! Saved all our asses yet again!"

The only reason he lived to see another dawn was that he was obviously drunk. "I'm not an Eskimo," she snapped, and shouldered him aside.

Bernie poured her a fresh Coke, the Bakers more Glenlivet, Bobby a bourbon and Dinah a glass of fizzy water with a twist of lime. Steven Seagal was still on the television screen, now getting on a horse in the company of a Chinese actress playing an Eskimo woman, although judging by the thickness of the tree trunks in the background, she should have been a Tlingit or a Haida or maybe even a Tsimshian. "Can you ride a horse?" asked our hero, and the actress glowed and replied, "Of course! I'm a Native American!" at which point Old Sam Dementieff alarmed all the other old coots at his table by going off into what appeared to be an apoplectic fit. "Horses!" he recovered enough to wheeze. "In Alaska! Yah sure, you betcha! Head 'em up! Move 'em out! Ride 'em cowboy! Yee-haw! Just let me hitch my dogsled up to those oat-burners, yawl!"

"I beg your pardon, but what is all this concerning an access road?" Mr. Baker said. The weighty and meticulous manner in which he put his words together caused Kate's eyes to narrow in sudden suspicion.

Bernie jerked his head toward the trio in the corner. "Those are the Jeppsens. They homesteaded forty acres on Mad Mountain six years ago." He jerked his head at the front door through which Wayne and Kay had disappeared, Dandy helping her down the steps and copping a discreet feel while he was at it. "Those are the Kreugers. They got the forty acres next door to the Jeppsens, five years ago."

"Most of the problem," Bobby said, "is that Kay and Wayne have master's degrees and Joe and Cheryl dropped out of high school."

"Yeah," Dinah said, "the Kreugers actually read books, can you imagine?"

"Dreadful," Mrs. Baker said, very much the dowager duchess.

"Deplorable," Mr. Baker said, eyelids closing and opening again in a long, slow blink, like an owl.

"And of course," Bobby said, "the Jeppsens are your ordinary, everyday born-again Christian fanatics, who think the Bible is the only book necessary. They home-schooled Petey," he added, "so they could keep him away from all those ungodly teachers at Ninil-tna High."

"And you see how well it took," Bernie pointed out, but then

Bernie, the local basketball coach, always resented any reduction in the available talent pool for his team, and Petey was almost five foot ten.

"It used to be funny," Dinah said with a sigh.

"Not anymore," Kate said, rubbing gingerly at the sore spot on her head.

"Absolutely not," Mrs. Baker said, even more stately than before.

"Indutipably—inbutibaply—nope," said Mr. Baker.

Displaying a fine, if fraying sense of discretion for which Kate loved them all dearly, the hippie, the hillbilly and the cheechako let this pass. "Then winter before last," Dinah said, "Bonnie Jeppsen, Joe's sister, got the postmaster's job instead of Kay."

"The latest installment in the saga," Bobby took up the tale, "is the access road between the two homesteads. The Kreugers are higher up the hill than the Jeppsens, and somehow the Jeppsens got to thinking that the access road crossed their land and the Kreugers ought to have to go around. But since the Kreugers going around would entail them going across Park land, Dan O'Brian naturally took a somewhat different view of the situation."

"I'll just bet he did," Kate said appreciatively. This part of the story was new to her.

Bernie added, "Of course, mostly they hate each other's guts because the Kreugers grow better tomatoes in their greenhouse than the Jeppsens do."

People in the Alaskan Bush have been shot for refusing offers for Boardwalk. "Breakup," Kate said, as if that explained everything, and perhaps it did.

"Breakup," Bobby repeated, without affection. "What the hell is it with breakup? We make it all the way through winter without going totally insane and it's finally spring and we're gaining daylight and the kings will be up the creek any minute and now we got to start shooting at each other?"

"It's because people make it through the winter that they lose it during spring," Kate said.

They looked at her askance. "Sure, Shugak, that makes just a whole bunch of sense," Bobby said, and rolled his eyes.

"Think about it," Kate insisted. "The winter's long and hard and cold and dark, but people can get through it by looking forward to spring—hell, sometimes spring is all they've got. It's so cold their water freezes, it's dark most of the day, maybe their spouse is sleeping around, maybe the kids are acting out, maybe they're broke, but they know spring is on its way, so they tough it out through the cold and the dark, knowing better times are coming." She drained her glass and set it down with a decisive snap. "And then spring comes, and their wives are still screwing around on them, and their kids are still shits and they're still broke. It's spring and nothing's changed, and something snaps."

"I would prefer that it did not snap in my vicinity," Bobby said with dignity, "thank you very much."

"Mine either," Bernie agreed.

"Nor nine meither," Mrs. Baker said.

"I'll too on it, pass," Mr. Baker said.

Dinah looked at the Bakers, a considering expression supplanting the dreamy one in her eye. "You know, Kate, I think you'd best come to dinner, and bring the Bakers with you. Caribou ribs and onions." She looked at Kate and waggled her eyebrows. "And Bobby's lemon meringue pie." She looked back at the Bakers. "And aspirin. And coffee."

Click! went a shutter, and they looked up to find the lady tourist from Pennsylvania and her husband peering at them over the top of their camera. "I hope you don't mind?" she said. "It's just that you all look so—" she hesitated, and then said with a rush, "—so *Alaskan*."

The two of them beamed.

Mr. Baker belched.

"Come to think of it," Dinah said, "maybe you all should just stay the night."

9

They reached the turnoff to Bobby and Dinah's, inches from a clean getaway, just as Mandy and Chick came barreling down the road on Chick's four-wheeler.

"Whoop!" said Mr. Baker, and rolled down the window to wave madly at his only child. He would have fallen out if Kate hadn't grabbed his belt and hauled him back in at the same time she jammed on the brakes. Miraculously, they were still working.

The four-wheeler slid to a halt just off the truck's starboard bow, squatting at the edge of the pickup's headlights like a malignant toad. It wasn't possible to make out facial expressions in the evening gloom, but Kate received the distinct impression that Chick was forcibly holding Mandy in the driver's seat.

Sitting very erect between Kate and Mr. Baker and always the critic, Mrs. Baker said, "She's supposed to be a musher. Where's her dogs?" Her severity was marred by a loud hiccup, brought on by a particularly large pothole five miles back.

"That's gy mirl!" Mr. Baker whooped exuberantly. He leaned across Mrs. Baker to inquire of Kate, "Did I you tell what a great musher is she?"

"Yes, you did," Kate said. Not a religious person, she was at this point heard to call on a higher power for assistance. She wasn't picky, she'd take anything. An earthquake would be good, something somewhere around 6 on the Richter scale, and the sooner the better. Unfortunately, the higher power appeared to have retired for the night. Somebody had to make the first move, so Kate shifted into second and turned to follow the blue Chevy's taillights down the one-lane game trail that passed for the access road to Bobby's homestead.

The toad fell in behind her.

The three vehicles rumbled across the plank bridge spanning Squaw Candy Creek and pulled up into a neat row in front of the big A-frame. Everyone filed inside, and Kate delivered Mr. and Mrs. Baker into the wrathful arms of their child and bent her head against the coming storm. It was not long in breaking. Mr. and Mrs. Baker sat at the kitchen table, meekly drinking down mugs of hot black coffee, and Chick, Bobby and Dinah hovered around the eye of the hurricane, trying for Kate's sake not to laugh out loud.

"I send them off for a lousy little sight-seeing tour of the Park, and you almost get them eaten by a bear, involved in a plane crash and shot by Cindy Bingley?" Mandy flung out a hand in her parents' direction. Mrs. Baker gave her a low five, and giggled into her coffee mug when Mandy's head swiveled around to stare incredulously.

Bobby abruptly wheeled his chair in a 180 and made for the console in the center of the room at flank speed. Chick hightailed it after him. Dinah stayed within earshot, pretending to assemble the ingredients for dinner. "And then, on top of everything else, you have the gall to take them out to Bernie's and get them stinking drunk?"

"She didn't get us drunk," Mrs. Baker said, sitting up straight in her chair, suddenly very dignified.

"Nah," Mr. Baker said with an expansive wave of his hand, unfortunately the one that held his coffee cup, and launched a spray of hot black liquid across the kitchen floor. "We wanted the trough. She just drink us to the led."

Mrs. Baker thought this so exquisitely amusing that she abandoned any attempt at dignity and positively guffawed. Mr. Baker chose that moment to erupt into poetry, and not just any poetry, either, but Vachel Lindsay going "boomalay boomalay boomalay BOOM!"

There was an outburst of snickering from the console, quickly suppressed. Dinah grabbed a sponge and bent down to mop up the spilled coffee, effectively hiding her face.

Mandy shifted her glare from Kate to Dinah.

"BEAT an empty BARrel with the HANdle of a BROOM!" Mr. Baker surged to his feet. "Be CAREful what you DO," he declaimed, forefinger raised admonishingly, "or Mumbo-JUMBO, God of the CONGO, Mumbo-JUMBO will HOO-DOO YOU!"

• • •

Dinner was served an hour later in an atmosphere redolent of caribou and restrained wrath. Dinah kept up a steady flow of mild gossip concerning various Park rats. Becky Jorgensen had passed away quietly in August, never having left the Alaska Psychiatric Institute where she had been resident since Roger McAniff had killed her husband and eight others in a one-day massacre two years before. Breakups really were better-than-average hard on the Alaskan Bush, they all agreed. After his fifth bad fishing season in Prince William Sound following the *RPetCo Anchorage* spill, Ethan Int-Hout, Abel's second son, was thinking of moving his family from Cordova back to his father's homestead and opening a bed-and-breakfast for fly-in customers. This naturally led to a debate on the merits and demerits of finishing the road from Ahtna to Cordova, a road in construction limbo since the Alaska Earthquake of 1964, which 9.2-on-the-Richter-scale event had taken out an essential bridge across the Kanuyaq River fifty miles north of Cordova. Kate, appalled at the thought of a paved, maintained road connected to the Richardson Highway passing within three quarters of a mile of her homestead, was adamantly against.

Jack Morgan, she remembered, delighted at the thought of a paved, maintained road connected to the Richardson Highway passing within three quarters of a mile of her homestead, was as adamantly for. Bobby pointed out that with the Prudhoe Bay oil field in decline and salmon stocks around the state in chaos, tourism was a lucrative, low-impact industry that ought to be given its chance.

"Low-impact?" Kate said, bristling.

Dinah hastily changed the subject, reporting that probate had finally gone through on the Gette homestead and a distant cousin from Plainville, Illinois, had inherited. No news yet on what he was going to do with it. There was yet another rumor that the Fish and Game, bowing to pressure from sports-fishing interests, was going to limit the red catch on the Kanuyaq, a potential disaster for the many subsistence families with fish camps along its banks. Rumor also had it that the Fish and Game was thinking of limiting the commercial catch at the mouth of the Kanuyaq as well. These two rumors had given rise to a third, that subsistence as well as commercial fishermen were arming for Armageddon, so that the fish hawks in the area were prudently avoiding any low flyovers.

Conversation inevitably came around to the morning's bear attack. "Guy was lucky," Bobby said. "Bear could have taken him out, too. You figure he ran?"

"Wouldn't you?" Kate shot a glance across the table at Mr. and Mrs. Baker. Food, drink and the accumulated events of the day had rendered them oblivious. They sat unheeding, shoulders slumped, eyelids at half-mast, dozing with their heads propped in their hands.

"Weird situation," Bobby said, ignoring the Bakers' potentially delicate sensibilities.

"Why weird?"

"Why didn't they have a gun? It's spring, for crissake, the bears are up, everybody knows that."

Kate licked her fork and put it down. "Bobby, how often have we had this conversation? Every time some transcendentalist type reads too much Rousseau and hikes out into the wilderness to become the neo-noble savage and starves to death, you get up in arms. Carol Stewart was in the wrong place at the wrong time. It isn't a pleasant way to die, certainly. But it isn't all that uncommon, either. There are a lot of bears in Alaska, and occasionally one eats somebody, usually somebody who has broken the rules of human-ursine cohabitation. And therefore," she added, "somebody whose loss can only benefit the gene pool. People are dumb, is all, even the experienced ones. Maybe especially the experienced ones." The memory of her own close encounter by the creek the day before lent an extra fervor to her words, and made Bobby give her a curious look. "What was it somebody said, you can't go broke underestimating the intelligence of the American people?"

"Human-ursine cohabitation?" Bobby said.

"So I have a vocabulary," Kate said. "Sue me."

After dinner Chick pretended an injury to the four-wheeler that needed immediate attention requiring assistance and dragged Mandy outside. Since Mr. and Mrs. Baker had passed out end to end on the long couch, oblivious of any future malign influence Kate might exert, she went. Bobby kicked back in front of his ham radio, shooting the breeze with King Hussein of Jordan, a regular correspondent and another avid ham.

He looked sublimely at home, and he should have, because he'd built the house to order when he came into the Park the same year as Dan O'Brian. It was one big square room without any dividing walls or doors, except to the bathroom, and no rugs, to accommodate his chair. The center was taken up by a pillar of electronic equipment reaching high into the peaked roof. A table buried in more electronic equipment encircled the pillar, from which Bobby talked to ham radio operators from all over the globe, took Park weather readings for the National Oceanic and Atmospheric Administration and broadcast his pirate radio station whenever he was in the mood. The rest of the house was arranged around the pillar; a king-size bed in the northwest corner, the kitchen in the northeast corner, the bathroom between. The living area of the house took up the south side east to west, a sprawling expanse featuring two armchairs and a ten-foot couch placed strategically in front of a huge stone fireplace flanked by triple-glazed picture windows framing a picture-postcard view, Squaw Candy Creek in the foreground and the Quilak Mountains in the background.

As Kate and Dinah were clearing the table, a third voice interrupted Bobby's conversation with the ruler of the sovereign state of Jordan. Bobby listened, replied and said, "Gotta go, King, I got visitors. Been nice talking to you."

King Hussein's deep, precise voice gave a courteous sign-off. The interrupt was KL7CC in Anchorage, with a telephone patch from Jack Morgan. "Well, hey, Jack. How are you?"

In Anchorage, Jack leaned back and propped his feet on a thick pile of case files, a broad grin spreading across his face. Bobby's voice wouldn't have sounded like that if Kate had been hurt. "Well, hey, Bobby, how you doing?"

"I'm fine, but Kate's looking a little flattened around the edges." There was a brief, startled silence and Bobby said quickly, "Just kidding, Jack. I guess you heard about the jet engine falling on her homestead?"

The relief in Jack's voice was palpable. "Bill did, on the radio five minutes ago. I've been stuck in the office all day, I didn't know anything about it." A note of humor crept into the deep drawl. "They said which park and they said the homestead belonged to someone named Shaktoolik, so I figured it could only be Kate. You sure she's okay?"

"Absolutely, but I'll let her tell you that herself."

"Hey, Jack," said Kate, who had drifted irresistibly into range of the mike. "I'm okay."

"I'm awful goddam glad to hear it, Shaktoolik. Bill says they're saying that engine weighed about eight thousand pounds."

"It used to. It weighs about ten pounds now. Per piece."

A chuckle. "So Chicken Little was right. Mutt okay? The homestead?"

In Niniltna, Kate, well aware of listening ears tuned in from Chickaloon to Chistochina, replied, "Mutt's fine, the homestead's fine and other than being sick of hearing about Chicken Little, I am too."

"I'd like to see that for myself."

"Strap on the Cessna and come ahead on up."

"Soon's I get the chance, I'll take you up on that invitation."

The sooner the better, they both thought.

"So," Kate said lamely. "What have you been up to lately?"

"Oh, we got us a doozy this morning. Drunk stabs a buddy to death and he feels so bad about it he tries to hang himself from the Captain Cook statue at Resurrection Park, but the knot comes undone. He falls down the hill through a bunch of devil's club and winds up in the mudflats."

A slow smile spread across Kate's face. "I like it so far."

"It gets better. He decides since he can't hang himself he might as well go to work—he's a burger flipper at some fast-food restaurant—so he climbs up the bank and walks down the middle of Fourth Avenue, covered with mud and devil's club stickers and the dead man's blood and, get this, with the noose still hanging around his neck." Jack paused expectantly.

Kate was willing to play straight man. "And?"

"And nobody notices."

"You're kidding."

"Nope. Seven city blocks, and nobody notices, not even a tourist. Not until he gets to the restaurant. They noticed him then, all right."

"I'll just bet they did," Kate said. Behind her Bobby and Dinah were laughing, too.

"Yeah, well, my life as we know it. Look, we're taking up airtime here. Just wanted to know you were okay."

Bobby said, "She's fine. There's a woman up here who ain't, though."

"I thought that engine falling didn't hurt anybody," Jack said, surprised.

With relish, Bobby said, "This one was taken out by a grizzly bear."

Jack was unimpressed. "Must be breakup."

Bobby scowled. Kate knew a warm feeling around her heart. "Gotta go, Jack. You interrupted Bobby exchanging pleasantries with King Hussein. Be talking to you soon."

"Be seeing you soon," he said, with feeling.

She avoided Bobby's eye. "Say hi to Johnny for me."

In Anchorage, Jack hung up the phone, a thoughtful crease in his brow. Kate had sounded distant, more distant than the two hundred miles between them would account for. It was probably his imagination. He shrugged it off, or tried to, and returned to the case file that had brought him into the office on a weeknight, a painstaking reconstruction of a ten-year-old rape-homicide in Wasilla that the Alaska state supreme court had kicked back on appeal. Because he knew how to concentrate, his unease over Kate faded into the background, to be brought back center stage in the wee small hours of the morning, the time when all one's chickens, Little and otherwise, come home to roost.

In Niniltna, Bobby exchanged cordial insults with KL7CC and signed off. A ham standing by in Tonsina couldn't resist keying his mike and making kissy-face noises into it. Kate Shugak's long-distance relationship with Jack Morgan was a byword in the Bush.

Bobby looked over Kate's shoulder. "Dinah! I told you to get off your feet!" He gave Kate a nudge. "Go do the dishes for her."

"I am perfectly capable of clearing the table and washing the dishes," Dinah said as Kate approached.

"I can see that," Kate said. "How have you been feeling?"

"I am feeling just fine," the blonde replied, raising her voice, "but if I have to answer that question one more time I won't be. You'd think this was the first baby to be born in the Park in this century."

Kate was pretty sure these bitter remarks had not been addressed to her, and when Bobby called from the radio console, "Have you got your feet up?" she was sure of it.

"Ignore him," she told Dinah.

"Easy for you to say, you don't live with him," Dinah muttered. She carried a load of dishes to the sink and ran water.

Kate found a dish towel threaded through the handle of the refrigerator door and started drying. "Need a ride somewhere?"

Dinah's hands paused in the dishwater. A smile appeared on her face. "Not on your life."

"Didn't think so."

They cleaned the kitchen while Bobby pirated a little radio wave, playing anything recorded on vinyl before Creedence Clearwater Revival broke up, interspersed with ads for a bake sale at the high school, a job offer for a gear mender paying minimum wage, sale items including a used freezer, a boom box and a 1964 Ford Falcon, and notice of the upcoming Niniltna Native Association shareholders' meeting.

When Bobby talked to people face-to-face, his voice was usually at its highest decibel level and the words tumbled out in a torrent; when he talked over the air, it melted into the mike like maple syrup. He sang the last lyric along with the Temptations. "Sorry about that," he said, as the last note faded away, "but cut me some slack, people, I'm soon to be married and raise a family, oh yeah, myself. Let's listen to what Bonnie Raitt has to say about motherhood." The beginning bass notes of "Baby Mine" reverberated up through the soles of their stocking feet. Kate was pretty sure that cut postdated CCR by about twenty years, but she wasn't fool enough to say so. Recently cuts from Mary Chapin Carpenter, Billy Joel and the Indigo Girls had also made it onto Bobby's playlist. The man really was mellowing out.

The women spoke in low voices, so as not to have their conversation broadcast all over the Park, the Sound and, depending on the skip that night, across the border into the next country. "I've never seen Mandy look so frazzled," Dinah said. "What's the matter? Mom and Dad giving her fits?" She looked over her shoulder toward the living room. Mr. and Mrs. Baker snored on, oblivious.

Kate smiled. "They aren't so bad, once you get to know them." Dinah looked at her. "Well, okay, at first you could tell they were thinking they were going up the river with Axel Heyst."

"The benefit of a liberal education," Dinah agreed, the beneficiary of one herself.

After Bonnie came the Beatles with "Baby, It's You."

Dinah washed a plate and handed it to Kate. "Jack sounded like he might be missing you. When's the last time you saw him?"

Kate thought. "New Year's."

"Yikes," Dinah said mildly.

"Yeah," Kate said, with feeling.

The moon was coming up over the Quilaks, large and nearly full. No ring, which meant the weather was going to stay the same for a while. There was a sudden movement in the bushes at the bottom of the yard but it was too dark to see what it was. Gee, maybe a bear.

Dinah said, "The two of you only see each other half a dozen times a year."

Kate came back into her body with a start. "Huh? Who?"

"You and Jack," Dinah said. "You don't get together that often."

Kate smiled. "Some men are like that."

"Like how?"

"Catch and release."

Dinah refused to laugh. "What keeps it going?"

On the air, the Fab Four were succeeded by Crosby, Stills, Nash and Young. Teach your children well. Kate hoped the kid didn't turn out to be a heavy-metal fan. Kiss didn't get a lot of airplay on the Bobby Clark Show. "What keeps you and Bobby going?"

"We live together," Dinah said, perhaps more bluntly than she meant to.

"What is this," Kate said, amused, "matchmaking? And you not even an old married woman yet." Dinah's blush revealed all, and she relented. "I like my privacy, Dinah. I like making my own decisions without compromise. I like coming and going as I please. There's no way I'm moving back to Anchorage, and I can just see Jack giving up his job and moving out to the Bush. Not to mention which, his son might have something to say about that."

"You did."

"Did what?"

"Gave up your job and moved out to the Bush."

"That was different," Kate said curtly.

Dinah's eyes dropped to the scar on Kate's throat. "True." She washed a plate, rinsed it and handed it to Kate. "You don't need him the way I need Bobby. The way Bobby needs me." Thoughtfully she added, "That probably comes from being orphaned so young. You had to become self-sufficient a lot earlier than the rest of us. Got you out of the habit of needing people." She dropped a handful of silverware into the rinse water. "Got you out of the habit of letting people need you, too."

Kate thought of Auntie Vi's request that she sound out Harvey Meganack on the health clinic, and of her reluctance to do so, overcome only by an elder's authority. An authority, she admitted to herself in the privacy of her own thoughts, that she avoided by living as close to the edge of that authority as she could get and still be in the Park. It wasn't the first time that Dinah, eleven years her junior, white and a cheechako to boot, had come uncomfortably close to plucking out the heart of Kate's mystery. "Thank you, Dr. Freud," she said. "Any other observations you'd care to make while you've got my id pinned to the drainboard?"

Dinah refused to be insulted. "I think you do love him, though."

"Him? Who him? Oh. Jack." She shrugged and stacked plates in the cupboard. "I like him, I respect and admire the job he does, he makes me laugh, he's great in the sack. And I do love the sound of his voice," she added, dwelling on the last morning that voice had woken her up. She closed the cupboard and cleared her throat. "What else is there?"

Dinah, looking ever so slightly crushed, said unwisely, "Sounds kind of cold-blooded to me."

"Cold-blooded?" Kate was surprised and maybe even a little hurt. "I love men," she said. "I love the shape of their bodies. I love the sound of their voices. I love it that they have to shave, and I love how their skin feels when they don't. I love it that they will not, on pain of death, ask for directions. I love it that they can make lifelong friends with another guy over a brand of beer or a game of basketball or the make of a pistol and never need to know another single thing about that person except that he drinks Full Sail Golden Ale or shoots a thirty-two percent average from the floor or owns a Colt Peacemaker. They're another race entirely and I find the study of them fascinating." She paused, and added, "I just don't expect a lot of them."

"Except for Jack," Dinah said, still bent on romance.

"Especially Jack. His hormones kick into overdrive whenever he's within ten feet of me. His forehead lowers, his jaw starts to hang, a club sprouts from one fist." Kate remembered her reaction to the NTSB man, to Mark Stewart, to Dan O'Brian for crissake. "Dinah, have you ever been physically attracted to a total stranger?"

The soapy dishwater stilled long enough for Dinah to give Kate an assessing look. "Just how long ago was it that Jack dragged you off to his cave?"

Their eyes met, and at the same time they said, "Too long." It made them laugh, and they finished the dishes with only an occasional admonitory roar from the DJ.

Jack Morgan would have slept better that night if he'd been listening to their conversation. He wasn't. He didn't.

10

Kate was awakened by the sound of an approaching helicopter. "No," she said, and pulled the sleeping bag over her head. After the alarums and excursions of the previous twenty-four hours she had slept long and hard, and she was in no mood for a one-on-one with Chopper Jim.

But the sound of the helicopter's engine got louder, and she heard the others stirring, Mr. and Mrs. Baker on the couch, Chick and Mandy in sleeping bags in front of the fireplace (the only warm spot on the floor, which Mandy had pointedly preempted the night before), and Bobby and Dinah in the monster bed in the back of the room. There were groans, moans and a whimper or two. Kate added a few choice words and unzipped the sleeping bag to wiggle into her jeans, feeling each and every one of her thirty-four years. The bandage over her temple had rubbed off during the night but the wound had crusted over and was barely sore to the touch.

Some stretches and toe touches limbered her up enough to let her move over to the front door and open it, just in time to see the all-too-familiar Bell Jet Ranger settle into the clearing, looming against the clear dawn like a gigantic black tarantula. She would have greeted the tarantula with more enthusiasm.

Jim Chopin climbed out, resplendent in blue and gold even at cockcrow. He was followed by a second man. It was with something of a shock that she recognized Mark Stewart.

"Good morning!" Jim said, all bright and shiny with good cheer.

"I don't want to know why you're here," Kate said. "I just want to know why you're here at the crack of dawn."

"Why, Kate," he said, hurt, "as a gentleman, it's my duty to return your calls."

"As a gentleman it's your duty to let me sleep in."

The grin, as wide and predatory as a shark's, should have been licensed to kill. "I'll mark that down that for future reference."

Kate refused to be lured. "How did you know I was here?"

The grin widened. "Heard you on the radio last night."

"Oh." She had said nothing over the air to embarrass herself, and therefore she refused to be embarrassed.

He gestured. "You remember Mark Stewart?"

"Under the circumstances, it would be difficult to forget," Kate said. "How are you, Mr. Stewart?"

"Fine."

The widower's expression was bland, his voice flat, uninflected. His grip was warm and tactile. Kate looked up to find him watching her, his face still, his dark gaze vibrant and compelling. She felt the hair on the backs of her arms stand up, and very carefully pulled her hand free.

Jim said amiably, "Mr. Stewart has agreed to accompany me up to the mine and walk me through yesterday's unfortunate incident, so that I can complete my report."

It was an odd enough request, thankfully, to free her from

Stewart's mesmerizing gaze. She looked at Jim and thought, What are you up to now, you sneaky bastard? "Why didn't you just go straight up there then?"

Amiability turned to amusement. "And hello to you, too, Jim," he said. "Beautiful morning, isn't it? Like a cup of coffee?"

Behind her there were noises, and with ill grace she held open the door. "You might as well come in, now that you've gotten us all out of bed."

"Who's all?" Jim followed her inside, Mark Stewart one step behind. A yawning Dinah was measuring scoops into the coffee-maker. "Morning, Jim."

"Morning, Dinah." The trooper doffed his hat, and raised an eyebrow as he took in the crowd. "What's this? A sleepover and I wasn't invited?"

"Mr. and Mrs. Baker, this is Sergeant Jim Chopin, of the Alaska State Troopers. Mandy's parents," she told Jim. "And Mr. and Mrs. Baker, you met Mr. Stewart yesterday."

Mr. and Mrs. Baker blinked up from the couch. Probably they had been expecting the maid with coffee, croissants and the *Boston Globe*. Mandy and Chick were rolling up their sleeping bags. Bobby was glowering at Jim from the kitchen table, but whatever pithy comment he had been about to make was forestalled by the sound of an approaching four-wheeler with the throttle all the way open.

"Jesus Christ," Kate said beneath her breath. Grand Central Station had followed her to Bobby's. She yanked open the door, this time to see Dan O'Brian roar up. He must have flown into Niniltna even before Jim was in the air to get to Bobby's this early.

"Hey, Kate!" he said, bounding up the steps. A morning person, obviously. So was Kate, but then usually she'd had more sleep.

"How'd you know I was here?"

"Why are you so sure I'm looking for you?" he said indignantly, and added, at the same time she did, "Heard you on the radio last night." He caught sight of Mark Stewart and his chin dropped. "Mr. Stewart?"

"Ranger O'Brian." Stewart's expression didn't change, but Kate received the distinct impression that he did not welcome Dan's appearance on the scene. For reasons she shied away from examining, she didn't want to be able to read Stewart that well, and deliberately stood where he would be out of her line of vision. Jim was finishing up the introductions with a placid air. "And this is Bobby Clark, Mr. Stewart. This is his house."

Bobby shot the trooper a malevolent look. Bobby was not a morning person. Dinah stepped into the apprehensive silence that followed his nongreeting with mugs of coffee all around. Mr. and Mrs. Baker accepted theirs in a manner strongly reminiscent of the Chosen seeing their first water after forty years of staggering around the desert. Mandy looked less ticked off than at lights-out the night before, but not much. Chick was still restraining a belly laugh.

Always at ease, Chopper Jim sat down across from Bobby and added milk and sugar, surveying them all with a glint of amusement in the back of his blue eyes, and something else Kate couldn't quite identify. "Thank you," Stewart said, and smiled at Dinah. Dinah returned the smile with equanimity, a certain curiosity and a purely female appreciation, which changed as Kate watched to a surprised understanding. She turned her head and looked at Kate. Kate nodded. Bobby sat up straight in his chair.

Dan O'Brian virtually snatched his mug from Dinah's outstretched hand and stepped out of range of Mark Stewart's vision. In a series of facial twitches, winks and head jerks reminiscent of an epileptic with Tourette's syndrome he managed to convey that he wanted to speak to Kate privately. Unless they went into the bathroom together, which might occasion some comment, there was only the porch. Resigned, Kate followed him outside, cradling the warmth of her coffee mug in her hands against the chilly dawn. Breakup was not known for its subtropical range of temperatures.

There were no clouds in the sky, revealing the sun as a dull gold disk low on the eastern horizon, outlining the jagged peaks of the Quilaks in the thin light of an Arctic spring morning. There was a steady drip of melting ice from the eaves, and the sound of a winter's worth of snow rushing between the narrow banks of the creek at the edge of the front yard. A mile downstream, the creek would merge with the silted gray expanse of the Kanuyaq, and from there the two would travel together to Prince William Sound and the Gulf of Alaska. Before long, the first king salmon would be beating its way upriver. Kate's mouth watered at the thought.

Dan was almost beside himself with impatience. "All right, all right, what?" she said.

He looked over her shoulder at the closed door, decided it didn't provide enough privacy and lowered his voice to a whisper that could probably have been heard on the next homestead. Subtle was not exactly Dan's middle name. "I called Anchorage last night and got a buddy to log on to Motznik for me. You know, the data base that accesses all state records?"

"Yes, Dan, I know what Motznik is."

"Okay, guess what?"

Kate took a deep breath and let it out. All she wanted to do at this point was go home and start reassembling the pieces of her life. There were supplies to be laid in, dip nets to be mended, caches to be repaired, snow-machine tanks to be patched, washing machines to be fixed.

Taxes to be filed.

On the other hand, it wouldn't hurt to drink Dinah's excellent coffee, enjoy the glorious dawn and listen to Dan carry on. He could be fun when he took up a cause, and his current mood had all the signs. "I don't know," she said. "What?"

"Mark Stewart has had a license for hunting everything on four legs in the state of Alaska for the last twenty years." He paused impressively.

Kate, in the act of swallowing coffee, did not choke in surprise.

That was all right, because Dan had more than enough enthusiasm for the both of them. "He applies for the moose lottery every year, Kate. He's got himself a tag six times and a moose five."

Since he so clearly expected a reaction, Kate said obediently, "So you're saying he is an experienced hunter."

Dan, losing patience, thumped the railing. "That's where I've seen him before, Kate! He was up last fall hunting sheep. He flew in with someone else and they stopped up on the Step for maps. I talked mostly to the pilot, guy name of, hell, what was it, Hooligan or something like that. That's why I couldn't remember Stewart at first, I didn't talk to him."

There was a crunch of twig and Kate looked across Bobby's yard to see a moose cow with a yearling calf browsing contentedly through a stand of diamond willow.

Dan demanded, "Don't you see? When I said I'd seen him before, he said he couldn't remember. He lied."

Kate sighed and turned to look at him. "Dan, it was five minutes six months ago. Maybe he's one of those people who just doesn't remember a face. And what does it matter anyway?"

"What does it matter!" At his shout the low murmur of voices from inside the house stilled momentarily. Dan whispered furiously, "It matters because that whole story about his wife and the bear attack is as phony as a three-dollar bill, and you know it, and it's even phonier if he's an experienced hunter, and you know that, too. Now, what are you going to do about it?"

Her lips compressed. "*Et tu*, Dan?"

Dan, bewildered, said, "What the hell does that mean?"

"It means you and every other mother's son in this friggin' Park thinks I'm in charge. In the meantime, I've got half a 747 scattered across my front forty, my cupboards are bare, my truck's been flattened and my dog probably thinks I'm dead. I'm going home." And she still had yet to talk to Harvey Meganack, a chore she was convinced was futile anyway, whatever Auntie Vi thought. "The situation's a little odd, I grant you, but—"

"A little!"

"Dan." She said his name with enough force to shut him up, at least for the moment. "Okay, so Stewart ran off on his wife. He panicked. It happens. So he outran a grizzly. Grizzlies aren't stupid, she probably stayed behind to feed on the wife." Kate controlled a shiver. "So Stewart doesn't look as frazzled as anyone else we've seen who survived a bear attack. Shock takes people different ways. None of it proves anything."

"He lied to me," Dan said stubbornly. "I don't like him."

"I don't, either," she surprised both of them by saying. "It still doesn't prove anything." She drained her mug. "If you want action, talk to the man. I've got my own problems."

The man chose that moment to open up the door and step outside. "Somebody call my name?"

"Ranger O'Brian, aka Sherlock Holmes, will be happy to fill you in." She waved a hand at Dan. "The game's afoot. Have at it."

Too excited to take offense, Ranger O'Brian did, promptly and thoroughly. In a minute, Dan was going to find a way to work the Trilateral Commission into the scenario. Kate turned to go inside.

Jim caught her elbow. "Kate."

"What?" Kate snapped, yanking free.

"Wondered if you'd do me a favor?"

"*Et tu*, Jim?" she snarled.

He blinked. "I beg your pardon?"

Kate took a deep breath and counted to ten. "What favor?"

"Come up to the mine with Stewart and me." He saw the answer in her face and said quickly, "You were first on the scene, you've spent a lot of time in the area and you know bears. I want you to listen to his story and pick all the holes you can. Dan's right. It's phony as hell."

"I didn't find anything, Jim," Kate said, with an awful patience she hoped neither he nor Dan would mistake. "And I told you, we saw the bear right after the attack. She'd been feeding, all right." She remembered the red-stained fur, the shreds of flesh between the claws, and again suffered through a flashback of the moments by the creek. She never wanted to look down the snout of a grizzly bear at that close a range again. What must Carol Stewart have felt her last few seconds, knowing there was no escape? Had she been conscious enough to feel the rip of the claws, the bite of the teeth? Had she— Kate yanked herself away from that thought and said briskly, "Believe me, that grizzly had been feeding, and recently. And she did come barreling down the hill from the direction of the mine."

Dan O'Brian couldn't resist. "And you took the All-White Enriched East Coast Couple up there anyway?"

Kate's eyes narrowed. "It was in the opposite direction from the way the bear was traveling at the time. It seemed like a good idea." Dan started to speak and she held up both hands, palms out. "Look, guys. If Mark Stewart wanted to kill his wife, it would have been a whole hell of a lot easier and a lot less risk to himself just to shove her into the Kanuyaq River and let the glacier calve on her."

"Unless she was already dead and he needed the bear to cover up how she really got that way in case the body was recovered," Dan hissed. "There's bear attacks and there's bear attacks, Shugak. That grizzly should have either run when she heard more than one voice, or taken both Stewarts out. At the very least, Stewart should have been wounded. And if he was an experienced hunter, he should have had a rifle with him."

"Even experienced hunters get brain cramps."

The door behind them opened and Bobby rolled out. "What's going on?"

With some asperity Kate demanded, "Is there anybody left in the house?"

She was ignored. Ranger O'Brian was more than happy to fill Bobby in. Bobby, who had taken an instant dislike to the tall dark stranger making eyes over the coffee mugs at his soon-to-be wife, entered into the discussion with enthusiasm, endorsing Dan's assessment of the situation without hesitation and heaping scorn on Kate for her steadfast dissent. The third time around, Dan O'Brian had Mark Stewart cutting up his wife with a hunting knife and feeding her to *Ursus arctos horribilis* one piece at a time.

Kate snorted and set her mug down on the railing with a thump. "Yeah, right. The first thing that bear would have done is take Stewart's knife away from him and jam it up his ass. Bobby, can I borrow your truck? I've got to make a supply run into Ahtna."

"But, Kate—"

"Dammit!" Kate turned on Dan so ferociously that he actually backed up a step. "Dan, there's the cop on this porch." She pointed at Chopper Jim, who had perched on the railing and was listening with a faint smile creasing his face. "You got a problem, take it up with him. Like I said, I've got my own to deal with. Bobby?" She held out her hand.

Meekly for him, Bobby fished keys out of his pocket. Kate fairly snatched them up and stamped down the stairs. Chopper Jim made no attempt to stop her. The trio of men watched as she backed the pickup around and thundered over the little bridge and down the road.

When the truck was safely out of earshot Chopper Jim remarked, "She's awful goddam cranky today. What's her problem?"

"Jack's in Anchorage and she's here," Dan said, the wisdom of the ages sitting on his leprechaun face.

Bobby, who knew her better than either of the other men, frowned and said nothing at all.

• • •

The old railroad roadbed was, if anything, in worse shape than it had been the day before. Driving Bobby's Chevy required relearning all the hand controls he'd had installed. Kate had them more or less mastered by the time she reached her own turnout, pausing just long enough to check on the cabin and fetch Mutt. The jet engine was still in the yard, unchaperoned; the go team was sleeping in this morning. This lack of attention didn't augur well for a quick reimbursement of funds, and Kate continued her journey in a gloomy frame of mind. Mutt, annoyed at having been left to her own devices the night before, rode shotgun in unforgiving silence.

They were home by one o'clock in the afternoon with a truck

full of groceries and a receipt bearing testimony to Kate's good credit with the Alaska Commercial Company, only to find the NTSB once more in possession of the clearing. Or so she assumed when she had to park fifty feet up the road because her turnout was full of vehicles. She recognized most of them, from which she deduced the population of Niniltna was exercising their right to a free market by renting their personal vehicles out to the go team at undoubtedly exorbitant hourly rates. Auntie Vi's Toyota Land Cruiser was first in line, which only confirmed her hypothesis.

Nor was the NTSB crew destined to be her last visitors of the day, more's the pity. She was lifting the first box of groceries out of the back of the pickup when the sound of an approaching engine filled her with foreboding. She raised her head to see her worst fears fulfilled: Mandy behind the wheel of her brand-new, newly battered Ford, its cockeyed front bumper making it look slightly tipsy. Mr. and Mrs. Baker were sitting next to her, erect and composed and looking as if they had suffered no ill effects from the previous day's strenuous activities.

Mandy didn't look happy. Kate had to resist the temptation to cross herself and she wasn't even Catholic. At least Chick wasn't along to titter in the background.

Mandy got out. The driver's side. She must have fixed the door. From the looks of it, probably with a crowbar. Whatever worked.

"Hi," Kate said warily, holding the box of groceries like a shield. It covered most of her major organs.

"Kate," Mandy said, voice curt. Great, she'd probably heard about the shoot-out at the Roadhouse.

"Ms. Shugak," Mr. Baker said, handing his wife out. "How nice to see you again."

"Indeed," Mrs. Baker added, unusually warm for her.

"Kate—" Mandy said.

"Mandy," Kate said, beating her to it, "I'm sorry about your truck but it wasn't my fault. That bear charged us, there wasn't a thing I could do about it. George ground-looped 50 Papa practically right on top of us, and there was no chance to get out of the way. And as for the bullet holes—you know what Cindy Bingley's like when she goes after Ben. There was nothing I could do, and nobody got hurt, not even Ben. At least the last I saw he was okay. And as for the Jeppsens and the Kreugers, hell, there's no way I could have—"

Without doing anything so vulgar as making a face, Mr. Baker wore an expression that nevertheless conveyed a distinct message.

"—no way I could have foreseen that, uh, Cheryl and Kay were going to have such a nasty argument," Kate finished weakly. So Mandy hadn't heard about the shoot-out. Yet. Kate thrust away the thought of what she might say when she did.

"Truck?" Mandy said, fastening on the one word in the flood that meant something to her. "Oh. Kate, don't worry about the truck. Besides, I told you. She's yours."

Kate blinked at her. "What?"

"You know." Mandy gave her head a tiny jerk in the direction of her parents, and winked reassuringly. "For what you did."

"Mandy—"

"That's why I'm here, actually," Mandy said, holding out the keys. "I already signed over the registration. It's in the glove compartment. And Mother and Dad wanted to say thanks for the tour." A faint grin crossed her face. "They enjoyed it, even if it did take them till this morning to dry out. Internally as well as externally."

She stood there holding the keys out, and was evidently prepared to stand there holding them out until Doomsday, so Kate awkwardly shifted the box in her arms and took them. "Well," she said. "Thanks." The one word didn't seem like enough somehow, and she added, "Come on down. I'll make you some coffee. Now that I have some."

Mandy looked at the boxes stacked in the back of the truck.

"Grocery run to Ahtna," Kate said.

"And you had to borrow Bobby's truck?"

"Well." Kate tried not to squirm.

Mandy looked at her, one eyebrow ever so slightly raised, and for just a moment the resemblance to her father was very pronounced. "You didn't believe me about the truck, did you?"

"Well," Kate said again, shifting from foot to foot. "I guess I just didn't know how right Fitzgerald was."

"How so?"

"The rich really are different."

Mandy's mouth turned up at the corners. "Yeah, and you know what Hemingway said in reply?"

"What?"

" 'Yes, they have more money than you and me.' "

"Glad to hear it," Kate said, regaining some of her composure. "If that's all the difference there is, you can help me hump these boxes down to the cabin."

They loaded up, even Mrs. Baker, and Mutt led her train of native bearers single file down the trail with her tail cocked at a lordly angle. "What's with all the traffic?" Mandy said behind her.

"I just got here, I'm guessing the go team is back."

At that moment a Sikorsky helicopter with a sling attached hove into view over the trees. "Great," Kate said, hastening her pace. "Now maybe they'll get that hunk of junk out of my front yard."

It was unfortunate that just before reaching the clearing Mandy tripped over a tree root and into a clump of alders, dumping her box of canned goods and making enough noise for three bears, two moose and a hoary marmot. Her subsequent crash and burn was loud enough to be heard even over the Sikorsky's engine, because it became immediately obvious that the Park Uninvitational Four-Footed Grand Prix across the homestead the previous morning had had a strong and lasting effect.

A shot rang out and a bullet thudded into a tree trunk a foot above Kate's head.

Mutt let loose with a ferocious bark.

Kate yelled, "Stay!" In a move that seemed almost routine by now, she dropped her groceries and dove for the ground, grabbing for Mr. and Mrs. Baker's ankles along the way, and none too soon, because in the next moment there was a *Whoosh!* and a cloud of spray hit the bushes directly in front of them.

Kate's eyes began to water and she pulled the neck of her T-shirt up over her face. Mutt whined and dropped flat, rubbing her face in her paws. Mandy sneezed violently. The whites of her parents' eyes turned a bright red and their noses began to run. Mrs. Baker began to cough.

Another bullet thunked into the tree trunk.

The pilot of the Sikorsky must have thought he was back in Da Nang and raised ship high and fast.

11

The noise of the engine faded.

Kate pushed herself up to her knees and yelled, "Hey! Who-ever's in the clearing! Cease fire, dammit!" punctuating her appeal with a tremendous sneeze.

"I *hate* breakup," Mandy said, choking and coughing.

"Amanda dear, don't you think we should—"

There was another shot and another spray and, incensed, Kate yelled again, "Cut it out, you guys! It's Kate Shugak, and you sons-abitches had better either shoot me on sight or have an awful god-dam good excuse for shooting and spraying at me before!"

The shots and spray ceased. "Kate?" A voice she recognized as John Stewman's spoke hesitantly. "Kate, is that you?"

Kate's reply was almost muffled by another tremendous sneeze. "No, asshole, it's the tooth fairy!"

She saw Mrs. Baker reach as if to rub her eyes and snatched at her hand. "No, don't rub it, that'll only make it worse." She stood, wet and muddy and furious. "Stewman, you disarm those people of yours or my dog and I will disarm them for you! And we won't care how gentle we do it, either!"

There was a brief pause, a rustle of movement. "All right, Kate. You can come out now."

They staggered down the path into the clearing to come face-to-face with Selina and Bickford, white-faced and trembling. Bickford was holding a rifle. Selina had acquired a bright orange can of bear repellent, still held at the ready. The rest of the team were clustered protectively together behind them. Kate couldn't imagine why, if the idiots had thought they were about to be charged by a bear, they hadn't at least run for the cabin.

A stray wisp of the pepper spray caught at her throat. "Put that down," she said, coughing. Neither Bickford nor Selina moved. Kate stepped forward and reached for the rifle. Bickford seemed disinclined to give it to her.

Kate looked at him and said very carefully, "Give me that rifle before I take it away from you and shoot you with it."

Bickford was not the stuff of which heroes were made. He surrendered.

She cleared the chamber and clicked on the safety. It was the .30-06 from the gun rack over her door. Now, that would have been downright embarrassing, getting shot on her own doorstep with her own gun. Another time Kate might have found the prospect mildly amusing, but considering the accumulation of events during the past two days, too many of which had offered bodily harm to her person, she was fresh out of a sense of humor.

All Selina's attention was occupied in trying to clip the can of bear repellent to her belt. Her hands were shaking so badly she wasn't having much success, and irritated as always at a simple job poorly done, Kate slung her rifle, snatched the can, yanked Selina's waistband away from her waist until she could see all the way down to her boots and jammed the clip over the belt. The elastic of the waistband snapped back and the can smacked into her belly. The other woman gave an inarticulate protest.

"Shut up," Kate said.

Selina shut up.

"The only reason you're still living," Kate told her, "is because you didn't score any direct hits." It wasn't easy to glare with watery eyes, but Kate managed it. "Now just what the hell is going on here?"

There was some shuffling of feet, a few inaudible mumbles and a great deal of staring up at the sky or down at the ground or off into space. After a moment John Stewman stepped manfully forward. "Well, Kate, some of us got a little nervous after the bear incident yesterday. And then we heard about what happened to that woman up to the mine—"

"That was thirty miles from here," Kate said. Nobody looked convinced. She shook her head and swore tiredly. "I didn't used to feel this old," she said, mostly to herself. To Bickford she said pointedly, "I assume that sky crane was to get that hunk of junk out of here once and for all?"

He nodded mutely.

"Good. Call it back. The sooner I see your backsides heading up that trail, the safer I'm going to feel. Mutt!"

There was a rustle at the opposite end of the clearing, and Kate looked around to find an extremely wary Mutt, yellow eyes turned an original shade of magenta, standing at the edge of the clearing in what could only be described as a tentative manner. Generally instinct and training compelled her to protect, but after the last two days Kate didn't know that she blamed Mutt if her first reflex was to run as far from the homestead as she could get. "It's okay, girl, it's safe to come out now."

Mutt wasn't entirely convinced, but she did come out of the bushes. Mandy, who had borne the brunt of the pepper spray, she gave a wide berth. "Thanks a lot," Mandy told her, and gave a convulsive sneeze, which was the signal for first her mother and then her father to follow suit.

"Come on," Kate said, and led the way into the cabin, where she pumped up a bucket of water into which Mandy immediately immersed her entire head, and emerged snorting and trumpeting like an elephant down at the local mud hole. Kate pumped up another bucket of water and Mandy's parents made do with a more refined rinse. Kate simply stood at the sink, head beneath the spout, and pumped. She wrung out her hair and groped for a towel. Head wrapped in a turban, she blinked at the room. Mandy had replaced the rifle in its rack over the door. The rest of the cabin looked much as she had left it. Lucky for the NTSB.

Mr. Baker had dried off and gone back outside, and through the kitchen window Kate could see him standing next to Kevin Bickford, who had his Earlybird cap pulled low over eyes that were darting nervously back and forth. The Sikorsky was back, and they were watching the sling being maneuvered around the engine. Kate just hoped the corpse didn't disintegrate when they tried to lift it into the air.

Mrs. Baker was standing next to the couch, staring down at the hole in it. Evidently she'd missed it the previous morning. She looked up to see Kate watching her, decided it would be a breach of good manners to ask and moved to the other leg of the couch to sit down, a little heavily, as if all this might have been just a little too much, finally. "Goodness," she said at last. "Amanda dear, you never told us how exciting life is in Alaska."

"It isn't always like this, Mother," Mandy said, but her voice was weak, and Mrs. Baker looked about as convinced as Mutt had when Kate called her into the clearing.

Mandy combed fingers through her damp hair. "We'd better get the rest of those supplies down the trail before it gets dark."

It took the four of them three trips, by which time the jet engine was gone. Stewman and the rest of the team remained behind for an hour or so, locating, photographing, cataloging and bagging any scrap of metal they had missed in the previous search that Kate could not immediately identify or claim, all under Mutt's bleak and intimidating eye. Kate gave her a piece of beef jerky in reward, and something about the sight of those large, sharp teeth ripping into the strip of meat made the investigators work faster.

The pickup looked even more flattened without the engine than it had with it. Kate resolutely turned her back on the mortal remains. Mr. Baker, chatting again with Bickford, beckoned her over. "Well, Ms. Shugak," he said in his best lord-of-the-manor air, "I believe you know Mr. Bickford of Earlybird Air Freight."

"We've met," Kate said, without enthusiasm.

"Splendid," Mr. Baker said jovially. "We've just been discussing your little, er, dilemma, in regard to compensation for this, er, unfortunate accident."

Kate opened her mouth to inform both of them that she didn't regard the situation as a "little, er, dilemma," but something in Mr. Baker's gaze stopped her. "Have you?" she said slowly.

Mr. Baker, hands in his pockets, rocked back on his heels and smiled at Bickford, who smiled back, a little sickly, Kate thought.

"Mr. Bickford and I have found much to discuss," Mr. Baker said, even more jovially. "It seems I am acquainted with his employer." He beamed at the two of them.

"His employer?" Kate said, drawing a blank.

"Yes indeed. Patrick O'Donnell and I are old friends. We manage to get in a game of squash whenever he's in town, and he's been out to the house for dinner quite often. A charming man."

"Who is that, dear?" Mrs. Baker came out of the cabin dusting fastidiously at her hands.

"Patrick O'Donnell, Margery," her husband replied. "You remember. The chief executive officer of Earlybird Air Freight."

"Why, of course," she said. She slid an arm through her husband's and bestowed a smile on the Earlybird man that was cordial without in any way encouraging overfamiliarity. "And how is dear Patrick?"

Bickford's expression indicated that he had about as much to do with dear Patrick as the parish priest did with the pope, but he struggled gamely to keep up. "The last I heard, he was fine, ma'am. He spends most of his time at corporate headquarters in New York, of course."

"Of course," Mrs. Baker agreed. "Will he be coming up to oversee this fuss, do you think?"

Bickford tried not to look appalled at the thought. "I don't think so, ma'am." He hastened to add, "I'm sure that he is in constant communication with the Anchorage office, however."

"A pity," she said. "It would be so nice to see dear Patrick again."

Mr. Baker patted her hand consolingly. The hand was adorned with a diamond solitaire the size of Plymouth Rock. Bickford noticed, and tried not to goggle. "I was just telling Mr. Bickford, dear, that I know Patrick would wish that every effort be made to redress this dreadful situation. No one hates litigation more than he does, and I'm sure Ms. Shugak would agree that there is nothing to be gained by action that would be most distressing for all concerned." He raised an expectant eyebrow in Kate's direction.

"Oh, of course," Kate said in a faint voice, mostly because it seemed to be required of her. Litigation? Like with lawyers? Lawyers cost money, and at this moment the one-pound Darigold butter can on the table in the cabin held less than two hundred bucks, and that much only until she filed her taxes. Mandy was watching from the doorstep of the cabin, a slight smile that was hard to read on her face.

"So I feel that, really, for the best interests of all concerned, a prompt, just settlement would be most beneficial. I'm sure Patrick would agree, aren't you, dear?"

"Certainly," said Mrs. Baker. "He would be most upset at anything less."

"Where do you bank, Ms. Shugak?" Mr. Baker said.

Kate stared at him with the fascination usually exhibited by a deer frozen in the headlights of an oncoming car. "Ah—"

"Yes?" Mr. Baker prompted.

"I really would prefer cash," she said, trying like hell not to sound apologetic and failing miserably.

"Cash?" Both of Mr. Baker's eyebrows went up. "Are you accustomed to keeping that amount of currency on hand?"

After a beat, Kate said, "How much—currency—are we talking about?"

"We were discussing an amount in the area of fifty thousand."

"Fifty thousand?" Kate's voice went up into a squeak, which what with scar tissue and a naturally low register was quite a feat. Mandy hid a grin. Kate cleared her throat and tried again. "Fifty thousand? Dollars?"

The eyebrows were still up, and Mr. Baker said blandly, "I believe so." He glanced at the Earlybird man for confirmation. Bickford gave a glum nod. "Of course, if there was some question—"

"No," Kate said, getting her voice back under control. "No indeed." She acquired a little blandness herself and sent some of it Bickford's way in a wide, bright smile. He looked even more glum. "I might be able to stretch fifty thousand to cover the damages."

Bickford cast a disparaging eye around the sixty-year-old homestead, including outhouse with ventilated door, cabin with patched roof, trashed garage, smashed cache, speared snow machine and squashed but obviously aged truck, and visibly restrained a disbelieving snort.

"Excellent," Mr. Baker said, and gave Bickford a warm, approving smile, beneath which Kate, now that she was looking for it, could clearly discern the feral grin. "There's no hurry, of course. Ms. Shugak will be happy to take delivery of her settlement—tomorrow?"

"Tomorrow would be fine," Kate said happily.

Mr. Baker extended a regal hand. "I'll be speaking to Patrick soon, Mr. Bickford, and I won't forget to mention how very helpful you have been."

"Thanks," Bickford muttered, and slunk off in the wake of the departing NTSB crew. Stewman came over to say goodbye, but Mutt, who had yet to forgive any of them for the bear repellent, wouldn't let him get within speaking distance of Kate, and he was reduced to waving a dismal goodbye. The Tom Sawyer grin was in abeyance. Kate, dollar signs dancing in front of her eyes, wouldn't have seen it anyway.

When the last of them had vanished up the trail, Kate regained enough sangfroid to look Mr. and Mrs. Baker over with a speculative eye. "Just how well do you know dear Patrick?"

Mr. Baker affected an elegant shudder. "Only too well. He sits on the board of my bank. A corporate genius, but—"

"He's a ruffian," Mrs. Baker said, with a slight but nevertheless distinctly disdainful lift of her upper lip. "He actually drinks his soup from the bowl at table."

So do I, Kate thought, but decided it politic not to say so. Instead, she said, "I think it's time you called me Kate."

"Why, thank you, Kate," Mr. Baker said, with a warm smile from which all presence of jungle had been banished. For the moment. "My name is Richard."

"And I am Margery," his wife said, and in her smile this time there was no repeat of the peer-to-peasant demeanor that had withered the speech on Bickford's tongue.

"Richard, Margery, would you and your daughter care to join me for a late lunch?"

"That sounds lovely, Kate. Thank you."

Kate stood to one side and let them precede her. "I should have known," she told Mandy once the couple was inside.

"Known what?"

"That your parents would be all right."

Mandy flushed a painful red right up to the roots of her hair. "Up yours."

"Bite me," Kate replied amiably, turning.

Mandy put a hand on her arm. "Listen, Kate? Thanks. Thanks a lot."

"For what?"

"I'm not sure. All I know is, Mother and Dad have really relaxed. This morning they were talking to Chick like he's a human being instead of something out of an old Western movie." She paused, and added, unable to conceal her surprise, "They've even been talking to me like I'm a grown-up instead of a ten-year-old. I don't know what you did—"

"I didn't do anything," Kate said honestly. "I didn't, Mandy." She added, "Unless you count nearly getting them eaten by a bear, almost getting them in a plane wreck and—" Almost too late she remembered Mandy didn't know about the firefight and swallowed the rest of her sentence. "Well. They won't go home complaining of an uneventful visit."

Mandy grinned. "Maybe that's what did it."

"Whatever. Anyway, if I helped, I'm glad. They're good people."

Mandy smiled, the slight smile she'd had as she watched her father go to work on Kevin Bickford. "He's something, my old man."

"Your old lady's not half bad herself."

"No," Mandy admitted. "She's not."

"And together they make one hell of a team."

"Yes," Mandy said slowly, and smiled. "They do."

The lines of Mandy's face had relaxed, and the anxious look in her eyes was gone. She looked ten years younger. Kate said, "Mandy, were you afraid they'd talk you into going home with them?"

The other woman, hands in her pockets, studied the ground and thought about it for a moment. "I guess I was," she said slowly. "I guess I actually was." She looked up at Kate and laughed. "What an idiot. Thanks, Kate."

"We do family therapy." Kate had held out her hand, palm up. "That'll be five cents."

Mandy made a production of digging a nickel out of her pocket, and then demanded a receipt for tax purposes.

Balance restored, they went inside, and were just sitting down to tuna fish sandwiches (with mayonnaise, diced white onions and sweet pickles on white bread, Kate's specialty) when from the clearing Mutt gave a sharp, warning bark.

Kate's newfound sense of harmony with the universe shattered. "Oh Christ, and what fresh hell is this?"

"*And* she reads Dorothy Parker," Mandy told her parents smugly.

Margery sniffed. "A vulgar woman."

Richard grinned. "You only say that because she insulted you at tea that day in New York."

"She insulted everyone, from what I hear," Mandy said, biting into her sandwich.

"You knew her?" Kate said, gaping. "You knew Dorothy Parker?" Mutt barked again. "Dammit," she said impatiently and crossed the room to wrench open the door. "Oh shit."

It was Billy Mike, coming down the trail as if the hounds of hell were at his heels, his round face flushed, his barrel-shaped chest heaving, his usually neatly combed hair standing up in tufts all over his head.

In a low voice Kate said a very bad word.

Her tribal chairman slid to a halt in front of her door. "What?" she snapped. Her tone of voice was inappropriate for speaking to an elder. She knew it and didn't care.

He knew it and took no notice. "It's Cindy and Ben Bingley."

Kate stiffened. "What about them?"

He gulped for air. "She's got him held hostage at their house."

"Their house? Their house in Niniltna?"

He nodded, panting.

Kate stared at him. "You drove twenty-five miles during break-up to tell me that? What the hell am I supposed to do about it? Chopper Jim's up to the mine, checking out that bear attack. Call him in."

He shook his head violently. "She says she'll only talk to you. She's got a rifle, Kate. Billy's hunting rifle."

Kate thought of the scene at the airstrip the previous afternoon. "So what's the big deal? Maybe she'll shoot him, maybe she won't. And if she does shoot him, maybe she'll miss. She did yesterday. Either way, it's no big loss." She turned to go back inside. "You want some coffee and sandwiches?"

Billy's voice was panicked. "Kate! She said she wanted to talk to you! Nobody else, only you! You've got to do something, you have to!"

Kate's outward indifference fooled no one, least of all herself. Her eyes closed and for a moment, for just one precious moment, she pretended she wasn't Ekaterina Moonin Shugak's granddaughter and anointed heir. The same vacuum that had yawned at her feet at the previous year's Alaska Federation of Natives convention yawned again, an ever-deepening chasm of obligation and responsibility that threatened to suck her in and rob her of her autonomy, her privacy, her solitude, her independence, everything that was important to her.

More important than family? Emaa's voice said in her head. *More important than your tribe? For shame, Katya. For shame.*

Damn you, old woman, she thought furiously, stay out of my head.

She opened her eyes and found the elder Bakers regarding her with curiosity, and Mandy with more than a little sympathy. Kate was going into town, and they both knew it.

She swore once beneath her breath. "All right, Billy," she said shortly. "I'll follow you in."

"Good," Billy said, although he didn't look convinced. He pointed over his shoulder in the vague direction of the road. "I'll just— I'll get my car."

"Fine."

Mandy smothered a smile.

"Right," Billy said. He backed up a few steps. Kate did not follow him. He paused to point over his other shoulder. "My car. I'll wait for you. I'll just— I'll follow you in."

"You do that," Kate said evenly.

12

The Bingleys lived five miles outside Niniltna, in a subdivision of a dozen houses whose construction had been subsidized by a low-interest loan program offered by the Niniltna Native Association in conjunction with the FHA. It was a pity the loan didn't extend to road maintenance, because there was a pothole the size of a lunar crater at the turnoff. There was no going around it, and Kate, calling curses down on Billy Mike's head, set her teeth and geared down. Mutt braced her front paws on the dash and dug in her claws. They climbed the opposite side of the pothole to emerge bumper to bumper with Billy's Honda Civic Wagovan.

Billy's wasn't the only vehicle present, and all of the front-row seats had long since been filled. Dandy Mike was there with Karen Kompkoff, his GMC long-bed Turbo Diesel V8 backed around so they could snuggle together in a sleeping bag in the bed and not miss any of the show. Auntie Vi, never one to miss an opportunity to make a buck, was selling Velveeta-topped pizza for a dollar a slice out of her second car, a brand-new Ford Aerostar, evidently too new to rent out to the NTSB. Old Sam Dementieff had Cab Calloway turned up to 9 on his tape player and both windows on his Dodge pickup wide open so no one would miss the beneficial effects of "Minnie the Moocher." Sergei Moonin moved from group to group, freely taking bets on whether Ben Bingley would survive the day.

Kate expected to see the Pace Arrow from Pennsylvania roll up at any moment. Too bad Mandy had talked her parents into spending what was left of the day at the lodge.

The sun, low in the southwest, cast a benevolent glow over the scene, which lacked only steel drums for a calypso carnival. Jimmy Buffett would have felt right at home. "I hate breakup," Kate muttered, but by then she had said it so many times it sounded too clichéd to be true.

Billy Mike came puffing up and yanked open Kate's door. Since she'd been in the process of opening it herself, he yanked her halfway out of the truck and she barely managed to catch herself before sprawling face forward into the mud. As it was, she went to her hands and knees with a solid splat.

Mutt peered at her over the side of the seat.

"Jesus, Kate," Billy said, staring down at her with a horrified expression. "I'm sorry. Let me help you up."

"No." Kate held up one filthy hand to ward him off. She sounded amazingly calm. "Mandy usually keeps a roll of paper towels behind the driver's seat. Will you check for me?"

Billy, terrified by her apparent tranquillity, scrambled around and found the towels and a plastic container of Wet Ones. Kate cleaned herself off, with Billy bleating distressed little apologies every few seconds.

"Billy."

"Yes, Kate."

"Enough." She looked at him; she even smiled. There was absolutely nothing in her expression to make him take a step back, yet take a step back he did. She stuffed the dirty towels into the plastic sack hanging from the ashtray knob and shut the door of the truck. "All right. Tell me what you know."

"Deidre—their oldest—came running over to my house with the other two kids in tow," Billy said rapidly. "They told my wife that Cindy had Ben at gunpoint and was threatening to shoot him if he didn't fork over the rest of the dividend money."

"I thought he blew it all in Ahtna."

"I think he did, and I think Cindy knows he did, but you know, Kate, I don't think Cindy cares." Billy's face worked. "The wife called me up to the office, so I came down here and tried to talk to Cindy. She ran me off with that .30-30 of his."

"Is it loaded?"

"I didn't ask her," Billy said indignantly, "and I sure as hell didn't wait around long enough for her to show me!"

"When'd she ask for me?"

Billy's eyes slid to one side.

Kate sighed. "You are a scum-sucking, brown-nosing, bottom-feeding, lily-livered son of a bitch," she observed, without heat. Even less of a tone to take when speaking to a tribal elder, but nobody heard except Billy, and he wasn't taking offense. She was pretty sure he wasn't even listening.

"Whatever," he said, patting the air. "You're the closest thing we've got to a cop, Kate. You used to be one, for crissake. Just see if you can talk her out."

"What part of the house are they in?"

"They were in the living room when I saw them," Billy said. "You familiar with the house?" Kate shook her head. "It's one of the prefabs the Association underwrote, so it's just like mine, living room and kitchen in front, bedrooms in back."

"Living room on the left or on the right?"

"Left."

"Can you see the front door from the living room?"

"Yes."

Kate sighed again. "Okay."

She closed her eyes for a moment and seemed to retreat inside herself. Billy watched, half apprehensive, half curious. When her eyes opened again, her chin came down so that she looked out from beneath suddenly heavier straight black brows, her shoulders squared, her hands flexed. Everything about her radiated the message, *Mess with me, motherfucker, and I will rip you three new bodily orifices before breakfast.* She was five feet tall and weighed 120 pounds, but the accumulation of power was obvious and intimidating, and ignored only at peril of, at best, one's dignity, and at worst, one's life.

Billy took another involuntary step backward.

"Keep everyone else out of the house," Kate said.

Unoffended, Billy nodded. What made him such a good tribal leader was his ability to pick the right person for the right job, and the self-control to stand back out of the way and let them do it. Besides, he'd already looked down the muzzle of Cindy's .30-30 once that day, and he wasn't eager to repeat the experience.

Kate walked through the crowd to the house, a buzz of speculation rising behind her. Sergei's odds shortened. Her muddy jeans clung clammily to her legs, an untimely reminder of the broken washing machine in her garage. And Cindy thought she had things bad. By the time Kate got to the front door she was mad all over again, and she thumped on it with a vicious fist. "Cindy? It's Kate Shugak. I'm coming in."

There was a pause, and then the sound of a distant voice. Kate couldn't make out the words. "Cindy," she said, raising her voice, "I can't hear you, I'm going to open the front door."

She opened the door and stuck her head in. "My head's in the door, Cindy. It's Kate Shugak. I'm alone, and I don't have a gun. I want to talk, so don't shoot, okay?"

Nobody did, so she chanced sticking a foot inside, followed by the rest of her body when no shots went off.

The hallway consisted of an anteroom between front door, kitchen and living room. All three were empty. Kate listened and heard nothing. "Cindy?" She took a step forward. "Cindy, where are you?"

Cindy wasn't in either of the bedrooms in back of the kitchen, she wasn't in the bathroom at the end of the hall. The door to the bedroom on the left was almost shut. Kate put her hand on it and pushed slowly. "Cindy?"

The light was dim through half-closed drapes. When her eyes adjusted, the first thing she saw was Cindy, squatting in a corner, hands clutching a rifle, cheek leaning against the barrel. She didn't look up when the door opened.

Ben was there, too, naked and spreadeagled across the queen-size bed, tied to the frame at wrists and ankles with what looked like black wire. He was also gagged, which Kate decided improved the odds of his surviving the day tenfold. She knew a moment's regret that there was no way to place a bet with Sergei before the booth closed.

Ben's eyes bulged at the sight of her, and he all but twisted himself into a pretzel to preserve his modesty. She allowed herself a long, cool look and a brief, pitying smile. He flushed. All over. Interesting.

She slipped into the room, Cindy on her right and Ben in front of her. Leaning against the wall, she let herself slide down until she, too, was squatting on her haunches, elbows resting on her knees, empty hands hanging loosely, unthreateningly, between them.

Minutes passed. She let herself become a part of the interior landscape, allowing her presence to seep into Cindy's consciousness. This landscape included the bed, a straight-backed chair and a closet with folding doors standing open to display Blazo boxes stacked side on side, shoes on the bottom shelf, socks, T-shirts, bras and underwear on the middle shelf, belts, hats, mufflers and boxes of cartridges and shotgun shells on the top. There was a nightstand on either side of the bed, each with a lamp. One was piled high with *Alaska Fisherman* magazines, the other supported a stack of romance novels, the top one featuring a cover with a spectacularly endowed young woman with enormous quantities of golden hair almost wearing a lavender gown. She was bent backwards over the arm of a bronzed young giant almost wearing buckskin pants. He, too, had enormous quantities of hair, only his was black.

Everything looked recently organized and folded and dusted. The hangers were lined up like soldiers in the closet, the books and magazines were in neat piles, the earrings on the dresser hung in neatly spaced pairs. A hardcore neatnik herself, Kate would have approved if she hadn't been so acutely aware that excessive outer neatness often indicated severe inner turmoil.

She glanced across at Cindy. Cindy's cheek was still pressed against the barrel of the rifle, vacant eyes fixed on nothing. Kate leaned her head back into the corner and gazed at the ceiling, letting her mind drift.

It had been an eventful thirty-six hours, to say the least. Airplane engines falling from the sky, bears on the attack, plane wrecks, shootouts, bodies lying around indiscriminately. Not to mention the Park's own generation gap in the form of Baker *père, mère et fille*. Park springs were always a little wacky but this one was pushing it.

She wondered if Jim Chopin was still in the Park, if Mark Stewart was still with him. She wondered why Jim had brought him. She wondered why Jim had come himself. He'd never been one to chase his tail. As the old saying went, and yesterday with more emphasis than usual, some days you get the bear, some days the bear gets you. The whole incident was cut and dried, there wasn't going to be any way to prove otherwise. A grizzly bear was one of your more efficient eradicators of evidence. There would be no way to tell if the victim had been dead before or after the bear attack. She forced herself to examine her memory of Carol Stewart sprawled in awkward death. The torn face and throat, ripped belly, shredded thighs. No. No way at all.

She swallowed hard, and as a kind of mental exercise retraced her route through the abandoned mining community the previous afternoon. Sunshine, brisk breeze, fluffy cumulus clouds. Roads muddy slush during the day, frozen over at night. Houses peeling paint. Windows broken, doors ajar, interiors stripped of anything useful long ago. Great view. Warm day.

And no claw marks. She had not seen any claw marks on any of the houses she passed, and she had walked down to the last one in the row before she found Carol Stewart's body. She had walked that far because Mark Stewart said—what did he say? His wife was on the roof of a cabin. But if he left her on the roof, and Kate found her in the middle of the road, the bear would have had to get her down, and the bear would not have been able to do that without leaving evidence of it behind. Kate remembered the matching sets of five-inch claws on the upraised, bloodstained paws, and thought, *Deep* scratch marks.

Come to think of it, there hadn't been any scuff marks on the peeling walls, either, such as might be left by the toe of a frantically scrabbling shoe. She tried to remember the kind of shoes Carol Stewart had been wearing. Wafflestompers, weren't they? Leather and Gore-tex uppers, Vasques, that was the label on the tongue. Decent brand, readily available at REI, characteristic choice of the urban hiker. Herself, she stuck to Sorels. Except in the winter, when she got out the bunny boots.

She looked at Cindy. Cindy hadn't moved.

Of course Carol Stewart, instead of climbing out of reach, could have tried to run for it. People are dumb, and Kate had noticed that the degree of dumbness increased in direct proportion to proximity to the Bush. After all, the victim hadn't had any kind of a weapon with her, either.

Kate would much prefer the bear attack that resulted in Carol Stewart's death to be one of those random occurrences that wake up everyone to the fact that they aren't in Kansas anymore, because the alternative was a hell of a thing to contemplate. What was the line from the old song? You always hurt the one you love, or something like that. Kate wondered if that included feeding the one you love to a bear. Could anyone deliberately inflict that kind of damage, that kind of pain on someone they once loved enough to marry?

She thought of the five years she had spent in Anchorage investigating cases of abuse inflicted by parents upon their own children. Yes, she thought. Only too many could do exactly that.

At that point she realized with no little annoyance that she was beginning to think there might be something to Dan and Jim's suspicions, and was glad when Cindy stirred.

The other woman gazed around the room with a dazed look on her face. "Kate," she said, on a note of discovery, as if she had only just realized Kate was in the room, which in fact she probably had.

Kate kept her reply low and calm. "Hello, Cindy."

Cindy became aware of the rifle. "Oh." She leaned it against the wall. "Sorry. I didn't mean to wave this thing at you."

Kate smiled without moving. The rifle was still within quick reach. "I didn't think you did."

Cindy sighed and shoved a hand through her hair. "I've really fucked it up this time, haven't I?"

"Not necessarily, Cindy."

As if she hadn't heard, Cindy looked at Ben and said, "I've just had enough, you know? Enough. Enough of you drinking up every dime that comes into this house, so that we don't have enough money to buy food for our children."

Her voice was rising, and Kate said soothingly, "It's okay, Cindy."

Cindy's head snapped around. "It's not okay!" Her face contorted. "It's not okay, Kate. It used to be, but it's not now, and it's never going to be okay again. It was bad enough before, but since Becky—" Tears filled her eyes and overflowed onto her cheeks. She snuffled and rubbed a sleeve across her face. "I love my kids!"

"I know you do."

"I never pretended to be any kind of a saint, but there has always been food on the table in this house!"

"I know there has."

"Now there isn't even that much!" Her head snapped around and she stared at Ben, her face twisted. "Maybe if I keep you tied to that bed, you asshole, maybe then I'll get to the mail before you do and to the checks before you do and keep some of the money you've been blowing on beer and whores!"

Cindy stood with an abrupt movement. Startled, Kate followed her, and the blood rushed to her head. It took a dizzy moment to reacclimate, and when she did Cindy had the rifle clenched in her hands again, lips drawn back from her teeth. "You can't treat us like this, Ben! Your sister might be dead but that's no excuse to pretend we are, too!"

Becky Jorgensen, née Bingley, had been Ben's sister, Kate remembered now. Ben and Becky had always been very close, and Becky had welcomed Cindy with open arms. All of Cindy's three children had adored her, too. Becky, one of Roger McAniff's victims two years before. Becky, she remembered now from the conversation at Bobby and Dinah's, who had died last August following two years spent at API trying to regain her sanity after the massacre. Thinking it over, Kate realized that Ben's present toot dated from the end of last year's fishing season, increasing in idiocy through the fall and reaching its nadir on New Year's Eve, so the story went, on which memorable night he'd been discovered in flagrante delicto with Nadia Kvasnikoff on the sink in the men's room of Bernie's Roadhouse. Kate, conducting a New Year's Eve celebration of her own on the homestead, had not been present for the denouement, but had it on good authority that Bernie had chased the both of them out into the frozen Arctic night with the baseball bat from behind the bar, and had only tossed their pants and boots out as an afterthought.

Ben had never been what anyone would call a model husband or father, but at Becky's death, something had gotten off the chain.

She looked at him. He had his eyes shut tightly; even so, tears seeped from beneath his lashes.

"Cindy," she said, "give me the rifle." She stretched out a hand.

Cindy didn't move, and Kate remembered years before when Ben, fresh out of the Navy, had brought his new bride home to the Park. Cindy had been a lovely, slender, fair-haired, young woman, with melting brown eyes and an open, friendly smile, excited at moving to Alaska, eager to learn everything she could about Bush life. She was ten years older than Kate. This afternoon she looked twice that, the light filtering in through the drapes to darken the pouches beneath her eyes and deepen the lines at the corners of her mouth. She looked old, and tired, her eyes dulled, her prettiness faded, her youth gone.

There was no hope left in her, Kate thought, and something twisted in her gut. "Give me the rifle, Cindy."

Without looking at Kate, Cindy handed over the rifle.

Kate emptied out the magazine and worked the action until the chamber was empty before standing the gun in a corner. She pocketed the rounds and said, "Let's turn Ben loose." Her hands went to the wire securing his left ankle. From the corner of her eye she saw Cindy move as if in protest. Her hands went on steadily unknotting wire, while she wondered where the 9mm automatic was. After a moment Cindy began untying Ben's left wrist.

When he was free Ben ripped the bandanna from his mouth and said in a husky voice, "Give me my pants." He sounded sober and shaken.

Without a word, Cindy went to the closet and pulled down a pair of Levi's. He grabbed them without thanks and stepped into them, a stocky man with a middle-age spread threatening his waistband, dark, straight hair thinning on top, eyes bloodshot, chin unshaven. Ben was Kate's second or third cousin, she couldn't remember which, but she remembered a visit to her grandmother's house as a child, when Ben, home on leave, had made her an admiral's hat out of newspaper, complete with cockade, and taught her six-year-old self her first sea chantey, "Rolling Down to Old Maui." He'd had a fine, deep baritone that rattled the rafters. Back then, there was always singing when Ben was around.

They weren't bad people, either of them, but they were going to wind up in jail and their kids split between foster homes if something wasn't done, and done soon. Kate waited until Ben got his zipper up before she said, "Guys, this can't go on."

They looked at her, faces numb to the point of exhaustion. She spoke slowly and deliberately, determined to get through to them. "You can do whatever you want to to each other, but you can't keep doing this to your kids. You know where they are right now? Annie Mike's. They ran there when you corralled Ben at gunpoint, Cindy."

Cindy stared at her.

"It's not the first time, either. Pretty soon they're going to decide they'd rather stay at Annie and Billy's than come home. And Annie and Billy have plumb run out of kids of their own to fuss over, so their house is probably feeling a little empty. Deidre's fourteen, Randy's twelve, what's Tom? Nine? Ten? Three kids, three kids just like yours, would just about fill up the cracks at the Mikes' house."

"They couldn't do that," Cindy said, her voice raw.

"Cindy," Kate said with as much force as she could muster, "how much more do you think it'll take to have the state declare you both unfit parents?"

Ben blinked at her. Cindy paled.

"How much, Cindy?" Kate repeated. "One more time getting caught out on a sandbar in the middle of the river with your jeans down around your ankles in the company of a man not your husband? Ben? How much more? Another score in the Roadhouse john? Another Association dividend spent on booze instead of food or clothes?"

Ben flushed. Cindy said, weakly, "The state couldn't do that. These are tribal lands."

"We don't have sovereignty yet," Kate said, "and DFYS doesn't take kindly to neglect. You patch things up between the two of you. I don't care how you do it, I don't care if you stay together or you split up, but you patch things up enough to provide some kind of stable home life for those kids, or, I guarantee you, they will find one for themselves."

She reached for the rifle. At the door, she turned to deliver a parting shot. "And I will help them."

She was almost to the front door when Cindy's voice stopped her. Kate turned to see her coming down the hall cradling a sliming knife, a filleting knife, a skinning knife and a well-worn Buck pocketknife. "Here," she said, thrusting them at Kate. "If you're taking the rifle, you might as well take these, too." She went into the kitchen and came out with a butcher knife and three mismatched steak knives. "These, too. Oh, and there's this."

She went to the coat hanger and fished around in the pockets of the worn pink plush jacket Kate had seen her in the day before, producing a Swiss Army Explorer knife flaking dried mud, complete with flat head and Phillips screwdrivers, saw, magnifying glass, scissors and, if they were lucky, maybe even a functional blade. "I tripped over this at the mine yesterday."

Kate accepted the hardware. "You chased Ben all the way up to the mine?"

Cindy nodded.

"I would like to have seen that," Kate admitted. "Where is it?"

"Where is what?"

"The nine-millimeter. The pistol you had yesterday."

"Oh," Cindy said. "Right. I forgot."

Kate saw the blank expression on her face and believed her. "Where is it?" she said, more gently this time.

"I tossed it."

Kate looked at her.

A bleak smile reached Cindy's eyes. "Really. I threw it in the Kanuyaq on the way back down from the mine. What do we need a nine-millimeter for? You can't bring down a moose with one unless he lets you walk right up to him and stick it up his left nostril." The smile faded. "It was just another one of Billy's toys."

The exhausted defeat in her voice pierced Kate to the heart. Juggling rifle and knives, she struggled to open the door and get out of that place of hopelessness and despair.

"Oh, here, let me," Cindy said, ever the polite hostess, and reached around Kate.

Kate paused on the doorstep. "Cindy—"

The bleak smile came back. "Don't worry, Kate. I'm all over my mad."

"Yeah." Kate wasn't convinced. "Next time, throw him out before you get mad enough to go for a weapon."

Cindy gestured. "Have to now. You've got them all."

13

The crowd parted before her like the Red Sea.

"What happened?"

"Yeah, Kate, what happened?"

"Did she shoot him?"

"Is he dead?"

"Of course he's not dead, you idiot, we didn't hear a shot."

"Maybe she knifed him."

"Kate, come on, talk to us!"

"Oh the hell with it, it's almost time for Alaska Weather on the TV. Let's go home."

"I hear it's blowing up a storm in the Gulf."

"No lie? Might mean some decent beachcombing for a change."

"Yeah, remember last breakup? Wish we could expect a Sea-land freighter to run aground every year. That was the best canned ham I've ever had."

The crowd had thinned, probably soon after Kate's arrival, since it signaled an end to the fun. Auntie Vi was among the missing, as were Dandy Mike and Karen Kompkoff and Old Sam. Billy Mike was still there, a very exasperated Mutt standing next to him.

"Okay," Kate told her, and Mutt sprang forward as if shot from a bow, almost knocking her over.

"Okay, Mutt," Kate said, juggling hardware, "I'm all right. I said okay!" Mutt retired with a wounded look, and Kate dumped rifle and knives into Billy's hands.

"What the hell—"

"Cindy thinks it's best she not have anything in the house with targeting capabilities or sharp edges. I agree."

Billy accepted knives and rifle awkwardly.

She had her hand on the door of the truck when the second voice said, "Kate."

She swore to herself, counted to ten and turned. "Jim."

The trooper was standing in front of the postmaster's truck. He must have landed the helicopter at the village strip and borrowed the truck from Bonnie Jeppsen to make the trip up to the mine. The mine was so overgrown there weren't a lot of landing sites for a chopper, even for a pilot with Jim's skill.

Mark Stewart was sitting in the truck's passenger seat. The windshield was too dirty to see his expression.

Mutt, who all too often demonstrated no sense in men, gave a welcoming yip and swarmed all over the trooper. "Hey, girl," he said, white teeth flashing, long fingers finding exactly the right spot between her ears and scratching hard. Mutt's legs nearly gave out under the ecstasy. Over her head Jim said, "Got a call there was a problem at the Bingleys. Thought I'd better check it out, since I was in the neighborhood. Want to fill me in?"

Billy Mike shifted his portable armory and cleared his throat.

The Swiss Army knife slipped from his grasp and fell with a splat into a puddle of melting snow.

Kate stooped to pick it up. "Ben's been on what amounts to a seven-month drunk. Cindy took exception."

"What with?"

"Yesterday it was a nine-millimeter automatic. Today it was a thirty-thirty." She jerked her chin at the rifle slipping from Billy's arms. "I, ah, I straightened things out. For now."

She paused, aware without looking at him of the unspoken plea in Billy's eyes. It wasn't as hard as she'd thought it would be to get the words out. "Jim, as a favor? Leave it alone."

"Is there abuse of wife or children?"

"No." Kate's voice was certain. "No spousal or child abuse." Yet, she thought. Where there was substance abuse of any kind, spousal and child abuse were never very far behind.

"Are the children at risk?"

Kate thought of Cindy crouched down in her marital bedroom, clutching the rifle, and of the three children running to Annie Mike for help. Yes. But if she said so, Jim would call in the Division of Family and Youth Services and the children would be placed in a foster home, probably in Anchorage or Fairbanks, probably not together. Would that be any better for the kids than what they had now? At least here they had Annie and Billy Mike, and the rest of the village.

And Kate herself.

She looked down at the knife she held in her hands, wet from its fall. Idly she began folding out all the implements, drying them carefully, one at a time.

"Kate?"

She looked up to meet Jim's steady gaze, and saw that it was her call. The trooper would be guided by her, would leave the children with their parents if she said so. She didn't want the responsibility, but it didn't look as if she had a choice. As if she'd ever had a choice. The words came out involuntarily, distant, as if formed by someone else and then placed in her mouth. "I don't think so," she said. "No," she added, more strongly.

It was the first time in her life Kate Shugak had sided for the tribe and against the law she had admired, respected, studied and sworn to uphold. To serve and to protect. She fought a sense of disorientation that threatened to overwhelm her, a dizziness that included a distinct impression of her grandmother's presence, transitory but strong.

She shook it off, almost angrily, and looked up to find Jim regarding her with an impassive expression. He held her eyes for another moment, before nodding once, very crisp, a conspicuous transfer of authority. "All right. If there's a problem—"

"I know, it'll be all my fault," Kate muttered. She closed the knife and pocketed it.

"Don't put words in my mouth," he said, mildly enough. "I was going to say, if there's a problem bad enough to remove the children from the home, call me and I'll see what I can do to get them placed somewhere without taking them out of the Park."

She felt heat rising up into her face. "Sorry, Jim." He nodded. It took an effort, but she got the words out. "Jim?"

"What?"

"Thanks."

The shark's grin was back. "Don't choke on the word, Shugak."

"Up yours, Chopin." The insult, freely given and as blithely accepted, restored the relatively noiseless tenor of their way and Kate's sense of equilibrium. Over Jim's shoulder she spotted Harvey Meganack, the ruby-eyed ram's heads on his gold nugget watchband flashing in the setting sun.

What the hell, if she had the Alaska State Troopers on the run she had to be on a roll. "Harvey! Hold up there, I need to talk to you!"

Harvey had started backing up as soon as he registered in her direct line of sight, but she was too quick for him. He halted, trying not to look like the stag at bay and not succeeding very well. "What?" he muttered.

"Nice to see you, too," she said blandly, and he flushed. She let him see her enjoying his discomfort before she said, "Auntie Vi wanted me to talk to you about the dividend the board is thinking about issuing for the Chokosna timber profits."

He didn't like the sound of that. "What about it?" he said guardedly.

"She and Auntie Joy think that some of it ought to be spent on a health clinic."

His face changed. "We've got a compact with the health clinic in Ahtna."

"Fifty miles away," Kate agreed.

"It's close enough for minor health problems," he said.

If he'd looked any more stubborn, she could have accused him of having a jackass for a father. Harvey Meganack had the high, flat cheekbones of his Aleut ancestors combined with the height of his Norwegian ones. He was further distinguished from his fellow Park rats by affecting the dapper in dress. True, he wore jeans, but they were pressed, as was his oxford shirt with the button-down collar. The latest in Eddie Bauer parkas topped the ensemble, and he wore a baseball cap with an Alyeska logo covering a bald spot he hid when the cap was off by parting the rest of his hair just above his right ear and combing it over. His smile was toothy and full of empty charm.

Harvey was a commercial fisherman and self-proclaimed independent businessman, whose pockets were frankly to let to the highest bidder when it came time to assign construction contracts on tribal lands, and who knew just enough about business to get the Association into real trouble. Kate was pleased not to be related to Harvey in any way at all, although that probably only held if she didn't climb her family tree more than two generations.

"Fishing was lousy last summer," Harvey added, "and it's been a tough winter. The money should go out to the individual families."

Kate held his gaze for a moment, and then deliberately looked beyond him to the Bingley house. When she looked back at him, he'd flushed again, the brown of his skin darkening to an uncomfortable bronze.

Unwisely, he attempted bluster. "Dammit, Kate, that don't happen all the time, it don't even happen most of the time. So Ben Bingley went on a tear with his kids' dividend checks, so what's new? All shareholders aren't Ben Bingley. Association money should go into the hands of the shareholders by as straight a line as possible, not be spent on some health clinic it'll cost us most of our logging profits to build and most of the yearly dividends for the rest of our lives to maintain."

It was the same line of reasoning he spouted at every Association meeting, an effective line that had gotten him elected to the board for four consecutive terms. Kate did not burst into applause, so he cast about for support. Demetri Totemoff stood stolidly at his elbow, looking at Kate out of tranquil eyes. A square-bodied, blunt-featured man with a permanently cautious expression, Demetri was a big-game guide who specialized in European hunters, spoke fluent German from his twenty years of Army service in Düsseldorf and was Kate's second cousin once removed.

"Maybe you'd better think this over, Harvey," Kate said. "And maybe you'd better talk it over with the board, the whole board, before you start spending your dividend." She nodded at the Bingleys' house. "We could use a substance-abuse counselor in Niniltna."

Involuntarily, he followed her gaze. He couldn't deny it, but he wasn't convinced, either. Fine, she hadn't expected de Lawd to pass a miracle; she had only promised Auntie Vi she would try. About to make good her escape, she was halted by Demetri's voice.

"Harvey, the girls are all out to the Roadhouse today, working on their quilt." Kate remembered that Luba Totemoff, Demetri's wife, had been one of the quilters the day before. "Joyce is visiting, so she'll be there, and you know Old Sam practically lives at the Roadhouse this time of year. Maybe we should head on out there, talk it over." He raised an eyebrow at the board's chairman. "Billy?"

Face as blank as a pane of glass, armed like Rambo about to head into the jungle—or Steven Seagal into the Alaskan Bush—Billy nodded obediently.

"Good," Kate said, "great," and headed for her brand-new, much-abused truck. "Good luck. See you all later." Later in the year, she thought, but didn't say.

"Kate." Again Demetri's voice stopped her in her tracks. Without turning she said, "What?"

"You've taken an interest in the subject. Seems only right you should attend."

Her tired brain chased itself in circles trying to find a way to get out if it, but her synapses were starting to close down, and besides, this was an elder making a request. "Sure," she said, turning and mustering up a smile, albeit one that could have used work on its sincerity. "I'm right behind you."

Harvey reluctantly and Demetri inexorably shepherded Billy into his pickup, and climbed into Harvey's brand-new Eddie Bauer Ford Explorer. They moved off down the road, the Yuppiemobile in the lead.

"You know, I think I'll come along," Jim said, readjusting the set of his hat. Beneath the brim his eyes laughed at her. "I'd like to see the end of this story." He looked back at the cab of his borrowed truck, where Mark Stewart still sat, motionless, expressionless, a graven image to loss. In a lower voice he added, "And I just might get to the end of another story while I'm at it."

In no mood to suffer gladly the all too often painfully observant eye of the Alaska Department of Public Safety's finest representative, still Kate could think of no way to prohibit Chopper Jim's attendance at what showed every sign of being a knock-down, drag-out family fight in which, if Demetri had his way, she feared she was meant to figure prominently. "It's a public bar," she said ungraciously. "Mutt! Come!"

Mutt, sitting in blissful inattention with her head pressed adoringly against Chopper Jim's knee, came awake with a snort and launched herself at the open door of the truck.

14

The convoy pulled into the Roadhouse parking lot and parked in the last row closest to the road. Kate sat for a few moments, examining the various vehicles and the surrounding area with care. Demetri, Harvey and Billy waited for a moment, shrugged and went inside. Mutt looked over, head cocked. "In a minute," Kate said. She completed her inspection, listened for shots and heard none, and decided it was safe to turn off the engine.

Silent still, silent all, and Kate relaxed and climbed out. The first thing she saw was Frank Scully's Cherokee Chief, brazenly sporting its green-and-white Washington plates. She approached for a closer look. Its out-of-date green-and-white Washington plates. That did it. She wheeled and went back to the truck. Aha. Like every good sourdough, Mandy had a tool chest built into the back. The key was on the ring.

Inside the tool chest was a pair of vise grips. Mutt looked a little alarmed.

Kate returned to Frank Scully's truck, fastened the vise grips to his back license plate and ripped it off. She went around to the front of the truck and performed the same service for the front license plate. Both plates went sailing across the road to disappear into a stand of alders.

"There." Kate strode to the truck, replaced the vise grips, closed and locked the toolbox. She dusted her hands. "All done."

Bonnie Jeppsen's truck pulled in next to hers, and Chopper Jim and Mark Stewart climbed out. "You took your time," Kate said.

"This thing needs a new gearbox."

"Oh. Good thing Bonnie's got a steady job."

"Yeah."

He started to head for the bar and Kate touched his elbow. "Look at this, Jim, here's a vehicle with no license plates."

"Why, so it is," Jim said happily, and extracted a book of tickets from an inside pocket. The Chief was unlocked, and the registration—Washington state, Kate noted—was in the glove compartment. Jim positively glowed. Chopper Jim was never so happy as when he was writing someone a ticket. He'd been ecstatic when two years before the state had changed the law so he could write tickets on private property.

For her part, Kate just loved keeping Chopper Jim happy, and her sense of well-being increased as she walked in the door of the Roadhouse and the first person she saw was Frank Scully.

"Ah, my good Eskimo friend," he said, lurching forward to drape a friendly arm around Kate's shoulders. "How ya doing, Katie?"

Oozing cordiality, Kate said, "I'm not an Eskimo, Frank, I'm an Aleut. Try to keep up."

Clearing a nearby table, Bernie blinked and poked a finger in his ear to see if it was still working.

Frank blinked bleary eyes. "Aloot. Right. Sorry. Keep forgetting." He weaved off to annoy someone else.

"Is it safe?" Kate said, peering into the bar's gloomy corners. "Have the Hatfields and the McCoys all gone home?"

"So far," Bernie said darkly. A new thought brought a hopeful sparkle to his eye. "Maybe they've killed each other and there's nothing left to do but bury the bodies."

"The sooner the better," Kate agreed.

Unfortunately, Demetri was right. Auntie Joy and Old Sam were both members of the Roadhouse quorum that evening, Auntie Joy sitting between Auntie Vi, who had abandoned Velveeta pizza sales for handwork, and Enid Koslowski, who was looking in a much better humor this afternoon than she had at the previous day's meeting of the quilting bee. Probably got lucky last night, Kate thought disagreeably, and didn't pause to speculate on whether that cranky little internal comment might arise from jealousy. Luba, Demetri's wife, rounded out the circle. Quiet, a little shy, she kept her neatly braided head bent over her work.

Harvey, Demetri and Billy sat at a table a safe distance from the quilters. The old women had a tendency to start in on the nearest man just for the pure enjoyment of it, and since Auntie Joy and Auntie Vi had changed all three men's diapers, a safe distance in this case meant all the way across the room.

Old Sam was seated at his usual table, surrounded by the usual suspects, watching more television. Today the arts had been abandoned for sport, in this case basketball, and from the hooraw going on in that corner of the room it would appear some money was riding on the outcome.

Ralph Estes was passed out with his head on the bar. Must be Saturday, Kate thought. If he was running true to form, he'd been drinking since Bernie had opened the front door at eight that morning, and had been asleep since three or four that afternoon.

In a far corner Dandy Mike licked the tip of one finger and ran it across Karen Kompkoff's collarbone. From the dazed look in Karen's eyes, it wouldn't be long before Dandy was beating feet out back. Dandy's custom alone probably paid the overhead on Bernie's cabins.

At Kate's entrance, Billy stood up and went over to murmur something in Old Sam's ear. The old man, eyes on the television screen, ignored him. Billy was insistent. Old Sam swore loud enough to be heard over the Unitarian congregation practicing their hymns in the opposite corner, and shoved his chair back. Meanwhile, Demetri went to talk to Auntie Vi and Auntie Joy. Auntie Vi gave her crisp nod, Auntie Joy her joyous smile, and both rose to follow him back to his table, from which he actually crooked his finger at Kate.

Chopper Jim, standing at her shoulder, exacerbated her irritation with a deep, rich chuckle. Mark Stewart, still the pillar of sorrow, stood at his side. They both watched as her chin came up, her shoulders stiffened and she all but marched across the room.

"Katya." Auntie Vi looked mildly surprised but welcoming. Auntie Joy beamed. Harvey looked apprehensive, Demetri stolid and Old Sam thin and gaunt and apparently immortal. He distributed his thin, gaunt and apparently immortally nasty grin around the group and straddled a chair from a nearby table, his hands on the back and his chin on his hands.

Kate looked slowly from face to face, as if she were seeing them all for the first time. Harvey, the self-important businessman and incipient dandy. Demetri, the guide, square and stolid and as monosyllabic as his wife. Billy Mike, the tribal leader and commercial fisher with the bright button eyes and the wide, cheerful smile. Auntie Joy, subsistence fisher, housewife, mother, grandmother, robust, laughing, her tubby figure dressed always in flowered, be-furred and rickracked kuspuks.

The fifth board member was its newest, Old Sam Dementieff, commercial fisher, tenderman, movie critic, basketball fan and father of twelve, who had outlived his wife and five of his children and three of his grandchildren and for whom Kate occasionally deck-handed in the summer. Old Sam had taken Kate's grandmother's place on the board, reflecting the shareholders' need for an elder of stature in the governing body.

Auntie Vi, the board secretary, acquired a lined school note-book and a pen with two spares, one behind each ear. Auntie Vi believed strongly in redundancy.

Kate stood around the perimeter of the group, unable or un-willing to bring herself to sit down. Harvey was the youngest board member at forty-five. Billy was what? Forty-eight? Demetri was fifty, Auntie Joy's entire family had just celebrated her sixty-fifth birthday, and Old Sam was a hundred and three if he was a day. Auntie Vi had been thirty for the last forty years and was deter-mined to remain so until she died.

Harvey was pro-development, period. Demetri usually sided with Harvey, Auntie Joy usually against him. Auntie Joy would vote for anything with the word "education" in it, Demetri for anything prefaced by the phrase "rural preference." Billy Mike changed sides so often there was no decoding his bias, and as for Old Sam—

She pulled herself up short. She had no business analyzing and measuring their characteristics, their prejudices, their strengths, their weaknesses. They were her elders and betters, who, like Emaa, always had looked and always would look at events through a local lens and would adjust accordingly their vision of what should be. These were Emaa's sisters and brothers, her daughters and sons, her mothers and fathers, and Kate would defer to them and to their wisdom. She would, she repeated to herself sternly.

Together, they had lived a total of more than three centuries and were at present marching resolutely toward their fourth. It was an impressive accumulation of wisdom and perspective. The dif-ficulty was that sometimes that wisdom and perspective hardened into a stance inimical to change, to new ideas, to fresh faces, to youth. Kate had been born and raised among them, but at thirty-four she was by far the youngest person in the group, and she knew that had she not been Ekaterina's granddaughter she would have had no place there.

In this, she was less than perceptive of the considerable regard in which she was held in the Park. Whether she knew it or not, she wore authority like a long cloak, with much was that swept up in its weighted hem of which she was unaware, including the undivided attention of the six people sitting before her now. Six pairs of sharp eyes watched her without seeming to, noticing the lines of control bracketing the usually mobile mouth, the fresh scab on her temple. None of them lingered over the scar on her throat, but then they'd all seen it before, and most of them knew the story behind it, or thought they did. Like the presence of the wolf-husky hybrid chowing down on beef jerky at the end of the bar, it only added to the accumulating legend.

The six elders sipped coffee brought by a self-effacing Bernie, who recognized a tribal council meeting when he saw one. They chatted in low voices, settling into their seats and getting comfortable with one another.

"Well," Billy said, setting his coffee down. Auntie Vi flipped open her notebook and retrieved one of her pens. Old Sam's bright eyes flicked from one face to another. Harvey frowned into his mug. Auntie Joy's needle flashed through a square of cloth. "I'd like to thank you all for assembling on such short notice." There were grave nods all around, except from Old Sam, who grinned his vulpine grin. "We've invited Kate to sit in on the meeting. She's got a proposal she'd like to lay before the board."

"What?" Kate said.

"Go ahead, Kate," Billy said encouragingly, and the other four board members swiveled their heads in unison to look at the youngster come amongst them.

On her best day Ekaterina Moonin Shugak couldn't have passed a better buck. You son of a bitch, Kate thought furiously, you set me up.

She sent a scowl across the table that should have fried Billy's brain in his skull. He took no notice of this lapse in generational respect, only continued to look at her, waiting, face schooled to an expression of innocent inquiry. So did the rest of the board.

The weight of their expectancy had a perceptible drag all its own, towing her in, sucking her under. She wasn't strong enough to resist, so she took a deep breath and waded in. "Cindy Bingley nearly killed her husband, Ben, this afternoon." Auntie Joy's beam vanished, and Kate waited for those who had been present to fill in those who hadn't been before continuing. "This wasn't the first time she's tried it. The next time he uses his and his kids' dividend checks to finance a drunk, she might get lucky. I don't think anyone here wants that."

Going immediately on the attack, Harvey went straight for the jugular. "So what are you saying, Kate? You want the Association to hold back Ben's and the kids' dividend checks?"

"I don't know, that's pretty extreme action you're suggesting," Billy observed without heat, "holding up a dividend for a lousy toot to Ahtna."

Kate hadn't suggested it, in fact hadn't even thought of it until now, but was willing to discuss the red herring Harvey had dragged across the trail just to get it out of the way. She might score some points of her own in the process. "It wasn't his first toot, Billy," she said, "and he isn't alone, as you very well know. Half the shareholders blow their dividends when they come in. Most of the time it's the wives and kids who suffer for it."

"They get their own dividends," Demetri said.

"Not if somebody beats them to the mailbox."

Harvey's glassy stare made him look as if he'd been stuffed and mounted, Auntie Joy beamed at her placidly, Old Sam examined Kate with a critical eye.

"I suppose we could hold Ben's and the kids' checks for Cindy to pick up," Billy said.

They studied that in silence for a while. From the expressions on their faces they were all entertaining visions of shareholders storming the Association offices for their checks and not relishing the prospect. "You know," Demetri said, "Cindy's not exactly blameless in this situation. She's done plenty of partying herself."

"She takes good care of those kids," Auntie Joy said.

"He'd sue," Harvey said flatly, because that was what he would do and don't any of them forget it.

"Not if he doesn't have any money to hire a lawyer," Auntie Joy said, because she hadn't had much use for Harvey since he hogged most of the fry bread at a dinner she cooked for the high school basketball team on which Harvey was a starting forward. That had been over twenty years ago, but Auntie Joy never forgot an act of greed or selfishness.

"Someone would take it on spec," Demetri said unexpectedly. "There are a thousand Philadelphia lawyers in Anchorage just drooling at the prospect of taking on a solvent Native Association for costs alone. They could drag the case out for years and run their billable hours into the stratosphere. We can't chance it."

Everyone was impressed by this professional assessment of the situation. Everyone also wanted to know where Demetri had come by the easy familiarity with legal jargon, but Bush manners prevailed and no one asked.

Personally, Kate didn't think Ben could leave off drinking and chasing women not his wife long enough to retain an attorney, so the point was moot. "Ben is a shareholder, like the rest of us," she said. "ANCSA funds were allocated by congressional act. It's probably a federal offense to interfere with their distribution. Ben gets his check, same as you, same as me, same as every other Niniltna shareholder."

They thought about that for a while. Tribal elders spent a lot of time thinking in silence, which led to rational problem solving and sensible decision making. It was one of their greatest strengths.

Demetri stirred. "She could divorce him. That way, she could attach his dividend for child support."

"If she hasn't divorced him yet, she's not going to," Billy said.

"He is a charmer," Auntie Joy admitted with a rueful sigh.

"What the Association could do," Kate said. Billy looked at her encouragingly. "What the Association could do," she repeated, setting her jaw, "is tackle it from the other end."

Bernie returned to refill their mugs and set a plate of Oreo cookies on the table, his inspired contribution to a harmonious meeting. Seven hands reached out, and everybody except Harvey opened up the cookies and licked the frosting off the inside.

"It's not just Ben and Cindy and their kids who need help. I'm sure you've all heard about the shoot-out the Jeppsens had with the Kreugers here yesterday," Kate said. "Some of you were present for it." Her hand moved to her left temple to finger the scab left by the too-close-for-comfort graze. Six pairs of eyes followed the gesture. Old Sam chuckled, and Auntie Joy looked at him, scandalized. "Three people were hurt. But," she said, and paused for effect. "But," she repeated, "because we had emergency medical technicians in the bar, we had treatment ready to hand."

"There wasn't anybody hurt that bad," Demetri observed. He'd had too many near misses with wannabe Great White Hunters for a couple of minor bullet holes to upset him.

Auntie Joy transferred her scandalized look from Old Sam to Demetri.

"True," Kate said. "But I believe the result would have been the same even if someone had been badly hurt. The point is, we had trained people at the scene to deal with the situation." She paused again. "People trained in Ahtna, by the Ahtna Native Health Foundation."

She held up her right hand. "I caught myself a splinter the other day, a bad one. Figured I'd need a tetanus shot. When I was in Ahtna this morning, I stopped by the health clinic and talked Irina Barnes into giving me a DPT booster. You all know Irina. She's the community health representative for the Ahtna Native Association, trained in town by the Public Health Service in emergency medical care and standard immunization and testing procedures." Kate paused. "A useful person to have around. We could do with one of our own."

This time it was Billy who broke the silence. "What are you saying, Kate?"

Kate took a deep, steadying breath and spoke her first words in an advisory capacity to the Niniltna Native Association board of directors. "I'm saying it's time we started some kind of clinic of our own, right here in Niniltna. Half the villages in this state already have some kind of health care clinic. Why not ours? Raven Corporation has a nonprofit health branch that's been trying to get a foot in the door here for years."

Harvey said, face set in taut lines of disapproval, "We don't want any outsiders telling us how to live. We can take care of our own."

Kate thought again of the Bingleys, of her cousin Martin's lifelong struggle with alcohol and drugs, of Chick Noyukpuk's, of her parents'. Of her mother's. Yeah, she thought, and we've done such a good job of it so far. She had to fight to keep from saying so out loud, and tried instead for a placating smile, but her facial muscles were unaccustomed to the effort and she gave it up. She did take a beat to rein in her temper, because abusing elders, especially in the presence of other elders, was no way to get anything accomplished in the village. On the other hand, she and tact were no more than passing acquaintances.

Learn, then, Katya, a stern voice said.

She closed her eyes. The board, watching and waiting, saw a shadow pass across her face, the usually smooth skin acquire lines that aged it into a harsh mask that had seen too much of suffering and sorrow. A mask that recalled the presence among them of an older, wiser woman whose deliberate and resolute speech echoed in the rasping voice of her granddaughter.

Kate opened her eyes and the mask vanished.

"We could try circulating a petition to go dry again," Auntie Joy said doubtfully.

Harvey rolled his eyes, but then Harvey liked a martini before dinner and a shot of Drambuie afterward. Niniltna had gone dry once, by a three-vote margin. Dry meant that no alcohol, not for retail sale or personal consumption or gin for Harvey's martini, was allowed on tribal land, none, zero, zilch, zip. The Association had hired shareholders to act as guards to check planes at the airstrip for incoming contraband, armed guards that were empowered to break up any intercepted shipments on the spot. It was a miracle that the Dry Act had passed at all, a miracle aided by a sagacious decision to hold the election during the summer, when most of the fishers were out in Prince William Sound.

When the fleet got back into town, another petition was circulated and another vote was taken, this time for the village to go damp, which meant alcohol couldn't be sold but it could be imported in small quantities for personal use. The second petition passed by a four-vote margin, having been held during the AFN convention, when all the dry votes were in Anchorage.

Everyone was afraid of what the circulation of a third petition might bring. No one wanted any bars opening up again in the village; at least the Roadhouse was twenty-seven miles away and Bernie was a responsible bartender. He didn't serve drunks or pregnant women, and he forcibly removed truck, snow machine and D-9 keys from driving lushes and bedded them down in one of the cabins out back.

For a nominal fee, of course. Social work came a long way behind capitalism on Bernie's list. "Certainly we can try, Auntie," Kate said, "but since the last vote went against us, maybe we should try something else. Like a clinic," she added doggedly.

"What's a clinic got to do with Ben and Cindy Bingley?" Harvey said.

"Everything," Kate said. "If we fund a clinic, we can hire counselors. If we have counselors on staff, locally accessible so our people don't have to go to town for treatment, which they won't anyway, we can tackle this problem at the roots. Other associations and corporations have already done so. Look at Ahtna. They've got a full-time substance-abuse counselor wired into the AFN sobriety movement."

"Our people won't go to Anglo doctors," Harvey said.

Kate said patiently, "They will if the board members are the Anglo doctors' first patients. In the meantime, why don't we set up some kind of additional funding to apprentice our own people to the staff of the clinic and, if they are so inclined, maybe pay to send them to medical school? They don't have to be doctors, they could be nurses, nurse-practitioners, physician's assistants, counselors. That way, eventually we would have our own people treating our own people."

"And," Auntie Joy added, "it might keep the kids home." All five of Auntie Joy's children had moved to Anchorage to pursue education and careers. Auntie Joy lived up the Glenn Highway from Anchorage, but it was a long, cold drive in the winter and she never saw enough of her grandchildren.

"Most of our money's tied up in capital construction or investments," Billy said, doubtful. "The sawmill at Chokosna. The salmon plant in Cordova. The market holdings Outside."

Auntie Vi glanced at Kate from the corner of her eye. "What about the dividend you're about to declare from the Chokosna logging profits? The shareholders aren't expecting that, so they wouldn't miss it."

Harvey bristled. Billy shook his head and said, "I don't know. The shareholders want money, and the Association has given it to them from the first year it showed a profit. They've been happy with that for a long time, going on twelve years now."

"And what do you think they are going to say," Harvey said triumphantly, "when we cut back on the quarterly dividends to maintain this clinic?"

"And this will be something new," Demetri observed, as dispassionate as always, "and you know elders. They like to move slow. And they vote."

Oh, Kate thought, *you mean like the six people at this table right now?*

"Shareholders are used to going to Ahtna or Anchorage for health care," Harvey said, and smiled at Kate. "I haven't heard any complaints."

"But then," Kate said, with a smile as false as Harvey's, "you weren't looking down the wrong end of Cindy's thirty-thirty today, were you, Harvey?" That was too close to impudence for her elders, and five different kinds of disapproval radiated in her direction. Again, Kate reined in her temper. "Where's Suzy Moonin going to get prenatal care for her and my cousin Martin's first baby? When Carl Stoff broke his leg, he had to be medivacked to Anchorage. When Eknaty Kvasnikoff's little brother—I forget his name—"

"Brian," Auntie Vi said.

"When Brian Kvasnikoff got appendicitis, he died because the weather was socked in and we couldn't fly him to a hospital in Anchorage. It's not just the substance-abuse treatment we need."

"The community is a small one, for the supporting of an entire clinic," Demetri observed.

"It isn't if you include everyone," Old Sam said, "Natives and whites."

Everyone was taken aback, especially Kate, since she'd been planning on saying that herself.

"Pay for white care out of Native funds?" Billy said, shocked.

"Nope." Old Sam shook his head. "Charge everybody on a sliding scale, a percentage based on their annual income. If they don't have any annual income, they don't pay. If they have a little, they pay a little. If they have a lot, they pay a lot. Harvey—" he grinned his desiccated grin at Harvey, who didn't grin back "—and, say, Bernie Koslowski, now, they'd pay a lot. Ben and Cindy, they'd pay a little."

He surveyed their startled expressions with tolerant contempt. "Else how we going to do it? We all live here, all together, Native and white and Negro or black or African American or whatever the hell Bobby Clark's calling himself this year. We're neighbors." He added, his sarcasm deliberately heavy-handed, "You all may be too young to remember the ructions we went through over ANCSA, but I'm not. Lot of resentment between the races because of it. Lot of it."

Billy opened his mouth and Old Sam raised his voice. "I don't want to hear it, Billy. It don't matter a hoot that we deserved restitution for getting our asses kicked around for three hundred years. We got money and land because we had brown skin and the people we'd been living next to for a century didn't. It's taken us twenty years and change to smooth over the bad feelings. No point in stirring it up all over again by starting a clinic—which idea by the way I like and will vote for—that only serves us Natives. Dumb." He met Harvey's glare with another of his patented nasty grins. "Dumb and divisive."

"Where'd you get the idea about payment, Uncle?" Demetri said. "I like it."

"Caught myself the clap the last time I was in town, over Fur Rondy in February," Old Sam said, and winked at Auntie Joy, who for once was not beaming. "Didn't want to stand in line at the Native hospital. Somebody told me about Family Planning. I went down there and they took real good care of me, and that's how they charged me. I was interested, so I asked." He grinned. "Got an awful cute little nurse behind the counter there, explained it all to me. Plan on visiting her again, next time I'm in town."

Kate's lip quivered at the fascinated way the rest of them sat staring at the wizened-up old coot. "Could the board maybe think about this for a while?" she said, sternly controlling the quiver. "Maybe you could meet next week and take a vote on whether to present it at the next shareholders' meeting."

Old Sam hooted. "Good God, girl, don't give them time to think. Make them vote, right here, tonight. If you don't, they'll talk it to death, just like Congress, and the damn thing'll never get built. The Association charter provides the board authorization for the creation of something like this, so we don't have to put it before the shareholders, which I for one don't think we should. I never noticed nobody in the Park ever voting for something just because it might actually be good for them."

After that comprehensive, scathing and unfortunately accurate assessment, no one could think of a thing to add, or they were too scared of Old Sam to try. Old Sam moved for a vote, Auntie Joy seconded it, and the measure to fund a community health clinic out of funds from the Chokosna logging project passed four to one, Harvey voting against, which was only to be expected.

Everyone looked as dazed as Kate felt as the meeting broke up. Auntie Vi, scribbling furiously in her notebook, said, "Who took over for Sarah Kompkoff as head of the local chapter of the sobriety movement, does anybody know?"

"Ethan Swensen," Auntie Joy said.

Surprised, Kate said, "Isn't he a little young?"

"He's twenty-two," Billy said. "He started drinking when he was nine. He's been sober three years. Who better?"

He jerked his head, and Kate followed him across the room to the bar. "What'll it be, Billy?" Bernie said.

"How about a beer?" Billy said.

"Coming right up. Kate, look what I've got." He reached beneath the counter and pulled out a six-pack of Diet Seven-Up. "George brought it in from Anchorage and dropped it off. Said he owed it to you."

"Bernie," Kate said, "I want you now."

"Kate," Bernie said, "I'm yours."

"You handled yourself pretty well over there," Billy said after Bernie had served them and moved on to another customer.

"You sandbagged me," she said. "You prick."

His smile was merry and totally lacking in remorse. "Yes, I did. And you handled it well."

"Thanks," Kate said, giving up for the moment any attempt to bring Billy to recognition of his bad behavior. "I think."

"No. It needed saying. The clinic's a good idea. I've been thinking a little along those lines myself. That's why I okayed subsidizing our people's EMT training in Ahtna out of the discretionary fund. Yes, we have one, your grandmother saw to that. I figured once the EMTs got back and showed their stuff, the board would be more receptive to the idea of a clinic." He saw Kate's look and smiled again, a movement that creased his moon face in two and made him look like a billiken. "I know, I know, it didn't sound like I thought so." His eyes were lit with mischief. "Let you in on a little secret, Kate. Sometimes I have to be against, to make everybody else for, just to get the job done." She looked at him, surprised, and he nodded, smile widening. "You helped the process along this evening, and for that I thank you." His smile faded. "Come a time, I'll want more. We all will."

"Come a time," she said promptly, "you'll whistle down the wind for it."

He didn't believe her, and smiled.

She didn't believe herself, and didn't.

He drained his beer and departed, leaving her with the uncomfortable suspicion that Billy Mike was much more than the part-time clown she'd always seen him as.

Of course, he was Emaa's handpicked choice to succeed her as chair. Kate would do well to remember that.

15

Kate was still staring after him when Auntie Vi spread her notebook out on the bar, finished off her notes, and dated and signed them with a flourish. "Well. That was one of our more interesting board meetings. You do know how to liven things up, Katya."

"It wasn't me, Auntie, it was Old Sam. He pretty much rolled right over the whole bunch of them."

"He did, didn't he?" Auntie Vi grinned. "It was fun to watch."

Kate had to laugh. "That it was, Auntie."

"Ekaterina—" Auntie Vi hesitated, and glanced at her greatniece.

Kate smiled faintly. "It wasn't the way Emaa would have done it, no, but she wouldn't have cared, so long as it got the results she wanted."

"Whatever works," Auntie Vi said, nodding. "Thank you, Katya."

"What for? Like I said, it was all Old Sam."

"No, Katya," Auntie Vi said firmly. "It was you. You set up the meeting because I asked you to talk to Harvey. Thank you. Now say, You're welcome."

"You're welcome, Auntie," Kate said obediently.

Old Sam was back at his original table, yelling, "Free throws win ball games!" as Michael Jordan bounced one off the rim. Kate looked across the room at him, watching as Jordan went up after his own missed foul shot and slammed the ball home for two. Old Sam pounded his approval on the table, upsetting several drinks in the process. Who would have thought that Old Sam, cantankerous old reprobate that he was, would step forward into Emaa's place so aptly, so ably, so opportunely? A sense of relief swept over Kate, and she turned back to Auntie Vi with a lighter heart. "How have you been lately, Auntie? I didn't get a chance to visit with you yesterday. I haven't seen you since—when?"

"Since you came in for starring at Russian Orthodox Christmas," Auntie Vi said.

"That's right, January," Kate said. It had been a crisp, clear night, and she had stood with her aunt at her aunt's front step to welcome and pass out treats to the carolers as they went singing from door to door. She'd ridden her snow machine in that afternoon, she remembered, which naturally led her to wonder now if she was going to be able to patch the gas tank on it. She hoped so. In spite of her new truck, the dwindling wad of cash in the Darigold butter can wasn't going to go far if she had to repair or replace all of her vehicles. So far the Earlybird settlement was just talk. Maybe she could work out a trade for the Great White Hunters' four-wheelers, both of which were still sitting in her front yard. Kate had no wish to learn how to mush dogs this late in life, and she'd never liked four-wheelers. It was a problem. She frowned, and then, when she felt Auntie Vi looking at her, shrugged off her woes. "You making good money off the feds, Auntie?"

"I made out okay," Auntie Vi said, which Kate took to mean she had made out like a bandit.

Chopper Jim was down at the other end of the bar, talking to Demetri. They'd both done time in Europe with the armed forces, and bored everyone very much with Cold War stories whenever they got the chance. Mark Stewart was sitting at a table against the wall, brooding over a bottle of beer. He was brooding so well that both Jackie Webber and Tina Moonin were trying to minister to his grief. He wasn't exactly beating them off with a stick.

"Auntie, did you know they were going up to the mine?"

"Who?"

Kate nodded imperceptibly toward Stewart. "The woman who died, and her husband. You said they were staying with you. Did you know they were going up to the mine?"

"Of course. I packed a lunch for them."

"Did Mark Stewart have a rifle or a pistol with him?"

Auntie Vi pursed her lips, and shook her head. "I didn't see one."

"What did their luggage look like?"

"I know what a rifle case looks like, Katya," Auntie Vi said tartly.

"I know you do, Auntie. But sometimes people put rifles in suitcases or duffel bags."

"Those ones had packs," Auntie Vi said firmly.

But you can break a rifle down, Kate thought. All it takes is a screwdriver to reassemble. Half the time the pieces will even pass through an airport security check.

"Why do you ask all these questions, Katya? He didn't have a rifle." She thought, and added, "He had a fancy knife, though. Had a screwdriver on it. He fixed the hinge on the door to their room." She grinned. "Good thing, too. They make lot of noise, and they were booked for all week." She saw Kate's expression. "What? What is it, Katya? Why you look like that?"

Kate's hand closed over the Swiss Army knife she had absent-mindedly put in her pocket after Billy dropped it in the slush. The one Cindy had found up at the mine in her mad chase after her errant husband. She pulled it out and gave it to Auntie Vi. "Like this one?"

Auntie Vi took it, and after a few moments' fiddling, managed to open out the Phillips screwdriver. "Yeah. Just like this one." She handed the knife back. "Why?"

"Did you warn them about the bear activity in the area?"

The old woman ruffled up. "Of course. Not my fault if they can't take a hint. I'm not their mother."

Kate turned away and caught a sly look in Auntie Vi's eye. "What?"

Auntie Vi took a ladylike sip from the glass of red wine that had replaced the mug of coffee with the council meeting's adjournment. "I see that woman before. That woman who died."

"Carol Stewart?"

Auntie Vi nodded.

Bobby and Dinah came in and were surrounded. Over the hubbub their entrance caused, Kate said, "Do you mean the Stewarts had been here before? When?"

"One year ago. Last spring. But that one was not with this husband." Auntie Vi's smile spread slowly across her face, her eyelids drooping so that she looked like the Cheshire cat. "But she make even more noise with him."

Kate stared at her, brows knit. "Wait a minute," she said slowly, "you were saying something like this last night when all the shooting started. Carol Stewart was in the Park last spring?"

"Yes."

"But not with Mark Stewart?"

"No."

"Auntie, I'm sorry, I have to get this straight. Carol Stewart stayed with you last spring, with a man who wasn't her husband?"

"Not this one. Maybe she change in the middle of the year." The old woman's eyes sparkled with mischief. Auntie Vi loved a good, nasty story, especially if it concerned no one she was related to, one reason she was a huge soap opera fan. She had had a satellite dish installed just so she could watch *The Young and the Restless* every day instead of waiting for the damn state to put it on Ratnet. In her presatellite days, she'd once had to wait two weeks to find out if Nicholas Newman had gone to jail for a murder he naturally had not committed. She was resolved never to let that happen again.

An argument broke out at Bobby's table. "Kate!" he roared. "Shugak, get your butt over here, they're ganging up on me!"

"Auntie," Kate said urgently, "who was it? Who was the man Carol Stewart was with last spring?"

"Vi!" Auntie Joy called from the quilting bee. "We need help with this stitch!"

Auntie Vi ripped her notes from the notebook, stuffed them into the hip pocket of her jeans for later transcribing to the Association computer and drained her glass. "I don't know, I don't care who they are or what they're doing here as long as they got cash."

"Try, Auntie."

Auntie Joy called again, and Auntie Vi huffed out an impatient breath, running a hand through her corkscrew curls. "I don't know. It was a fish name, or something like that. Sardine?" She frowned. "No, that's not right. I just don't remember, Katya."

"What did he look like?"

"It was a year ago, Katya. Skinny guy, I remember thinking he weigh less than she did."

"Was he dark? Blond? How old was he?"

Auntie Vi shrugged. "Brown hair, maybe. About her age, I guess, maybe couple years older. Look, I have to go help those ones finish that quilt. If I don't, they sew it to their laps."

Kate watched her cross the room with her bouncy, birdlike step. She turned back to the bar to find Chopper Jim lying in wait. He'd taken his hat off, which meant he was available to talk other than business, his dark blond hair smooth and shining. "I don't see any blood on the floor," he said with a grin.

"Where's your prisoner?" said Kate, who knew perfectly well where he was but didn't see any reason not to rag a little on Jim.

"He's not my prisoner."

"Why'd you bring him back?" she said bluntly.

"I told you, I wanted to walk over the ground with him."

"What did you find?"

"Nothing."

"Did Stewart show you which roof his wife was on?"

"He was a little confused," Jim drawled. He looked over her shoulder at Mark Stewart, and the blue eyes narrowed. "He couldn't remember which roof it was. Said he was in kind of a hurry at the time."

"There are a dozen houses back there," Kate said with acerbity. "Did he manage to narrow it down to two or three? Or maybe even just one, with a few scuff marks from the sole of a hiking boot or a few claw marks from a grizzly?"

"You noticed that, too," Jim said, satisfied. "Nope. He sure couldn't."

Dan O'Brian stamped inside. Kate saw him and waved vigorously. He looked right through her and joined the group around Bobby and Dinah.

"Still mad from this morning, I guess," Chopper Jim, a trained observer, said.

Kate set her glass down on the bar with a bang and stalked across the room to tap Dan on the shoulder. "O'Brian."

He sent her a cool look. "Shugak."

"You said you had a friend look up Mark Stewart on Motznik."

Dan almost sniffed. "I thought you weren't interested."

"I'm not. Did your friend happen to mention if Stewart has a pilot's license?"

Dan pushed back from the table and regarded her. "You're not interested, but you want to know if Stewart flies."

Kate felt the creep of warmth up the back of her neck. "There's no law says I have to be consistent," she snapped. "Does Stewart have a pilot's license or not?"

"No, he doesn't. I told you, when I saw him last fall the other guy was flying. Hooligan, or something like that. What's this all about, Kate?"

"Were he and Carol married in Alaska?"

"Yes, what—"

"Did you get the date on the marriage license?"

"Yes."

"Well? When? When did they marry?"

"Six years ago," Dan said. "Why the sudden interest?"

She stood still for a moment, frowning. "No reason," she said. "Excuse me."

Dan, sputtering, half rose to his feet to go after her. "Goddam that Shugak! Who the hell does she think she is! I oughta—"

"Don't," Bobby said. "I've seen her like this too many times. Don't bother."

Dan watched Kate halt in front of the trooper and start talking rapidly. He settled back into his seat, fuming. "Women," he said, and the word was not complimentary.

"I hear you," Bobby said, one hand massaging the back of Dinah's neck. Dinah looked dangerously close to breaking into a purr. "I hear you, boy."

Across the room, Kate said, "Jim, how does Stewart say he got here? Him and his wife? Dan says he doesn't have a pilot's license."

"Air charter out of Merrill Field."

"Did he say which one?" Jim shook his head. "I think you should find out which one."

"Why?"

"So you can ask the pilot if he had a rifle with him."

"Did somebody tell you he had one?"

"No."

"Did he even have a bag that might look like it could hold a rifle?"

Reluctantly, she shook her head. "No, I asked Auntie Vi. Both Stewarts carried packs."

"Than what makes you think he had a rifle?"

"You can break a rifle down, Jim. The individual pieces don't take up much room. You could pack for a romantic week for two and still have room left over for a barrel, a stock and a trigger."

"Not to mention ammunition."

"Not to mention."

He looked down at her and quirked an eyebrow. "I thought you weren't interested."

"I'm not, goddammit," she said.

He continued to look at her, saying nothing.

"Oh hell," she said. "Bernie! Can I have another of those Diet Seven-Ups?"

The noise in the room grew to the point that Old Sam let loose with a vivid curse and turned the volume on the television up to 9. One of the pool players was in the process of running the table and she offered up an even more vivid curse, which Old Sam applauded politely before sitting back down. Luba glanced sideways at her husband and said something and Enid, Auntie Joy and Auntie Vi threw back their heads and laughed. Demetri, Harvey and Billy shifted uncomfortably in their chairs. In the far corner, the Unitarians were trying "Amazing Grace" on for size and finding it fit their soprano profundo section, if there was such a thing, rather well. Through it all Ralph Estes snored peacefully.

Bernie refilled Kate's glass with ice, popped open another can, served Jim another beer and, in response to a slight jerk of the trooper's head, drifted back down the bar.

Kate took a long, reviving drink. "Auntie Vi said something else, Jim."

"What?"

She had to raise her voice over the music. "Auntie Vi said Carol Stewart was up here last spring, too."

Jim was quick. "Alone?"

She shook her head. "With another man."

His brows rose. "Hmm. I suppose she could have been married to someone else a year ago."

"She could have been, but she wasn't." Kate nodded in Dan's direction. "Dan's Motznik buddy pulled up a marriage certificate for Mark and Carol dated six years ago."

"Really," Jim said, glass arrested halfway to his mouth. "Did Viola know who the other guy was?"

The jukebox blared out Aerosmith and Kate winced. "She can't remember his name. It reminded her of fish. She said sardine, and then she said that wasn't right."

"Description?"

Kate shrugged.

"Great." Jim drained his glass, and regarded Mark Stewart over the rim of it. "You ever been charged by a bear, Kate?"

Kate took another drink. "Does day before yesterday count?"

"I thought the three of you were in the truck."

She shook her head. "I got charged on the homestead the day before that."

Jim gave Kate a sharp look that held the beginnings of under-standing. "Tell me."

She told him. When she came to the part where the bear stood up and snapped its teeth, Jim didn't go all manly-man on her and try to hide his shiver. "I hate that sound. Did you go for your rifle?"

Kate was silent.

"Kate?"

She raised her eyes, the expression in them rueful. "I didn't have it. Both the rifle and the shotgun were back in the cabin."

He closed his eyes and shook his head.

He hadn't said anything, but she agreed anyway. "Yeah, I know. Dumb. Especially for someone who is supposed to know what they're doing out here." She remembered the conversation at Bobby and Dinah's table the night before and one corner of her mouth curled in self-mockery.

He shook his head. "Close."

"Too damn close," she agreed.

"You gonna take the shotgun down to the creek when you go fishing from now on?"

Kate gave a short laugh. "From now on, Jim, the shotgun goes with me to the outhouse."

"Good." He paused. "So that's it, huh?"

"So that's what?"

"You got charged and survived. Carol Stewart got charged and didn't. Could have been you and wasn't. That's why you're finally asking questions. You want to find out what happened."

She shifted uncomfortably and didn't reply.

He looked over her shoulder, and she knew he was looking at Mark Stewart again. "I got charged once myself, hunting on Montague Island. Big male. Real big, and there was snow on the ground, which as you know makes 'em look twice as big as they already are. False charge, he stopped about fifty feet away from me and reared up like a goddam jack-in-the-box. He ran off after he let me know I was someplace I shouldn't be and he didn't like it and he was sure I knew he didn't like it. I've never forgotten it." He dropped his eyes to Kate's and added in an even tone, "I've never forgotten what happened afterward, either. It took twelve hours to come down off the adrenaline high, and I was still jumping at noises a week later."

Kate nodded. "It's not something you get over overnight."

They both looked around at Mark Stewart. Evidently Tina had ceded the field to Jackie, who had Stewart's hand pressed between hers, soothing away whatever strain might remain from grizzly-induced nervous trauma. The treatment appeared very effective. Tina was across the room, flirting obviously and outrageously with Frank Scully. One of the Moonin boys—Sergei, or was it Tom?— didn't like that any more than he'd liked her making up to Stewart.

"Of course," Jim said thoughtfully, "if you were expecting a bear charge—"

"—like if somehow you managed to provoke one—"

There was a brief pause, broken by Jim. "He said he'd gotten her up on the roof before he ran for help, but he didn't have a mark on him, like the bear had taken a swipe at him, or like he'd gotten in between the bear and his wife."

Kate remembered the long strips of paint peeling back from the clapboard sides of the buildings. "I didn't see any trace of anybody climbing up any walls to a roof."

"Me either, and I looked pretty carefully this morning."

There was another, longer pause, broken again by Jim. "Well, if he did what I think he did, he took one hell of a chance."

"I wouldn't care to hand-feed a grizzly myself." She drained her glass and frowned. "You'll never prove it, you know. If there's no forensic evidence, all you can prove is that the two of them came into the Park and acted dumb, and unfortunately, dumb is not a capital crime." She drained her glass. "No, you'll never prove it."

"Aside from finding the rope he tied around her neck with the stake attached to it, that is." He saw her expression and gave an apologetic shrug. "Sorry, Kate. Remember, by the time I saw her, she was no longer a woman. She was just a hunk of leftover meat."

"Me, too," Kate said softly.

"Bears," he said. "They wake up cranky, the way everyone does when they wake up hungry. If they stumble over a patch of horsetail first, fine. If they stumble over a nicely decomposing body instead, that's fine, too. If they run into a couple of idiots setting themselves up as the main course, all the better. Hell, no-body ever got mad at Binky—God rest his ornery little soul—when somebody tried to crawl into his cage at the Alaska Zoo. If you're the kind of person who thinks crawling into cages with polar bears would be, like, totally rad, dude, you're doing the whole human race a favor when you do."

"And if the bears get an assist on the goal?"

"As you so astutely pointed out, Kate, we don't have any evidence." The quickly bitten off words indicated that he was not as resigned to the situation as he would have her think. "Hell, we don't even have motive." He brooded for a moment. "Thought I'd give Jack a call, have him run a make on Stewart. Purely unofficially, of course."

"Oh, of course," Kate said courteously, and wondered what Jim's boss would have to say if he thought for one moment that

Sergeant James M. Chopin, pride of the Alaska Department of Public Safety, was treating a random bear attack as a murder investigation.

Dan O'Brian had bellied up to the bar and was holding forth on the trails, trials and tribulations of a ranger's life for the edification of one Amy Kasheverof, a medium-size brunette with flashing dark eyes, a dimple in her right cheek and an impressive cleavage displayed to advantage in a tight scoop-neck T-shirt.

Kate caught sight of Ben Bingley, sitting alone in a corner, nursing his head and a beer. "Only one so far," Bernie said in answer to Kate's inquiring glance.

Old Sam Dementieff caught her eye and raised his Irish coffee in salute; she bowed slightly in return, feeling unsettled that he evidently regarded them as being somehow in cahoots.

Karen Kompkoff's husband had shown up in time to rescue her from a fate worse than death and Dandy Mike was now hustling Shirley Inglima around the pool tables (didn't the man ever let up?). The four Grosdidier brothers, who at one point had constituted four of the starting five of the Kanuyaq Kings, had joined Old Sam beneath the television monitor, dwarfing the old man, who more than made up in noise what he lacked in size. The Unitarians had moved on to "The Old Rugged Cross" and were making an even better job of it than they had of "Amazing Grace." The quilters were doing finish work. Kate wondered if Dinah knew the end product had her name on it.

All in all, kind of slow for a Saturday night, but then it was early.

"Not to change the subject," Jim said, "but Nathan Harrigan is your DB. Ring any bells?"

"I don't have any DBs," Kate said instantly, but something nagged at the edge of her consciousness. She puzzled at it for a moment and got no change. "You mean the body the go team found near to but not on my place yesterday?"

He nodded. "I talked to the coroner this morning. It's too soon for a positive identification, but the body matches a missing person description. Guy from Anchorage, electrician, contract hire for

Northern Enterprises—now there's an imaginative name—anyway, he didn't come in for work one day last October. After three days' no show and no call—apparently Harrigan was the responsible type—the boss got worried and sent his secretary to check out Harrigan's apartment. Nobody home, nothing missing except maybe a few clothes, truck parked in the lot. Nobody's heard from him since."

"No family?"

He shook his head. "There was a girlfriend a while back, last summer sometime according to the apartment manager, but he couldn't remember much about her except that he thought she was blonde. Or maybe brunette. I love eyewitnesses. Almost as much as I love breakup. And of course he didn't know her name or anything about her. Nobody at work did, either."

"A man who kept himself to himself," Kate murmured, still trying to scratch the little itch at the back of her brain. "How'd he die?"

"Coroner says he's got a crack on the back of his skull, and his right femur is cracked about halfway down."

"So he fell down and broke his leg and hit his head while he was at it?"

"Something like that."

"Did you find a rifle or gear or anything at the scene?"

Jim shook his head again.

"Then what the hell was he doing out there?"

Jim smiled his carcharodonian smile, all teeth and appetite. "I was hoping you'd check around a little, take Mutt, see if the two of you can sniff out something."

She opened her mouth to tell him exactly and precisely what she thought of that idea when the window to the right of the door shattered, and the neon Rolling Rock sign with it.

"Shit!" Bernie said, and dropped for cover.

16

The second bullet shattered the mirror behind the bar.

Chopper Jim clapped his hat on his head and performed a neat, economical, 5.4 swan dive over the bar to land with a breathless thud on Bernie's other side. Bobby had his chair in overdrive with Dinah in his lap as he skidded around the other end. Dan was left sitting, open-mouthed, where he was, one arm around an equally befuddled Amy.

Kate tackled the gray streak as it launched itself from beneath her stool. "No, Mutt, no! Stay!" Mutt, growling and barking, was an inch away from fighting free when Kate got a headlock on her. "No! Calm down, girl, calm down. Dammit, stop that!"

She got to her knees and knotted a hand in Mutt's ruff. "Come on, sweetheart, there's a good girl. Come on, dammit!" With a mixture of curses and endearments she managed to crawl around the bar, hauling Mutt behind her. They took cover next to Bernie.

The door banged open and a figure backed in. Kate, sneaking a look over the top of the bar, saw that the figure, which looked ominously familiar, held a rifle at waist level and was firing point-blank into the parking lot. For the moment the target had shifted, and she motioned to Jim and together they rose to grab Dan and Amy and haul them over the bar to safety, where they landed on Bernie, hard. Bernie complained.

All around the bar, tables and chairs overturned as everyone in Bernie's Roadhouse dove for cover for the second time in two days, with the exception of Ralph Estes, who remained head down on the bar, snoring peacefully. The six Unitarians charged off in six different directions, uttering loud cries to the Lord. Dandy Mike wound up on top of Shirley Inglima, which was what he'd been trying for anyway, and all four Grosdidier brothers were jammed into the same corner.

Mark Stewart and Jackie Webber were on the floor beneath their table. Harvey, Demetri and Billy Mike had sought refuge with Old Sam, whose gleeful expression was clearly visible from where Kate crouched. The quilting bee rose to its collective feet, folded and stowed their work and made for the back door in calm, orderly procession, bullets flying all around them. Kate, furious with fear, saw the door close safely behind Auntie Joy and suffered a wave of relief that had her sagging weakly against the bar.

"GodDAM!" Bobby roared. "We didn't use this much ammo at Hue!"

"Do something, Kate!" Bernie said, shoving her.

Kate shoved Bernie. "It's your bar, you do something!"

Bernie shoved Dan. "It's your Park, you do something!"

Dan shoved Jim. "It's your state, you do something!"

The trooper might have been able to hold out against everyone else, but Mutt barked an endorsement of their views right in his face. Until then he had regarded Mutt as his love slave, but sometimes love is not enough. He cursed, thrashed around until he got his .357 out and very slowly and very carefully got his feet under him to hoist a wary eye over the top of the bar.

The next round took his hat off.

Chopper Jim sat back down again and said very calmly, "I think we'll wait a bit longer before we mount a frontal assault."

"What do you mean we, white man?" Bobby said.

Kate cursed them all with impartial fervor. "Bobby, hold Mutt." Mutt didn't like it, neither did Bobby, and Jim said sharply, "Kate!" but she was up on all fours and peering around the end of the bar before he could stop her.

The figure in the doorway was reloading and a positive hail of bullets smacked against the outside of the building. Kate recognized Cheryl Jeppsen feeding shells into the stock of a Winchester. She ducked back. "It's the Hatfields and the McCoys again."

"Gee, why am I not surprised?" Dinah said wearily.

Bernie swore loud and long. "Goddammit, why do they always have to come and shoot up *my* place? Why can't they stay home and shoot each *other's* places up! I *hate* breakup!"

"Give it up, Kay!" Cheryl shouted. "Go on home and I'll forget you started this!"

"*I* started it!" a furious voice yelled from outside. "Like hell! You started this, you bitch, I was driving down the road minding my own business, and you shot my husband!"

"It's not your road, and it's not your land!"

"Bullshit! We've got a right of way!"

A shot was her reply.

"Can't you throw them out of the Park or something?" Kate said to Dan.

"You tell me how, legally," Dan said grimly, "and I'll be more than happy to oblige."

Another flurry of shots and everybody ducked. "I don't know, get creative, take their land back or something!"

"What land?" Dan hissed back. "Their homesteads? It's not federal land anymore, it's state land, or it was until the Jeppsens and the Kreugers won it in the lottery, now it's private property.

Both families have already proved up, it's theirs, nothing the Parks Service can do about it now," Dan said, adding with heartfelt sincerity, "thank God."

"You think maybe you guys could discuss who owns Alaska some other time?" Bobby said politely, adding in a ferocious bellow that could probably be heard in Whitehorse, "LIKE AFTER SOMEBODY COLDCOCKS THOSE TWO CRAZY BITCHES OUT IN FRONT OF THIS FRIGGIN SALOON!"

Kate swore ripely—there'd been a lot of that going around lately—and raised her voice. "Cheryl? Cheryl, it's Kate Shugak."

"What do you want?" the woman with the rifle snarled without turning around.

"You think you could kind of take it easy? There are a lot of people in here who don't use your land to get to their homestead. No reason for them to get hurt."

"I don't have any intention of shooting anybody, except that red-haired, brass-plated bitch outside!"

Cheryl's Christian charity was slipping along with her language. As if to underline the thought, there was another loud *Bang!* and Kate flinched. So far, it had been the noisiest spring in the Park in her memory. "Cheryl," she tried again, "this is silly. Are you and Kay just going to keep shooting at each other until you run out of bullets?"

Cheryl fired, Kay fired a return volley and a bullet hit the bar right in front of Kate with a businesslike thud. Another shattered a bottle in back of the bar and showered them all with glass and liquid. Kate sat down.

"Offhand," Dan said, picking brown glass out of his hair, "I'd say the answer to your question would be yes."

Dinah tasted the back of her hand. "I always did like a shot of Grand Marnier after a meal. Settles the stomach, promotes digestion, gives you that nice little glow, you know?"

Bobby slapped her hand away. "You're pregnant, you're not supposed to be drinking."

There was another shot and almost simultaneously another

bottle shattered on a shelf in back of the bar, raining tequila and shards of glass mostly on Bernie. A second later a withered finger dropped to the bottom shelf and rolled off into Bernie's lap. Dan and Amy both let out involuntary yelps.

Bernie's sense of outrage swelled to heroic proportions. "There goes the Middle Finger bottle! Goddammit! I just refilled it, too, and with Jose Cuervo Gold! This bullshit's starting to cost me money!"

He leapt to his feet and started around the bar. "All right, you two, that is just about enough!"

Cheryl swiveled and brought the rifle up. "Don't move, Koslowski! Don't take another goddam step!"

"Such language, Cheryl," Bernie said mildly, but he froze where he stood. One of the Grosdidier brothers said, "Oh hell," sounding more disgusted than alarmed. "I can't look!" Frank Scully screamed from beneath a table, and buried his head in his arms. While Shirley Inglima's attention was distracted Dandy Mike slid one hand beneath her blouse. She didn't object. As far as Dandy was concerned, Bernie ought to throw a shoot-out every day.

Kate rose to her feet to give Cheryl two people to cover. "Cheryl, this has to stop." There was a furtive noise from behind the bar and she knew Jim was crawling down to the opposite end. She raised her voice to cover the sound of his movements. "Put the rifle down, and maybe the Parks Service can get some kind of arbitrator in to resurvey the land and reroute that road."

Dan O'Brian might have had his own ideas about that but he kept quiet, for which Kate was profoundly thankful.

It didn't do any good. "You go to hell," Cheryl said tightly. "This has gone way beyond some arbitrator." The muscles in her shoulders tensed, the barrel of the rifle began to rise, and in that moment Old Sam Dementieff lunged forward to grab hold with both hands, gnarled knuckles gleaming against the dark metal.

Cheryl was around five foot ten, weighed in at 160 pounds and was a hale and hearty forty years old. Sam was five foot one, weighed maybe 100 pounds with his boots on and had at least forty years on Cheryl, but he had a grip like the big claw on a king crab and he hung on like grim death as Cheryl tried to throw him off. The barrel swung first to the left and then to the right and then back again, this time all the way around in a circle so that it pulled Old Sam into a smart trot.

Kate and Bernie both took a step forward, but Old Sam's palms were sweaty and his grip slid down the barrel and off, right over the sight, which must have been fairly painful. Centrifugal force did the rest: Old Sam, moving by then at a medium gallop, slammed into Ralph Estes's back, which caused Ralph's gut to slam into the bar. Rudely awakened, Ralph sat up with a disbelieving snort, turned green and blew chunks across the bar, showering Dan and Amy with predigested popcorn and beer. It was as efficient an example of projectile vomiting as an admiring Kate had ever seen, but then she was out of the line of fire.

Cheryl, momentarily stunned, was motionless for one second too long, just long enough for the basketball fans to switch sports and sweep down in a group tackle. She fought hard, letting out a primal scream that Kay must have heard outside and correctly interpreted, because when Kate crashed through the front door and skidded to a halt in the middle of the parking lot, all she saw were the taillights of Wayne's old International bouncing down the road to Niniltna.

Kate swore in disgust and was turning to climb back up the steps to Bernie's front door when it burst open and Cheryl came flying out. She knocked Kate flat, left the footprint of a size-nine shoepac on Kate's chest and made tracks for an ancient and filthy white Econoline van.

Kate sat up, only to be knocked flat for the second time that evening by the Grosdidier flying squad in hot pursuit. The door to the Econoline slammed, the engine started and the van fishtailed out of the parking lot and onto the road, moving at about the same pace as the now long-gone truck.

The Grosdidiers stamped and kicked and cursed, and only be-latedly remembered Kate, still prone at the bottom of the Road-house's front porch trying to catch her breath. They stood around in a circle peering down at her, identical expressions of gathering concern on their nearly identical faces. "Are you okay, Kate?" Peter said, stretching out a hand.

Her breath returned with a great whoosh and she took in grate-ful gulps of cool night air. Ignoring Peter's hand, she got to her feet, wincing a little on the way up. "I hate breakup," she said, very quietly but with great feeling.

"She is hurt, guys," Luke said in an odd voice. "Look." He pointed.

Everyone looked, including Kate. Her right bicep was soaked in blood, and she became aware of a throbbing ache in the same area.

"Holy shit," Peter blurted, and the Four Musketeers exploded into action.

"Help her up the stairs!"

"Pressure, we've got to apply pressure directly to the wound!"

"Antiseptic, we need antiseptic!"

"Shock! She's going to get shocky!"

"We need to lay her down, put her feet up!"

Four pairs of hands reached for her.

"No!" Kate yelped. "I'm fine! Really! It's no problem. Don't touch that arm, Luke!"

Johnny said earnestly, "It's okay, Kate. We're just trying to help."

"I know," she said, still fending them off. "And I appreciate it. But please don't. I'm begging you. Please." The stairs rocked gen-tly beneath her feet. Wet mud seeped through her shirt to her skin. Her left knee thought about giving. She strengthened it with a mental threat. "I'm fine, guys. Really. I'm fine." She turned and took the steps at a slow limp, followed at close range by a four-Grosdidier escort.

Inside, Bernie was surveying the shambles of his bar. He closed his eyes and shook his head. "*Breakup,*" he said with loathing. Resentfully, he cracked the seal on a new bottle of Jose Cuervo Gold. The withered, slightly yellow middle finger floated down through the amber liquid to rest gently on the bottom.

Mutt left a handful of hair in Bobby's fist and bounded over to Kate, placing her paws on Kate's chest. Kate would have fallen right over if Paul, bringing up a close rear, hadn't slapped both hands on her shoulders. A rough tongue slurped the side of Kate's face, once, a second time, followed by an inquiring yip.

"I'm okay, girl," Kate said, not at all sure that was the case. "I'm all right. Settle down now."

Jim reholstered his pistol, which he had never fired. His eyes narrowed on Kate. "Is that blood?"

"I caught one in the arm," she muttered, sitting down heavily. "It just creased me. You got something I can tie it up with, Bernie?"

"Sure," Bernie said, long-suffering. "I got nothing better to do with my linen inventory." He produced a clean square of worn cotton sheeting, and the four Grosdidiers jumped forward as one.

"Hold it!" Kate barked. They halted, identical expressions of disappointment on their faces. Kate handed the cloth to Bobby and sat down so he could reach her.

Behind them furniture shifted as tables and chairs were righted. The back door opened and the quilting bee filed back inside in effortless dignity. Auntie Joy and Auntie Vi saw the blood on Kate's arm and hurried over to exclaim and offer Bobby advice. Bernie handed out broom and dustpan, and someone dropped change into the jukebox. The first song to play was, appropriately enough, Jimmy Buffett's "Boat Drinks," which made everyone laugh, a little shakily, and feel better.

"Doesn't look too bad," Bobby said, tearing the cloth into two strips.

"Bullet or glass?"

He scrutinized the wound. "If you made me pick, I'd choose

glass." He looked at her and smiled, without much more humor than Mutt showed baring her teeth. "Another battle scar for you, Shugak."

"Yeah," she said, closing her eyes for a moment, "now I can strip my sleeves and show my scars with the best of you."

"Whatever." He folded one of the strips into a pad and used the other to tie the pad to her arm, his hands deft and gentle. It smarted, and Kate winced. When he was done she said to Bernie, "You got some aspirin?"

He produced an economy-size bottle of Bayer. At her look, he said, "After the last two days, you don't think I need this much aspirin to run this place?" Kate took four and washed them down with warm Seven-Up.

"That's twice, Kate," Bobby said, his outward calm belied by the rage simmering beneath. "That's twice those bitches have taken their best shot at Dinah." They hadn't been shooting only at Dinah, but under the circumstances Kate respected his tunnel vision and didn't comment. "They've managed to clip you both times."

"Not to mention what they've done to my bar," Bernie growled.

"Not to mention," Bobby agreed. "Maybe it's time for a little executive action, you know?"

"Kate?" Jim said, studiously polite.

"Yes, Jim?"

He had replaced his hat, adjusting it so the brim formed a level line just above his eyes, which were steady and very, very cold. The bullet hole through the crown, above and just a little off center of the gold braid tie, lent a certain emphasis to his calm, precisely spaced words. "Would you drive me out to the Kreugers' and the Jeppsens' homesteads, please? I'm afraid I don't know exactly where they are."

"What are you going to do, once you're there?"

"Gee, I don't know," Jim said, descending momentarily into mild sarcasm. "Arrest them?"

"What for?"

"I'll think of something," he said, very dry.

Bobby's roar was back, with interest. "Yeah, attempted murder kind of leaps to mind!"

The wound on Kate's arm throbbed painfully. She looked past the trooper to see Mark Stewart standing very close to Jackie Webber. His chin was up, his shoulders back, the rangy, youthful body held gracefully erect. His clothes fit well, his face was clean-shaven, his smile swift and charming. He was a looker, and he knew it. He was accustomed to the adulation of the female of the species, and expected it.

His eyes met hers with easy, unworried self-possession.

He smiled.

Something inside her clicked into place.

Something else snapped in two.

It was the last straw. It was the final nail, it was too much on the plate, it was too many irons in the fire. It was jet engines falling out of the sky, it was bear charges, it was plane crashes, it was bodies revealed by melting snow, it was wives shooting at their husbands and too-heavy duties assumed too soon and it was murder most foul and it was overload, it was too much, it was breakup, that was all, the breakup of winter, the breakdown of marriage, of the social fabric, not to mention the very fabric of modern technology itself, and there was no shelter from the fallout.

Kate felt disoriented, frayed at the edges, and in self-defense she withdrew, took a step back, out of herself. It changed her perspective, as if she were perched on her own shoulder.

"At the very least, aggravated assault," Jim added. "With intent. So let's go."

Kate's second self whispered in her own ear. "I've got a better idea," she said.

Bobby was inspecting Dinah for wounds over her exasperated protests when the tone of Kate's voice got through to him. His head snapped around. "Kate?"

The second self whispered again. Kate got to her feet and smiled across the room at Mark Stewart. "Mr. Stewart? Would you like to come with me?"

She sounded like Mae inviting Cary to come up and see her

sometime, like Circe convincing Odysseus to stay an extra year on Aeaea, like Eve encouraging Adam to take just one bite.

Dan sighed.

Bernie shivered.

Jim Chopin, not a fanciful man, felt the hair rise on the back of his neck.

"Jesus, Kate," Bobby muttered.

"Down, boys," Dinah said, and wondered if Kate was aware of the power she had, when she bothered to use it.

Jackie Webber gave Kate a dirty look.

As the events of the past forty-eight hours—of the past year— had demonstrated, Mark Stewart was not a stupid man. Careful, methodical, a planner, he was a man who did nothing on impulse, a man with no nerves to speak of and no conscience to bother him after the fact. He had to know what Kate suspected, why the trooper had asked him to return to the mine, that they had learned at least some of the truth and guessed at the rest. But they had no proof, and as long as he continued to say as little as possible, they never would have. It would be foolish to go anywhere but back to Anchorage by the first available transport, and sheer madness to accompany this woman anywhere else.

But he was still a man who saw himself reflected in every woman he met, and the challenge in Kate's invitation made his hunting instincts sit up and howl.

As she had been certain they would. "I think you might enjoy it," she added, and smiled, a lush, lavish smile that promised him everything.

"Kate," Bobby repeated, this time a wealth of warning in the single word.

Her second self stopped her ears. "Stay," she said to Mutt, and sauntered to the door. She turned to look over her shoulder at Stewart, and smiled again. "You coming?"

No fool, Mark Stewart wasn't a coward, either.

And she was only a woman, after all.

He picked up her gauntlet and followed her into the night.

17

The road wasn't much more than a tractor trail, full of deep ruts, yawning potholes, treacherous glaciation and the occasional malevolent washout. It didn't help that it was now full dark before moonrise, but by that time Kate's second self had firm hold of the scruff of her neck and was whipping her unrelentingly onward. Lights flashed in the rearview mirror, showing one vehicle faint but pursuing. Branches scraped against metal. Tires cracked through thin layers of ice to splash into puddles beneath. The cab of the truck rocked back and forth.

In the passenger seat Mark Stewart rode silently, one hand braced against the dash. A thread of tension, taut and humming, quivered between the two of them, but he didn't speak. Neither did she. The challenge had been made and accepted, and they were both infected with a kind of reckless madness.

Twenty minutes later the convoy pulled up in front of a snug little cabin next to a two-story barnlike structure at the base of a hill. Halfway up the hill was the timbered entrance to a mine; from the entrance ran a wooden sluice that was falling apart, one twelve-foot plank at a time. The sluice ended in a creek, next to where an old steam engine stood, shedding flakes of rust into the water.

Bobby's truck pulled up next to her, and people literally poured out of both doors. Kate walked past them as if they weren't there, marching up to the large building like she owned it and tugging at the doors. They gave but wouldn't open all the way. Her second self noticed the Yale padlock hanging from the hasp, and whispered to her that the key was probably in the cabin.

The cabin door was unlocked, the cabin itself unoccupied, Mac Devlin probably away on a mission to strip-mine an especially scenic part of the Park. Inside, a key rack hung from the wall next to the door. She sorted through them until she found a Yale key and brought it back to the barnlike structure. The key slid smoothly into the padlock and turned without a hitch. The padlock snapped open, and she folded the double doors back one at a time.

Her second self began to hum the "Hallelujah Chorus."

It was a D-6 Caterpillar tractor. The body was a bright and gleaming yellow, the ten-foot blade a ton of shining silver steel. Two, almost three years before, Mac Devlin had been enjoined from excavating mining claims on Park lands, grandfathered or otherwise, and since then this gleaming monster had not been used for its original purpose. Mac never failed in the hope that one day restrictions would ease, or in cursing the memory of Park Ranger Mark Miller, whose murder had been, in Mac's view, timely, if not downright providential. In the meantime, the Cat paid for its keep by building access roads and digging foundations for construction.

The perfect weapon, and in excellent repair. Kate checked the gas tank. Full. Her opinion of Mac Devlin rose. She went back to the cabin, traded the garage key for the ignition key and clambered up into the Cat's roomy seat.

Mark Stewart stood next to the right tread. She held out an imperious hand. "Well, Mr. Stewart?"

A smile spread slowly across his face, a smile that, again, physically jarred her with its appeal. It was almost enough to kick her second self out of the driver's seat, but not quite. "It's Mark," he said, and took her hand, following her up.

Lined up outside the barn, waiting for what they hoped might be a little less than Armageddon, Bobby, Dinah, Dan, Bernie and Chopper Jim watched Kate and Stewart settle into the cab of the Cat.

"I want to make one thing perfectly clear," the trooper said.

"Which is?" Bobby said.

"I am not here."

"Shit, Jim," Dan said, "none of us are."

The key in the master switch turned easily and just in time Kate remembered to preheat for thirty seconds. The engine turned over on the first try and a cloud of black smoke issued from the exhaust. A great throaty bawl rattled the rafters in the roof and the teeth in Kate's head. Her heart thumped in her breast, and there was such a rush of blood to all the extremities of her body that she felt even more light-headed than she had before. All she could feel was the shuddering, rumbling beast beneath her, straining at the leash.

The sense of power that comes with sitting up on a Caterpillar tractor is absolute. At the controls of 31,000 pounds of metal with the power of 140 horses behind it, you become unstoppable, invincible, omnipotent. In a day you can alter the course of a river, in a week you can demolish an entire forest, in a month you can move a mountain. You can reshape your entire physical world with the shift of a lever, the roll of a track, the bite of a bright, sharp blade. It is the ultimate toy in the biggest sandbox of them all.

With a D-6 Caterpillar tractor and enough gas, you might even be able to demolish a blood feud by building a road to nowhere and back again. In the driver's seat of this growling yellow monster, neither Kate nor her second self had any doubts. She reached for the master clutch.

There wasn't one.

Kate had driven a Cat only once before in her life, the summer she was sixteen, when Abel had apprenticed her and his third oldest son to a miner outside Nizina for casual labor. The miner had been in the process of shoving the bottom of a creek down the maw of a sluice box with a D-5. At first he wasn't going to let Kate drive it, but he needed Seth to cut supports for the tunnel he was digging into the hill above the creek, so, mumbling and cursing and spitting a lot of tobacco juice, he put Kate up on the D-5. She learned to drive it and drive it well, because the old miner had a habit of shoving her off the seat and taking over himself whenever he was displeased with her performance. It wouldn't have been so bad if they hadn't usually been in the middle of the creek at the time, but then she wouldn't have learned so well or so quickly if they'd been on dry ground, either. Kate really did hate getting her feet wet.

Cat skinning was not a skill forgotten in a moment, or even in years, but an old D-5 was not a new D-6, and it took some time to figure out the controls, long enough for some of her audience to become restive. "Kate," Bobby said, raising his voice over the sound of the engine, "maybe this isn't such a good idea."

"Yeah, Kate," Dan said, "maybe we ought to—"

Jim said nothing, because he wasn't there.

Dinah said nothing, because she knew it wouldn't do any good.

Bernie said nothing, because he was beginning to have an idea of what Kate was going to do, approved whole-heartedly and wasn't about to do anything that might cause her to think twice.

Her second self scoffed at all of them and instructed Kate to pay no attention. She obeyed without question. It seemed there was no master clutch on this Cat. A pedal in front of her right foot acted as a decelerator and allowed her to change gears. There were still two tracks, right and left, and two steering levers, one for each, and two brakes, one for each. The hydraulics on the blade control lever took some getting used to and after she dropped the blade for the second time she was glad Mac hadn't put a floor under his tractor shed.

She stepped on the decelerator, raised the lockout bar to put the tracks in gear and let out the decelerator. The wide metal tracks began rolling beneath the bright yellow body of the machine, right out the door. She found a switch for the lights. In the sudden glare people scattered like marbles.

"Shugak," Bobby yelled, "you are out of your fucking mind!"

The Cat rolled forward, in a direct line for Mandy's truck. After all it had been through during the last two days, Kate could almost hear it give a pitiful moan. At the last possible moment she stopped grabbing for the nonexistent master clutch, stepped on the decelerator, thought her way into a left turn, pulled back a little on the left track lever and pushed forward a little on the right lever, took her foot off the decelerator and started forward again. The Cat swerved abruptly away from the truck and onto the tractor trail leading from the mine, leaving no more than a six-inch gouge down the right-hand side of the pickup. Not fatal, not even serious, and she accepted her second self's congratulations with pride.

Everyone else ran for the trucks. They all thought she was insane but nobody wanted to miss a minute of it, not even Chopper Jim, who removed his hat and jacket and tie so as to be less identifiable as the enforcement arm of the law.

Choking from the exhaust, deafened by the engine, eyes straining to see beyond the floodlights mounted on the cab, Kate took the Cat down the tractor trail that separated Devlin's mine from the road and roared into an enthusiastic left turn that doubled the size of the intersection with one swipe.

The light-headed feeling persisted. She laughed once, a mad sound that should have alarmed her but didn't. It should have alarmed Stewart, too; instead, he laughed back at her, a husky, deep-voiced sound of pure male enjoyment. "Jesus," he said. "You really are something."

A responsive shiver traveled up her spine. The aches and pains of her various wounds were hushed. She didn't question what put her in the Cat's seat, she didn't try to rationalize inviting Stewart along for the ride, she didn't attempt to talk herself out of any of it. She couldn't bring Carol Stewart back to life; worse, she couldn't bring Carol's murderer to justice. Ben and Cindy Bingley might kill each other before the solution she had set in motion this evening reached them. She couldn't unwreck George's plane, she couldn't give Margery and Richard Baker the society babe daughter they had always wanted, she couldn't make the jet engine not fall off the 747, she couldn't make spring be over and summer begin.

She couldn't bring her grandmother back to lighten her own increasingly heavy load.

But there was something she could do to make things a little safer for her family and friends and neighbors, to restore a little order to the Park.

She laughed again.

Stewart's deep voice was amused. "Ride 'em cowgirl."

A bright, slashing smile was her reply. His grip tightened on the dash.

It was two miles up the old railroad roadbed to the turnoff to the homestead area, and along the way Kate practiced moving the enormous steel blade on the front of the machine up and down, remembering as she did most of the vocabulary required to skin a Cat, some of which would have put George Perry to the blush. She even tried her hand at grading a section of the roadbed, digging up fifty feet of it before she got the hang of just where the bottom edge of the blade was in relation to the controls.

"She really is out of her fucking mind," Bobby said, wrestling his pickup over one of the speed bumps Kate had inadvertently left behind.

Dinah and Dan did not disagree.

Jim, right behind him in Kate's truck with Bernie riding shotgun, had an inconvenient attack of responsibility and wondered if perhaps, after all, he ought to stop this before it went any farther. "Think I should stop her?" he asked Bernie.

"Think you can?" Bernie said.

They looked at each other. "Nah," they said in unison.

The turnoff to the homestead area appeared and Kate cautiously negotiated the Cat onto it. By then it was purring beneath her hands, the purr of a Bengal tiger, one prepared to turn on her the minute her attention was distracted, but a purr nonetheless.

She remembered pretty much how the homestead area was laid out and who owned what from the flyer the state had mailed everyone in the Park. The sixteen forty-acre lots were crazy-quilted over a short, broad valley and a gradual rise ending in a small plateau. The plateau dropped off to the Kanuyaq River, into which all the streams in the area drained. The Jeppsens were lower down and on the left, the Kreugers a little higher and on the right. The only place their properties touched was northeast corner to southwest corner. According to the terms of the sale, the disputed road was supposed to have right-of-way over both borders, as was standard in state land transactions—Kate was pretty sure that it was in fact the law—but the Jeppsens had in their infinite wisdom decided to deny the Kreugers access to their own property; that is to say, access over the portion that belonged to them, right of way or no. This would have entailed the Kreugers building an entirely new road from some other access point, an access point located on Park land, a plan to which Dan O'Brian could be expected to take instant and vociferous exception.

It was obvious where the Jeppsens' land ended and the Kreugers' began, even in the lurching light of the Cat's floods. As soon as the one-lane track crossed into Kreuger territory, the scenery changed from overgrown Alaskan bush to near lunar desolation. Kate stepped on the decelerator and paused to size up the situation, the Cat rumbling a protest.

The Jeppsens had dug holes big enough to float a boat, and a winter's worth of snow had melted inside them, the water in several coming up almost to the top of the Cat's treads. Breakup, with its twenty-four-hour freeze-and-thaw cycle, had nibbled around the edges of the original holes and doubled the size of some of them. Entire trees, not an asset frivolously uprooted in the Bush, had been felled across the track, trunks splintered by an inexpert but indisputably thorough hand. Several crooked man-made ditches traversed the width of the road, and in one stretch the floodlights winked off a scattering of metallic objects. Kate didn't stop; if someone had sprinkled a handful of screws or nails—galvanized steel, from the silver reflection—across the path, it wouldn't matter to the Cat's metal treads. She hoped.

Even in a Caterpillar tractor the ride was rough and rocky, as much because of the attempts made at repair as the initial sabotage. The Kreugers had used the felled trees and what loose, unfrozen gravel they could find to fill in the holes, rerouting the track around the ones that weren't stable enough to drive over, but it looked as though they were fighting a desperate rearguard action against a superior and much more destructive force, with little hope of victory.

"No wonder they went to the mattresses," Kate said out loud, a fine phrase she'd picked up from Mario Puzo.

Stewart chuckled, and again she felt that shiver of response ripple up her spine. She dropped the Cat's blade with a solid CHUNK! and let out the decelerator.

The enormous blade scooped up mud, snow, dirt, boulders and trees regardless of size, weight or shape, filled in holes and tamped them down again beneath the crushing weight of the tracks. This continued all the way up the gentle incline past the turnoff for the Jeppsens' homestead and well into the Kreugers' front yard, where Kay and Wayne Kreuger, one holding a rifle, shirt bulging from the bandaged shoulder beneath it, the other with a bandage around his head, stood on their front porch, faces white with shock.

Kate swept into the yard, taking out a corner of garden fence along the way, and remembered just in time where the decelerator was. The Cat rolled to a halt, shuddering and shaking unhappily in neutral, tugging at the reins. Raising her voice over the noise of the engine, she shouted, "This is the end of it, do you hear? You've got a road now. This fight between you and the Jeppsens is over, as of today."

Wayne, a stocky, olive-skinned man with a jutting chin and a scowl, recovered from his shock and yelled, "That depends on the Jeppsens! They started it!"

"I'll take care of the Jeppsens! You've got your road! Put away those frigging guns and start acting like civilized human beings, or I'll be back with this Cat and I won't stop until this valley has been returned to its natural state!"

The Cat made known its intentions to start forward again, with or without Kate, and she grabbed the controls and hung on for dear life. The right side of the blade ripped the rear bumper off the old International pickup parked in front of the porch and the tractor swept out of the Kreugers' yard and back down the trail, nearly sideswiping Bobby's blue pickup.

It was a lot smoother going back, Kate noted with satisfaction. Her second self radiated warm approval.

The turnoff for the Jeppsens came so fast she almost missed it, and it was considerably wider than it had been once the Cat passed through. She kept the blade down, mowing down everything that got in the way, including a raspberry patch, an empty drum of thirty-weight and a boy's bike, right into the Jeppsens' front yard.

Stewart laughed again. He sounded excited, even aroused, and why not? He would revel in outlawry, in destruction.

In murder.

As Kate herself was reveling in this very moment. The realization should have stopped her, at the very least given her pause. Instead, she pushed both levers forward with a cry that raised an answering yell from the man next to her.

The sound of the Cat's 140 horses must have been audible for miles, because the floodlights caught Joe and Cheryl Jeppsen standing on their front porch with much the same expression on their faces as the Kreugers had had on theirs. The Cat gave Kate just enough time to notice that Cheryl's twin shiners had achieved a yellowish purple of truly historic hue.

More practiced now, she drew the tractor around in a magnificent sweep, barely nicking the bottom stair of the porch steps, and stepped once more on the decelerator. The engine idled and the yellow monster slowed to a reluctant halt, its menacing growl muted.

"What the hell do you think you're doing, Kate?" Joe yelled. He was a thin, bony man with a cadaverous face and dark, burning eyes. One calf was in a cast, one hand held a shotgun. Cheryl had a rifle. The edge of the lights reached just far enough to illuminate Petey on the throne of the one-holer outhouse, reading a copy of *Road and Track*. Stunned, he gaped through the open door.

"I think I'm building a road," Kate yelled back. "You people have taken enough shots at me in the last forty-eight hours to run out my luck for a lifetime! You put those goddam guns away and start trying to get along with your neighbors!"

"They started it! They—"

"I don't give a rat's ass who started it! It stops today!"

Forever after, Kate would swear she hadn't meant to do it, that she'd once again forgotten the lack of a master switch and the substitution of a decelerator, not to mention that it was pitch black at the time and she couldn't really see where she was going. No one ever believed her, but whether she meant to or not, the Cat took the turn too wide. Petey, with a front-row seat, so to speak, recovered from his stupefaction in time to leap for safety, although it was difficult for him to move very fast with his jeans around his knees. His ass flashed white in the Cat's mercilessly bright halogen floodlights, denim hobbling his steps as he hopped awkwardly out of the way, as the wide steel blade mowed down the thin walls, the tracks crunched over them and the aromatic fragrance of eau d'outhouse filled the clearing.

To Kate's profound relief the Cat did not founder in the hole left behind. She pulled back on the left lever and pushed on the right and the Cat turned left. Joe and Cheryl, joined by Petey, pants up now, stood watching in open-mouthed silence as she passed in review before them and rolled out of sight. No one shot at her, probably, she decided, because of the two truckloads of people following her, not that that had ever stopped the Jeppsens before.

The air was cool on her cheek. A few stars were beginning to peer warily through the torn wisps of April clouds. The now full moon emerged from behind Angqaq and threw the peaks of the Quilaks into jagged relief against the eastern horizon. Deaf from the noise of the engine, hoarse from shouting over it, Kate was exhilarated and drunk with power.

"I love breakup," she told the full moon rising up over the Quilaks.

The noise of the engine overwhelmed the words, and Kate half stood and shouted out to the entire Park, "I *love* breakup!"

A warm, firm hand settled on the back of her neck. She didn't so much as jump, merely turned her head to meet Stewart's eyes. He smiled at her, his teeth a white slash in the dark cab. She smiled back.

If anything, the trip back to the Cat's garage was even faster and more reckless than the trip out. Kate knocked down three cottonwoods and graded a five-hundred-foot section of roadbed along the way. She pulled into Mac Devlin's yard with a grand flourish and drew to halt in front of the open doors of the garage.

She didn't turn the Cat's engine off, liking its dangerous growl, as if at any moment it might throw off the leash and head out on its own.

The warm, heavy hand on the back of her neck tightened. She felt rather than saw the almost feline ripple of awareness that ran over him, and smiled to herself.

"That's how we take care of problems in the Park, Mr. Stewart," she said, leaning back against the seat, and with the words her several selves merged back into one. Her mind felt extremely clear. She turned toward the man seated next to her, her left hand resting casually on the gearshift, her other moving to lie almost naturally along the back of the seat, causing his to drop away. A breeze rippled through the tops of the trees, and in the distance they could hear the sound of the two trucks laboring down the track toward them.

"We have a problem, and we take care of it. We don't bother the troopers if we don't have to. We try not to have to."

"So I see." His voice was thick, and he shifted in his seat. He began to lean toward her.

"The way I figure it happened is this," she said.

He paused, his face in shadow.

"When you found out your wife was screwing around, you decided to teach her and her lover a lesson they would never forget. The last lesson they would ever learn." She began to sound less and less like the Lorelei and more and more like the big trooper with the cold blue eyes. "And you decided to teach it to them where you were surest of your ground."

He didn't move, and she couldn't make out his expression. "So, last fall, you brought her lover up here, probably on a hunt. And you left him here to die."

She raised her left hand and tucked back a stray lock of hair that had come free during their wild ride. The motion pulled the fabric of shirt and windbreaker tight against her breast, and she saw his eyes drop involuntarily. If he were standing in front of a firing squad and one of the shooters was a woman, he would die taking her measurements with his eyes. Kate knew a sudden sympathy for his dead wife.

She let the hand lying on the back of the seat slip down to his thigh. He started. "And then you went back to town, and you watched your wife grow frantic at the loss of her lover, and you were probably just sympathetic enough to keep her from leaving you altogether." Something in the quality of his silence changed, and she said quickly, "Or perhaps you smothered her with affection. It's always fun to make someone who has wronged you feel guilty."

She felt a muscle flex beneath her hand, and was satisfied. "Of course. So that this spring, you could seduce her into coming to the Park for a second honeymoon. To get away from it all, I think you said yesterday. And you took her up to the mine. For a picnic lunch, you told her."

Her voice was like sandpaper, scraping at all the rough edges. "You killed her there, and you made enough of a mess to fetch every bear within ten square miles."

She gave his thigh a gentle squeeze, and dropped her voice to a raspy whisper. "And then you came looking for me, or someone like me, to tell your sorry story to." She paused, waiting.

He wanted to test her. She could see it in the set of his shoulders, feel it in the tension of his thigh, could almost taste it on the tip of her tongue.

The wind was increasing in volume, a real chinook by the warm feel of it, the leading edge of the storm brewing in the Gulf. A cloud crossed the face of the moon. The trees rustled, snow melted from branches like rain, and a chunk of ice slid suddenly from the cabin to crash to the ground beneath.

It broke his spell. He reached for the hand on his thigh and flattened it against his crotch. He was hard, but then she'd known he would be. "You can't prove anything."

"No, I can't," she said. The first ray from Bobby's headlights hit the clearing. She tightened her hand and he gasped. "I don't have to prove anything, Stewart. I know what happened. I've told you because I can't bear the thought that you think you're so smart you've committed the perfect crime and gotten away with it. You haven't."

Her hand tightened further. "Hey," he said, alarmed, and tried to pry her loose.

She squeezed, hard, with her right hand and with her left

grabbed for a handful of his throat, her nails sinking deep into his skin.

Stewart's whole body jolted with shock, and the first inkling of how much he had underestimated her. This was not how he had imagined this prolonged period of sexual titillation would end. The shock was closely followed by fury, with the sudden realization that she'd played him like a harp to just this end, but the fury was quickly supplanted by fear. Her grip was unbelievably, terrifyingly strong for such a small woman.

He went limp, like an animal playing dead so the bear won't be interested. It didn't work all that well with bears, as he had cause to know, but it was the only option he had.

It wasn't working with this woman, either. Kate chuckled, and he shivered at the sound. She tightened her right hand, and he whimpered. She leaned closer, her lips brushing his ear, and dropped her voice. "You think with your dick, Stewart. Not all that impressive an organ, is it? After all, it led you here."

That stung his pride, and he choked and tried to twist away. She tightened her grip again. He was still erect, he didn't seem to be able to help it, but the skin of his throat gave beneath her nails, and a warm trickle of fluid ran between her fingers. "This is how we take care of problems in the Park, Stewart," she repeated. "We see something wrong, we fix it. Don't come back here, or I'll fix all your problems, once and for all." She squeezed again. "Got it?"

He gave a half-gasping, half-choking kind of gurgle. She took that as a yes. "Good boy," she said, for all the world as if she were praising a not very bright pet dog. She smiled at him for the last time and, one hand on his crotch, one at his throat, raised him up and pitched him out of the cab of the Cat.

He fell hard, and lay still for a moment, long enough for the trucks to slam to a halt and empty their occupants into the yard. "Jesus Christ, Shugak," Bobby said, trying to unfold his chair and stay between Dinah and Stewart at the same time.

"He's not dead, is he?" Dan said, aghast.

"No," Jim said with more assurance than he felt, and was immensely relieved when Stewart staggered to his feet.

When Jim would have helped him to one of the trucks, Kate's voice, a low rasp of sound, came clearly over the sound of the Cat's idle.

"No. Let him walk."

Jim's hand dropped as he stared up at the dark figure in the cab.

The full moon was up high enough for the rest of them to watch in silence as Stewart limped shakily out of the clearing, shoulders hunched, hands clasped protectively over his crotch, something dark staining the front of his shirt.

He bore only the very slightest resemblance to the tall, good-looking, confident ladies' man who had left the Roadhouse two hours before.

18

The next morning she finished her taxes and made an early trip in to the post office to drop her tax form into the mailbox, a whole day before the deadline. She exited the post office feeling efficient and virtuous and every inch the franchised American, and very nearly saluted the flag.

She got the hell out of Dodge unambushed by anybody bent on drafting her to do good and returned to the homestead to rebuild the base of the couch with plywood and two-by-fours. There was no more of the blue canvas she'd used for upholstering fabric when she'd built it years before, so she improvised with a piece of olive drab Army blanket. She hated sewing; consequently her stitches were small and neat, so as to get the job done as fast as possible and not have to go back and redo it later. Finished, it looked like a splotch of pond scum floating on a blue lake. Or, if she squinted, maybe a lily pad. She'd have to check the Sears catalog for new material and reupholster the whole thing. Oh. Right. There was no more Sears catalog. Great.

She set up the ladder again and sanded the Spackle on the ceiling patch. There was a little less than a gallon of the flat white latex paint in the garage, left over from the last time she'd painted the interior of the cabin, more than enough to cover the area involved. She had been right; the paint had faded and she had to paint the whole ceiling to make it match. Fortunately, the cabin was only twenty-five feet square and the loft ceiling was easily reached. At noon she took down the ladder for what she devoutly hoped was the last time and trundled everything back out through the slush to the garage.

The chinook had blown itself out by six that morning, leaving temperatures in the upper forties and climbing. The roar of runoff down the creek had increased and she climbed down the bank, shotgun in hand, to assess the boulder situation. It looked solid, and a good thing, too, because there would be no muscling of rocks against the force of that water. Her judgment may have been influenced by the rustling of brush she heard across the creek, and the infrequent grunts and groans of her local grizzly, letting her know he was there.

The Park was just lousy with bears this spring.

Bad news for Carol Stewart.

The grizzly gave another grumble of discontent and Mutt barked sharply from the top of the bank. "All right, all right, I'm going," she told the grizzly. "All right, all right, I'm coming," she told Mutt.

There was no salvaging the Isuzu. Even the metal of the wheels was bent. She started up one of the four-wheelers and towed the corpse to the garbage dump a thousand feet from the clearing. She'd bury it as soon as the ground thawed. At least until then it would be out of her sight.

A hammer and a fistful of nails and the cache was almost as good as new. Two of the four legs were intact and quickly reattached. She fetched the axe from the garage and shoved through the brush to a stand of slender birch about a quarter of a mile from the cabin. She found two of the right diameter and length, and felled them and hauled them back to the clearing, where she stripped them of bark and let them sit. It took fifteen minutes and a quarter of a can of Goop to clean the sap from her hands.

"Oh to be anywhere else, now that spring is here." Mutt, curled up in a patch of sunlight on the one dry piece of ground in the clearing, gave her a quizzical look and tucked her nose back beneath her tail.

Like burying the truck, setting the cache back up would have to wait for the ground to thaw. She checked the meat in the root cellar beneath the garage. It was still mostly frozen. She pulled out a package of caribou backstrap steaks for dinner. It was too much for her to eat alone, but she felt she had earned a treat, and she didn't want her tenderest cut of last fall's moose to thaw and spoil.

After lunch she pushed the snow machine into the garage and was draining the tank of its remaining fuel so as to begin work on a patch when Mutt gave a sharp warning bark from the yard. "What now?" she asked the rafters, and went to see.

It was Bickford. He apologized for not making it out sooner. The thick manila envelope held fifty thousand dollars exactly, in cash, half in hundreds, half in fifties. Kate went dizzy at the sight of so much green and hoped it didn't show.

She made Bickford wait while she counted it. He made her sign a receipt. Honors about even, he departed, and she sincerely hoped that was the last she was going to see of anyone for a while.

She went inside and sat down at the kitchen table to admire the cash and think warm fuzzy thoughts of Mr. and Mrs. Baker. After a nice long while she tucked the money back in the envelope and got out pen and paper to write two letters, the first a list of books to Rachel at Twice Told Tales in Anchorage, the second a list of cassette tapes to Susan at Metro Music, also in Anchorage.

She peeked in the manila envelope again. Surely there was enough there to finance a trip into town. She could get a new tape deck and a supply of batteries at Costco, have a Reuben at the Downtown Deli, check out the latest in snow machines.

Spend quality time with Jack.

Blood suddenly humming with anticipation, she added notes to Rachel and Susan not to mail her orders, she would pick them up in person.

The second envelope had just been sealed when Mutt barked again. Kate swore. Was she never to be left in peace?

She went to the door and beheld Bobby jouncing into the clearing on his wheelchair, Dinah trotting along behind.

Kate frowned at her. "Take it easy, you're walking for two now, you know."

Around Mutt's enthusiastic licks of welcome—every now and then her taste in men showed signs of improving—Bobby managed to say, "I keep telling her," and Dinah rolled her eyes.

"You got coffee?" Bobby demanded. At her nod he roared, "Well, don't keep us standing out here in the cold, woman, pour it out!"

It wasn't cold, it was in fact getting fairly close to the Big Five-Oh, as the much anticipated fifty-degree mark was known, but Kate resigned herself to the inevitable and led the way inside without comment.

When they were all around the kitchen table, Bobby stirred in creamer with a decisive hand and fixed Kate with a piercing stare. She met it with a bland expression. "We've been playing this game of Clue," he said.

Kate raised an eyebrow.

"And we thought we'd try out one possible solution." He looked at Dinah.

"Carol Stewart," Dinah said.

"In the Park," Bobby said.

"With a bear," Dinah said, and giggled.

Bobby looked at Kate. "Well?"

"Well what?" Kate sampled her own coffee, rejoicing in the

fact that she had coffee again, not to mention corn Niblets and Darigold butter, which would go fine with tonight's backstrap. She'd better boil up some rice, too, seeing as how it looked like she was going to have company for dinner.

More company than she'd thought. "Hi," Dan O'Brian said from the doorway. Behind him could be seen the distinctive outline of a round-crowned, flat-brimmed trooper hat.

Kate sighed. "Jim, it's breakup, you have to have business somewhere in the Park other than on my homestead."

"Kenny Ellis in Glenallen's got me covered for today," he said, stepping inside, immaculate as always.

"Bernie coming, too?" Kate said as she poured out.

"No, he's busy, puttying up the bullet holes in the bar." Jim pulled out a chair and sat down.

Dan found an empty Blazo box and perched on it. "We had to promise to stop in on the way back, though, and give him the straight scoop."

They all stared at her expectantly.

"So," Bobby said.

"Carol Stewart," Dinah said. "Actually Mark, because you're supposed to say whodunnit first."

"In the Park," Bobby said.

"With a bear," Dinah, Dan and Jim said together.

Nobody laughed this time. After a pause, Jim added, "We know he did it, Kate. You know how. Tell."

She rubbed a hand over her face and sighed again. "I never would have figured it out if Earlybird hadn't dropped that engine on me," she said. "But it was the sardine that really put it all together. Finally."

"Sardine?"

"Sardine?"

"You didn't tell me about any sardine," Dan said accusingly.

"Wait a minute," Jim said. "Last night, when Viola—"

"Yes." Kate nodded. To the others she explained, "Auntie Vi

said Sardine was the name of the guy Carol Stewart came to the Park with last spring. But then she said no, that wasn't right, and then she couldn't remember what was."

Bobby thought it over and didn't get it. He said so.

"I didn't, either, at first. Then there was the shoot-out." She fortified herself with a Fig Newton. There was a forty-eight-ounce bag of chocolate chips in the cupboard but what with one thing and another she had yet to get around to baking. With luck, she could seduce Jack into baking for her, chocolate chip cookies being his specialty.

"And," Jim prodded.

"And, I've always found that flying bullets really focus my attention, you know? I was lying there in back of the bar, and I remembered sardine is a kind of herring."

The other four exchanged speaking glances. "Hooligan," Kate said, unperturbed, "is also another name for herring, right?"

"Yeah," Dan said, brow furrowed, "or it's a family member, or something like that."

"And hooligan sounds pretty close to Harrigan, doesn't it?"

"Yes."

Kate leaned back and stared at him. "Ring any bells?"

Dan stared back, bewildered. "No, I—"

"Kate—" Jim said.

"Wait a minute!" Dan said, sitting bolt upright. "Of course! Harrigan, Nathan Harrigan! That was the name of the pilot! The one who flew Stewart into the Park last fall!"

"Yes." Kate waited for Dan to fill in the rest of them on his first meeting with Stewart and Stewart's pilot.

Jim's brows snapped together. "Wait a minute. You mean Nathan Harrigan, your DB"— he pointed at Kate —"was the same guy you"— the trooper pointed at the ranger —"saw with Mark Stewart in the Park last fall?"

Kate refrained from repeating yet again that Nathan Harrigan wasn't her dead body, and simply nodded. "Yes. And, according to Auntie Vi, Harrigan was also in the Park with Carol Stewart last spring. According to Dan, he was back, this time with Mark, Carol's husband, six months later." She drank coffee. "And Stewart, Dan informs me, has had permits for moose, caribou and bear, not to mention fishing licenses, in this game management unit for the last ten years. You were right, Dan, he's an experienced hunter. There was no excuse for him to go up to the mine unarmed."

"Wait a minute," Jim said. "Wait just a damn minute. Are you talking about a double homicide here? You think Stewart killed his wife and Harrigan, too?"

"I know he did," she said, and polished off the cookie and reached for a second. "You said the coroner said Harrigan was an electrician in Anchorage. Bernie says Mark Stewart is a long-time contractor, also in Anchorage, one of the good old boys who went into business during the oil boom in the seventies. He put up the Roadhouse back when they were both starting out."

"I didn't know that."

"Bernie was telling us about it, day before yesterday," Bobby said.

Kate nodded. "Anyway, Anchorage isn't that big a town, so my best guess is Harrigan probably worked for Stewart at one time or another. Probably how Harrigan met Stewart's wife, too."

Bobby and Dinah and Dan exclaimed together, but Bobby's stentorian bellow naturally won out. "Harrigan, who you're saying is the dead body got found out here the day the sky fell, was screwing Carol Stewart?"

Kate nodded again. "Yeah, and right here in the Park, too. Auntie Vi said she'd met Carol before, on a visit to the Park last spring, only she wasn't with Mark, she was with some guy called—"

"Sardine!"

"Only she remembered by association, a sardine is a hooligan, and hooligan sounds close enough to Harrigan."

"Let me get this straight," Jim said. "You're saying Harrigan actually came out hunting to the same place he'd been screwing the wife of the guy who invited him on the hunting trip?"

Kate shrugged. "I don't know much about Harrigan, but I do know enough about contract hiring that he'd think there might be a job in it if he accepted Stewart's invitation."

"He was taking an awful chance," Dan said.

"Dumb," Bobby said. "Dumb to come back to the Park with Stewart, dumb, dumb, dumb."

Kate's smile was thin and noticeably lacking in amusement. "Stewart probably insisted on it."

The three men didn't get it, but Dinah did. "Returning to the scene of the crime?"

Kate nodded. "First with Harrigan, then with his wife. Rubbing their noses in it."

They thought about that for a while. "If you're right, this guy's some kind of sadist," Dan said.

"Some kind," Kate agreed.

Dinah shuddered.

"Dumb," Bobby insisted. "If I'd been Harrigan, I would have run a mile from the guy."

"Maybe," Kate said. "Maybe not. You read the papers. The state economy hasn't been the same since the pipeline years. Construction jobs are few and far between. If he needed the work, and if he thought the hunting trip meant work, Harrigan would want to believe Stewart knew nothing of the affair. He'd will himself to believe it."

"You're guessing," Jim said flatly, leaning back in his chair. He sounded disappointed.

"About all the Anchorage stuff, yes," Kate said. "Did you get a positive ID on the body?"

Jim nodded abstractedly. "It came in this morning. It is Nathan Harrigan. But—" He fell silent.

Kate finished her cookie. "Two wounds, the coroner said. One blow to the head, hard enough to knock him unconscious, not hard enough to kill him. While he was out, another blow to his leg, hard enough to break it, to incapacitate him, so Stewart could walk away and let it look like an accident."

Jim thought about it, and gave a slow nod.

"Maybe Stewart waited until Harrigan woke up, maybe he was gone when Harrigan woke up, and so was anything Harrigan could have eaten, or used for warmth, or for shelter. So Harrigan lay where he was and waited for death."

Her voice lowered, her words taking on an unconscious rhythm.

"Maybe Agudar was kind, and let him slip into the long sleep in peace with the cold of the night.

"Maybe Raven led the bear or the wolf there first.

"I don't know."

She paused. "All I know is it took a while, and during that time he knew who, and he knew why, and Stewart wanted it that way."

The room was silent. In the distance a raven croaked at a squirrel, and got a chatter of outrage in return.

Dan stirred. "The murder weapon?"

"I imagine the coroner's report will say a blunt instrument of some kind." Kate looked at Chopper Jim. "Used properly and with enthusiasm, the butt of a gun is a fine offensive weapon. They teach you how to use one in the service, I hear. Stewart didn't need any special tools. Enough fools out here already fall over their own guns and shoot themselves; it doesn't take much imagination to turn one into a murder weapon."

Dinah shivered, all trace of fun wiped from her face. "It's so— so cold."

Kate nodded. "Literally." She reached for another cookie.

Incredulously, Jim said, "Did Stewart admit all this to you last night?"

"God, no." Kate shook her head. "He's too smart for that. This guy diagrammed the whole operation, like a military exercise. You might want to check on that, Jim," she added dispassionately. "Be interesting to know if he's ever seen military service, and if he did time in tactical command."

Jim's expression was pained. He hated it when a soldier went bad.

"Yeah," Kate said, thinking it over some more, "he was smart enough to take a rifle when they went up to the mine—"

"But he said—" Dan burst out.

"He lied."

"You don't know that."

"Yes," Kate said. "Yes, I do." And she did. "He's too smart not to. He broke it down and carried it in his pack. He waited until they were out of sight of the village, maybe pretended he heard a noise and stopped to assemble it. Carol Stewart probably watched him do it. For their protection, I'm sure he said. For his protection, really. So whatever he suckered out of the woods to eat on her wouldn't turn on him." She used a swallow of coffee to wash the bitter taste out of her mouth.

"What did he do with it?"

"He tossed it. Probably used it first to scare the bear off. We never would have heard the shots over the noise of the road or the truck's engine."

Dan sat up straight in his chair. "Remember, Kate, when we said we'd called the trooper? Stewart was surprised. He didn't think anyone official could make it to the scene so quick."

"He was probably counting on it," she agreed.

"Maybe we could go back up there," Jim said, "run a search pattern, see if we can dig that rifle up."

"You know that nine-millimeter Cindy took out after Ben with?" At their nods, Kate said, "She told me she pitched it into the river. Hell, it's right there, all you have to do is step to the edge of the cliff and let go. Stewart's rifle is probably offshore of Port Dick by now, and probably the pack with it, so we can't look for gun oil or anything on the fabric."

"But—"

"It's in the river," Kate said flatly. "I'd bet every dime I've got on it."

Her eyes fell on the fat manila envelope reposing innocently on one shelf. Well. Maybe not every dime.

There was no dragging the Kanuyaq, which emptied into the Gulf at a gallop during a spring thaw with heavy runoff. "So," Jim said heavily, breaking the glum silence, "Harrigan and Carol Stewart were having an affair."

"His landlord said there had been a girlfriend," Kate said. "He said she was blonde. Carol Stewart was blonde."

"The landlord also said the girlfriend might have been a brunette," Jim said. "So, Stewart finds out about Harrigan and his wife, and he plans his revenge. He brings Harrigan up last fall, breaks his leg and leaves him for dead, and brings his wife up this spring and feeds her to a bear? This what you're telling me here, Shugak?"

"Yes."

"How did he kill her?" Jim asked. "He couldn't have used the rifle, there's no way you could hide that from the coroner. You're the one says he's so smart, he'd have to have known that. So how did he kill her? You hardwired into that, too?"

She ignored the sarcasm in his tone because she knew it wasn't really directed at her, and reached in her pocket. The Swiss Army knife clattered to the table. They stared at it, mesmerized. "Auntie Vi says he had one of these. Maybe even this one. Cindy stumbled over it the morning of the attack, when she chased Ben up the road."

Chopper Jim picked up the knife and located the blade. Over it, his eyes met Kate's. "You didn't think to bag it?"

"At the time, I didn't know it might be important. Besides, it'd been lying in the slush and the mud before Cindy found it. Cindy's handled it, I've handled it, Auntie Vi's handled it."

"Hell, I remember now, I watched you clean it yesterday afternoon."

She nodded.

"Not much of a killing machine," Dan said, examining the two-and-a-half-inch blade critically.

"One slice from behind." Kate's hand went to the scar on her throat, a thin ridge of roped flesh that had healed badly and now would never fade. "You take the victim by surprise, you're stronger than she is anyway—" Her hand dropped. "You don't need a bowie knife to get the job done." She added dispassionately, "He would have waited to kill her at least until he heard the bear. Fresh blood, hungry bear. Unbeatable combination."

Dinah shoved her chair back. "Excuse me," she said, and left the cabin.

Bobby started to go after her. "Don't," Kate said.

He scowled at her.

She shook her head. "Don't," she repeated.

He looked at the open door, hands resting on the wheels of his chair. With an oath, he brought them back up to the arm rests. "And if Stewart hadn't heard a bear?"

Kate's shoulders rose and fell. "It didn't have to happen the first day. Auntie Vi said they were booked in for a week. He had time to wait for the perfect opportunity. He just lucked out the first day. A bear showed up on schedule, Stewart killed Carol, let the bear chew on her enough to obliterate the evidence." She reflected. "Then he heard us coming, and either chased the bear off or it ran off. Stewart didn't have time to break the weapon down again, so he pitched it into the river and came to meet us." She frowned down at her coffee. "Too bad we couldn't have tested his hands for residue."

"I don't know." Dan crossed his arms and frowned. "Seems awfully iffy to me."

"Then he would have fallen back on plan B."

"There was a plan B?"

"Dan," Kate said with finality, "there is always a plan B for the Mark Stewarts of this world."

"Hell." Jim sat back, lips flattened into a thin line. "It doesn't matter much whether he used the knife. Even if we found his fingerprints on it, which we won't, and traces of her blood on it, which we won't, it wouldn't be enough."

"No." Kate shook her head. "It wouldn't."

"Especially if he's as smart as you think he is, and loved her up in front of all their friends in town. No motive."

"Oh yes there was," Kate said. Sex or money, she thought, the two most popular motives for murder. She was pretty sure it was one of Morgan's Laws, but she couldn't remember which one. She'd have to ask Jack the next time she saw him. Soon, she thought. Tomorrow would be good. "Whether anyone saw it or not, there was motive up the wazoo."

"Come on, Kate," Dan said. "A lot of wives screw around on their husbands. A lot of husbands don't take them out and feed them to bears."

"A lot of husbands don't have Stewart's ego." Kate remembered Stewart forcing her hand against his erection. It had been a taunt, a blatant provocation, his response to her challenge. He must have thought she just wouldn't be able to resist all that male pulchritude and would fling herself on him. She'd met men like him before, men whose certain, unwavering belief in their own irresistibility formed the pillar of their existence. It was imprudent to disillusion them, imprudent and dangerous and potentially fatal. As Carol Stewart and Nathan Harrigan had discovered, at the cost of their lives. "It's all ego with him."

"And how," Dinah said from the doorway. Her face was pale, but she met Bobby's questioning look with a reassuring smile. "Mr. Stewart thinks *very* well of himself. What was it Bernie called him? Something movie star–ish?"

"Redfordy," Dan supplied.

Dinah nodded. "Right. And he'd encourage the resemblance. King stud. He'd take adultery as a personal affront. Especially if the guy worked for him."

"And especially if they did it here," Kate said, waving a hand to indicate the Park. "Stewart's very own personal hunting ground. Adding insult to injury."

"I wonder," Dinah said thoughtfully.

"What?"

"If maybe Carol Stewart didn't bring Nathan Harrigan here for that very reason. Stewart's kind always screw around. Maybe she was making a point, taking her lover on her husband's own ground."

Kate's mouth twisted up at one corner. "If she did, her revenge was very short-lived."

Jim tossed the Swiss Army knife down in disgust and folded his arms. He didn't want to believe any of it, not because it wasn't true, but because he was afraid that it was and he had not a shred of hard evidence to back any of it up.

"He make it back to Niniltna?" Kate said.

"Stewart?" At her nod, the trooper nodded.

"Too bad. I was kind of hoping that bear would show up again." Her smile was cold. "Mandy's dad, who has been big-game hunting in Africa, assures me that once a lion tastes human flesh it won't eat anything else. Be nice if the same held true for bears. In this one case, anyway."

"Where is he now?" Dan said. "Stewart."

"Back in Anchorage," Jim said. "No help for it, Dan," he said in response to the ranger's disbelieving look. "No probable cause, no hard evidence of foul play. He cooperated fully. Couldn't hold him."

"As a matter of curiosity," Kate said, "was Carol Stewart insured?"

"Yes, but just a standard policy through his business. He had an identical policy, and they both took them out years ago."

"Ought to pay for both trips, out and back," Kate said coolly. "Like I said. Smart."

Dinah made an inarticulate protest, quickly smothered. Bobby caught her hand and glared at Kate.

"Son of a bitch," Jim said suddenly, and brought his fist down hard on the table in an uncharacteristic display of temper. Everybody jumped. "Son of a *bitch*."

Kate thought of Pastor Seabolt, and of the long, hot June days in Chistona. "Something I learned last summer, Jim," she said.

"What?"

"Sometimes? There's just no cure for a situation."

He didn't like it. None of them did.

Dan broke the silence this time. "What did Stewart say to you last night, Kate?"

"Nothing," she said, with perfect truth. "Nothing at all."

Bobby said shrewdly, "What did you say to him?"

She chose her words with care. "I suggested he make this his last visit to the Park."

"Breathing the air here might be hazardous to his health, is that it?" Bobby barked out a humorless laugh. "So might riding shotgun on that damn D-6 with you on the throttle. Jesus, Shugak, when I said you should take executive action, I didn't mean you should take it on a Caterpillar tractor. You got a death wish or what? My eyes about dropped out of my head when you took off outta that barn." He looked her over critically, and added, "You sure that was really you in your body last night?"

"Maybe it was her evil twin," Dinah suggested, recovering enough to join in. "Brought out by the full moon."

"I figured the Antichrist," Dan said.

"Nah, pod person," Jim said, adding hastily, "Not that I would know, since of course I wasn't there."

The taut atmosphere of frustration and anger eased to where laughter and friendship might be possible once again.

Kate drained her mug and pushed back her chair. "It's moose backstrap for dinner. Who's staying?"

• • •

They were gone by nine, and there was still enough light left for Kate and Mutt to walk out back and sit down on the large, smooth boulder embedded in the edge of the creek bank. Overhead the sky turned from blue to pink to orange to red and back to blue again. The stars came out one at a time, Venus first, brighter than every other body in the sky, save the sun and the moon.

Soon the stars would be burned out of the sky by the light of the midnight sun, and Venus would fade into the east for the summer. Kate had an affinity for the stars, for the constellations, especially for Orion. As a little girl she had pictured him standing, harpoon in hand, poised at the water's edge, intent on spearing his next meal. Much later, in Masterpieces of World Literature at the University of Fairbanks, she had learned he was supposed to be carrying a sword and shield, and still later that he raped one of the Pleiades, or maybe it was Artemis, the first in a long line of the disillusionments that come with growing up and leaving the magic behind.

Breakup certainly qualified. The season was supposed to be one of hope and renewal, spent gathering rosebuds while ye may. Instead, it all too often degenerated into destruction and despair. It had been a clear, cold April night when her mother had begun the long walk home from a party, only to pass out at the side of the road and die of exposure.

Well, she thought with cold satisfaction, it might have taken thirty years, but she had paid back for her mother, in spades. It had been a long time since they'd had a bootlegger in the Park.

Her satisfaction was fleeting. People got away with murder during breakup. People got away with murder and then got away. First Lottie Gette, now Mark Stewart. Kate shifted restlessly on her rock. Failure was not an option open to her, and yet here it was, staring her in the face, and for an instant panic clawed at the back of her throat.

She beat it down before it could take over. All right, it had been three days of frustration, personal and professional. And sexual. This last was going to be the easiest to relieve; as soon as the homestead was in decent enough shape she was headed into town in her brand-new, slightly bruised truck. She would go into Niniltna to tell Bobby to call Jack and let him know she was coming. Jack was a smart man; by the time she managed the two hundred–odd miles into town he would have farmed his son out to a friend's house for the duration. She had a sudden vision of going through his front door like a conquering army and her need was so great she couldn't even smile.

Hormones had even more to answer for than Charles II and Walt Disney. But it was the personal and professional frustration that nagged at her most. What was her profession nowadays? She'd been absent from the DA's staff for, what, four years now. In the blank marked "Occupation" on her tax form she had written "private investigator" for the first time, mostly because the bulk of last year's income had been earned in that capacity, but the truth was she didn't even have a PI's license. Hell, in Alaska, there wasn't any such creature, there was only a state business license, available to anyone who could fill out the form and produce fifty bucks. That was it, that was all you needed, bing, bang, boom, you were in the peeper business.

But if she wasn't a private investigator, what was she?

And then there was the acute personal frustration of being thrust into a position of responsibility for the tribe, of shouldering duties and assuming obligations she had never sought and had certainly never wanted. It wasn't just the tribe, either, it was the whole goddam Park, Native and white, cheechako and sourdough, ranger and miner and homesteader, fisher folk and fish hawk. Predicaments R Us, You Bring 'Em, We Fix 'Em, K. Shugak, Proprietor. Meetings Mediated, Marriages Counseled, Murders Solved. She didn't even have to advertise, they came, bringing their baggage with them, whether she wanted them to or not.

The first shoot-out at Bernie's flashed through her mind. Nobody had told her to break it up. There had been fifty, sixty people in the Roadhouse that night. Any one of them could have taken the initiative, could have restored the peace, but no, Kate Shugak had ridden to the rescue yet again. Or crawled, in this case. And of course she had had to answer Mandy's *cri de coeur*, and there was no denying Billy Mike, invested with all the weight and majesty of tribal tradition, and Dan seemed to take it for granted that it was her job to bring Mark Stewart to justice, and how could she stand by and let Bernie get shot up a second time, and even that prick Jim Chopin regarded her as Tonto to his Lone Ranger, and . . . oh, the hell with it.

The hell with all of it.

Twenty feet below, cold, crystal water rushed downstream between narrow banks. From beneath a budding salmonberry bush, a snowshoe hare poked its head out, coat already turning brown for the coming season. An eagle passing high overhead called out a melancholy good night.

A passing breeze caught at the branch of a fir tree. It reached down and brushed her cheek, the needles scratching gently at her skin.

"Emaa?" Kate said softly.

At her knee Mutt stirred, looking up at her with patient yellow eyes, and unthinkingly she knotted a reassuring hand in the coarse ruff.

The bark of the branch smelled strongly of resin. "Emaa," Kate said into the gathering night, "they lean on me. All of them, they lean on me. How do I stand against it? How did you, all those years?"

The silence was the silence of the living land, water tumbling stone, wind through the trees, the chatter of squirrels, and the song was almost lost in it.

She sat up straight, watchful, waiting, listening. It came again, three pure descending notes, floating to her on the wisp of a breeze. The golden-crowned sparrow, the spring-is-here bird, the first one of the year.

It sounded again, nearer this time. Her eyes groped for it in the dusky twilight, and after a moment there it was, six inches long, light brown with darker streaks on its plump body and a golden one on its head. It perched at the end of an insubstantial alder twig, swaying a little as it cocked its head, looking at Kate alternately from each bright eye.

The song sounded again, Spring is here, here is spring. That was its job, to usher in spring in song. That was what it had been made for, what it was best at. It might dream of being an eagle, soaring, aloof, detached, but it was the spring-is-here bird, and it sang the news from the branch of an alder.

Kate let out a breath she hadn't known she was holding. "All right, Emaa."

She got to her feet, and in a flutter of wings the sparrow was gone. "I love you, Emaa," Kate said, raising her voice. "I miss you."

Mutt trotted ahead. Kate paused, shotgun cradled in the crook of one arm, and looked over her shoulder at the fading outline of the mountains, the lambent glow of the rising moon.

"I need you," she said, almost whispering the words.

Her only answer was the song again, three notes, coming clearly over the wind in the trees, the howl of a distant wolf, the drip of melting snow.

It was enough.

It would have to be.